My Dearest
Barbara ~
It has been many
good years of friendship
~ not a one gone to waste.
God is good & you have been
such an inspiration.

Love Imani
McClendon
AKA

MOURNING GLORY

by

Imani McClendon

Bloomington, IN  Milton Keynes, UK

authorHOUSE™

AuthorHouse™
1663 Liberty Drive, Suite 200
Bloomington, IN 47403
www.authorhouse.com
Phone: 1-800-839-8640

AuthorHouse™ UK Ltd.
500 Avebury Boulevard
Central Milton Keynes, MK9 2BE
www.authorhouse.co.uk
Phone: 08001974150

First published by AuthorHouse 4/27/2006

ISBN: 1-4259-1062-9 (sc)

Printed in the United States of America
Bloomington, Indiana

This book is printed on acid-free paper.

This novel is based on the true-life story of Imani McClendon.
The places are real. The events and situations are real.
The characters names are imaginary.

"He whose mind is stayed on me,
I will keep in perfect peace."

Isaiah Chapter 26 Vs. 3

PREFACE

I am a product of a hapless cycle of disillusion, bestowed upon a depraved bunch of folk to whom my beginnings and the red of my blood make me kin. I have been torn by the sins of my father's past. Pockmarked by the sins of my mother's past and degraded by my own doing.

Embrace the children of my flesh, Dear Lord, and shower grace upon the babies of my womb. Cradle them in arms of forgiveness and let not their joys be trampled for the wrongs I've done. The yearning to spread their wings is intolerable, and their wanting for a better way will never cease.

There is a little girl inside me who speaks as a child, but because she is all grown up now, there will be times when she also speaks from the heaving breasts of a woman. Yet somewhere inside - there is still that little girl. Our thoughts, this little girl's and mine, overlap sometimes as we attempt to bring you our story, which before we could never bear.

Soft spoken in the meekness of her youth, this broken child has arrived to have her say. To all who watched and did not see and to all who listened, but never heard, look at the side of a milk carton or hold a candle to your cheek and look inside a mirror. Do you know where I might find – this little girl?

You know the lyrics to my life's song,
Dear Lord.

You know the melody
in the absence of mere words.

Thank you for this longing in my belly
and for the words to color these pages
with a stroke of truth.

Thanks for a forgiving spirit
and may these writings be your will.

To God be the glory.

TABLE OF CONTENTS

CHAPTER 1

FAMILY SNAPSHOTS

LETTER TO DADDY

When I think of you, Daddy, my tangled thoughts perplex me like my matted nappy hair, unraveling, but hard to comb.

Where are my sisters and why ain't 'dey home? If not for ignorance, there would be no streamers, Daddy. 'Cause' it ain't no celebrating a life dropped in a toilet bowl on Christmas Eve.

You beat her. The bigger her belly, the more you beat her. Then how brazen of you to dump the fetus in the garbage pail like it was a piece of trash. I thank God you will be prosecuted and I hope they cage you under the jail.

"Bzz – bzzz"
"Grandma," Cedric whispers. "You got a fly."
"Bzz—zzz. Bzzz."

"Grandma, a fly on your nose." Grandma's nose wrinkles - and that's when my brother Cedric SMACKS that fly.

"Look at her," Celia says. Grandma springs from her chair. Eyes wide open.

"Yup," Minnie nods, "she drunk"

"Um hmm – and look at 'dem eyes. Don't she look like a fish – jumped outa' water?" They fall out laughin' like 'dey is at a circus.

"Who you?" she hollers. Cedric's mouth drops.

"Cedric – I'm Cedric, Grandma."

"Bertie's boy?" Grandma frowns – looking outa' one eye.

"No – Annie Belle."

"Ohh –" Her eyelids flash. Bottom lip hangs low, like a wad of dough on a chicken pie, glasses slapped cockeyed. Cedric stands quiet, watchin', until Grandma's eyes close. Her head drops back.

"Grandma," he whispers. "Can you see me, Grandma?" He grabs her chin with his little fingers. "Grandma, pick your face up."

Cement cylinder blocks pile high and an old oven rack is stacked on top. It's summertime! Everybody is here and not one invited guest. My mom's got ten brothers and sisters and they pack a yard full. Not even Mr. Ellis, the red faced white man from across the way, gets an invite. He just drags his saggy rear over from the row houses on the other side of the street.

"Boy," Aunt Bertie yells. She's my mom's sister. "Go on and play with the other kids and leave your grandma alone." She carries a big bowl of potato salad to the table and slides it down right next to the collard greens. Aunt Bea shuffles across the graveled lot barefoot, carrying a big plastic water pitcher, full with lemon-iced tea. My Daddy sits watchin', hands resting and folded in his lap. He looks down to her feet and sniggers at the sight of her, then shakes his head in disbelief.

"You is one flat footed woman," he says. "I swear 'fore God, I ain't never seen no sucha thing in all my days."

Aunt Bea is a large woman who don't never wear no shoes. Mommy says Aunt Bea's got velvet slippers, when really it's just crust building up underneath.

"Woman, your feet so hard you could walk on hot coals and never feel it." He clowns her without a smile on his face.

"You mind your damned business," Aunt Bea tells him.

"You ought' be shamed", "walkin' 'round barefoot – lookin' like an ol' yard-dog."

Aunt Bea rolls her eyes and shoves her nose in the air. Daddy's face cracks with silent laughter. His eyes tear up with water and his shoulders shake.

Big bottles of liquor sit tall on a cloth-covered collapsible table. Folk are guzzling pickled tonic-water, too fast to realize they are already drunk. Uncle Leroy, he's married to Aunt Bertie. He juggles a glass, eats a hotdog and flips burgers all at the same time. His eyes move closer together each time he sets the glass down.

"Hi baby," Aunt Tootsie smiles, showing spaces in her mouth where teeth used to be. "Come 'mere and give your Auntie a kiss. I wuv you." She giggles and falls over to wrap her arms around me. Her head trembles and a grin stays plastered to her face.

"Ya better watch it 'der, Tootsie. You look like you ain't feelin' no pain."

"I'm alright." Auntie giggles and Mom reaches into the ice-bucket and pops a beer of her own.

"You feelin' pretty good 'der yourself, Annie Belle." Aunt Tootsie jokes.

"All right now," Mom laughs, before both sisters turn their cans upside down.

"Every time I look at you, Annie Belle, you're pregnant."

Uh-oh, that's Aunt Trudy. NOBODY can talk so loud. She's my grandpop's sister.

"Aunt Trudy, – h-e-e-e-y!"

"Hi Tootsie! Aunt Trudy says. Everybody is excited. Aunt Tootsie and my mom reach to hug Aunt Trudy, but Aunt Trudy reaches to put her hand over my mom's belly.

"Annie Belle, I'm gonna tell you the truth, you look like you're pregnant to me."

Really I don't think my mom wants no more babies. Her belly stays big from the nine of us she's already got. When Mom tells Aunt Trudy she's not pregnant, Aunt Trudy hollers, "Well, thank God for that!" and laughs out loud. Aunt Trudy fires questions like a semi automatic and talks faster than a moving train.

"When you comin' to church with me Anne Belle – AND BRING THEM KIDS with you, too! Somebody oughta' tell 'em about the Lord. SOMEBODY!"

"Hey – Aunt Trudy!

"Hi Lonzo!" Aunt Trudy smiles. "Boy you are the spittin' image of your father. You look just like Pop, where is Pop, anyway?"

"He's over there." Aunt Tootsie points the way to where my grandpop is sittin' under a tree and bitin' into an onion, like he's eatin' an apple. At the same time Uncle 'Lonzo reaches his arms, but Aunt Trudy smacks him and draws back.

"Uh-uh," she says. "Boy, you smell just like you been rollin' 'round in a distillery." She giggles, playfully. "You can kiss me some other time. I don't know what's wrong with you people. Ya drink too much for me. And why your pants so tight?" She laughs out loud. Uncle 'Lonzo laughs louder.

"What you mean – why my pants so tight? 'Dis is what 'dey wearin'." He spins around on his toes to show off his skinny legged pants, snapped tight around his waist. Then Uncle 'Lonzo licks his hand and slides his palms across his straightened hair to fix it back in place. Everybody bursts out laughing, 'cept Uncle Buster.

"Damn, 'Lonzo! If you can't hold your liquor – don't drink. – Faggot." Uncle Buster don't like it when nobody step on his new shoes. He's young, buck wild and don't mind a good fight.

"Fuck you," Uncle 'Lonzo says - after Uncle Buster walks away.

"What da hell you niggas' got to do all 'dat swearin' fer?"

"Fuck you old man." That's what Uncle Buster thinks. My daddy just look at em wit' his nose turned up, like he's smellin' somethin' foul.

Aunt Trudy grabs her pocketbook. "Come on Tess, Mildred!" She hollers for her sisters. "Let's go. Where's Mae?"

"You'll leavin' already Aunt Trudy? Mom asks. "You just got here."

"I can't stay 'round here," she laughs, "these niggers fight too much for me. I guess its time for me to go. Annie Belle," she yells, "I'll have to come see you some other time," and she turns to walk away.

"What's 'dat you say 'der nigga'?"

"Shut up ol' man – 'for I put my foot up your ass."

Daddy springs to his feet. He don't care nothin' 'bout them brothers. He says they drink too much and they're good-for nothin'. He calls 'em lazy and says they wouldn't work in a pie factory shewing flies. "If I had my way," Daddy says, "I would blow all 'dem no good niggas' brains out, 'cause 'dey too stupid to know 'dey ass from a hole in the ground." Thanks to God, my daddy don't have his way, and I pray he never do. Daddy's fists ball up like he wanna' punch somethin'. Uncle Buster's hand reaches inside his pocket. Now a bottle flies across the table. From where I sit or from where I hide, it looks more like a bar room brawl. One of 'dem old stick-'em -up cowboy movies. The only things missing are the ten-gallon hats and maybe stirrups for 'der boots. Sometimes I wish for a stallion or two hitched to the back porch. That way they could ALL ride off into the sunset.

"They did a nice job on him." That's what Aunt Tessy say.

"Um-hmm", Aunt Mae cries and wipes the water from her eyes.

"If I didn't know no better," Aunt Mildred sniffles, "I'd say he was sleep."

Aunt Trudy raises the veil on her velvet church hat and looks 'em all in the eye.

"I don't know what you all are cryin' bout'." Her voice echoes through the sanctuary. "Daddy is gone home to glory. PRAISE GOD!" Everybody turns and looks.

"Oh Lord," Uncle Buster says, "der go Aunt Trudy – who got her started?" He looks at her wit' a long drawn face. "That's why I hate funerals," he whispers. "All 'dat hollerin' ain't needed."

"Preach!" Aunt Trudy shouts, "preach Pastor!" Her feet pound the floor and the pews shake. Uncle Buster rolls his eyes and sticks a finger in his ear. Uncle 'Lonzo giggles and Aunt Tootsie smirks. "HALLELUJAH! THANK YOU JESUS!" Aunt Trudy's church hat trembles side to side with the motion of her head, swinging forward and falling back. "YEAH! YEAH!" She rallies him on. "All right, now!" she hollers louder. "YES LORD! HALLELUJAH!"

Suddenly, the pastor gets quiet. He mops the sweat from his forehead, wipes the spit off his mouth and takes a sip of water. The lid on the casket goes shut.

"One, two, three." Mom says we should never count the funeral cars. "Seven, eight, nine." And she says that doing so will only bring us bad luck. "Twelve, thirteen, fourteen, fifteen, sixteen … "Today is great-granddaddy's homecoming. Well, ain't death in itself, bad luck? "Don't let a black cat cross your path," she says. "Don't break a mirror, it brings seven years bad luck. If a spider spins a web before you, more bad luck – and when your left eye twitches …" I don't get it. Mommy never explained how I was to go about getting good luck.

I raise myself from my seat at the rear of the vehicle to see the beaming headlamps from a mighty rumbling caravan. All the funeral cars suddenly stop in a line, one in front the other.

"Why we stoppin'?"

"Just be still, we'll be goin' in a minute."

A police officer motions, but the cars keep driving through. Then one minute goes by and two more. All of a sudden the rear car door flies open and Uncle Buster takes off. He runs down the middle of the street and across the parking lot, weaving in between the cars, before entering the front door of a liquor store.

"Uncle Buster gonna git left." Now 'dat's what I think. The big hearse drives forward and the family car moves behind. Then I see Uncle Buster with a brown paper bag tucked under his arm, running like one of them famous football players heading for a touchdown. Just in time, with the door hanged open and one foot skatin' the gravel on the ground, Uncle Buster drags his other leg inside. The car door slams and the slow moving car rolls away.

An entire lamp-lit motorcade of mud-logged tires meanders down the stretch of a slick path, before resting at the roadside. Drivers and passengers remain in their vehicles to witness a shiny brown casket slipped from the back of a long hearse, then into the able arms of several stone-faced men, dressed in black. The hefty box is lowered onto the ground, right beside a fresh mound of soft dark dirt. Only moments pass until a mob of mourning onlookers, including me, surround the site of another plot belonging to another family member laid to rest. It is a different sort of gathering under the pitter-patter of a rainy sky. Aunt Tess says her mother is buried here and her brother Bodine, and on she goes. It is sort of like a family reunion, the only gatherings we have now, since the family fell apart. Uncle 'Lonzo, Uncle Melvin, Uncle Buster, and all my grandpop's sisters are here.

Aunt Tess is all the time fussin', when beneath all that talk is a soft ol' lady, just trying not to get her heart jerked. Everybody says Aunt Mildred is crazy. Some say she even spent time in the crazy house. But, I don't care that she talks to herself or that she wears a winter coat and scarf in the summertime. I like the way she giggles. Aunt Mae pinches my arms, and twists my skin and Aunt Trudy just likes talking about the Lord. But to hear it told, Aunt Trudy is even crazier than Aunt Mildred. I don't listen much to all that talk about my Aunties. I'm just glad they are here.

"Annie Belle, you all are comin' to the repast now, ain't cha'?"

"Yeah, Aunt Trudy, we'll come by for a little bit."

"Please – come on by," Aunt Trudy says, "and have some cake and coffee."

"Cake and coffee? Hmmph," Mom says, when Aunt Trudy ain't lookin'. "I'll drop by for a minute or two," she whispers to Uncle Melvin, "then I'm goin' home and git me a drink."

"I know that's right." Uncle Melvin laughs hoarsely and nods a simple grin. When all is through, I hug my Aunties, say goodbye to Uncle Buster and we go about our way.

❄

A few days ago we packed our belongings in cardboard boxes. Mommy said we were movin' up, when really we just moved to the other side of town. Pink and white magnolia petals spray the ground, and a weeping-willow tree marks the center of the yard. There is a rock garden and miniature peach tree that grows real fruit, lilac bushes and a grapevine weaving in and out of a long pathway. I like the morning glories best of all and the double-sided shed. If I had my way, I would make it a playhouse with real curtains and a table and chairs. My mom likes the built-in barbeque grill, and she's the best cook ever. But my daddy says her spoil comes in the bottle.

He's bullheaded and has the evil eye of a humped-backed cat with hairs on end and waiting to strike. But nobody knows that better than sweet Annie Belle. My daddy is old enough to be her daddy, with eighteen years between them. But, I think my mom Annie Belle loves him better than she loves her last breath. She lived in a one-room garage with a dirt floor, until she met my daddy. Now she's got a house all her own and still she stays sad most times, drinkin' and frownin'. It used to be my mom wouldn't drink a lick. Now she tucks a whiskey bottle in her pocketbook, so Daddy won't see.

"Look at you – you nappy headed so and so." She wears an old, print housedress with pockets in the sides and her hair stands like a dust mop on top her head. "Why don't you comb ya' hair and put some clothes on." Daddy yells, then plucks her upside her head like a coconut. He marks her face with lumps and embarrasses her in public. Her face stays broken in hives, half from worry and some from drinking. She's tired, trying to please him, like anybody would. He done run all her family away. When school opens again, I'm gonna be a third grader and I didn't' see Uncle Buster, not since I was in kindergarten. I think my mom is maybe missing Uncle Buster.

It's ninety-seven degrees, and it don't matter to Daddy that it's Independence Day. The sun shines hot and he layin' on the ground and working under his car. It don't matter 'bout the grass, neither. He parked the car on top of it. Nobody shows up much no more, ever since that big fight. If it weren't for Uncle Melvin, there wouldn't be visitors at all. He comes every Sunday with a pocket full of silver dollars. Mom's family cut the fool a lot, making cracks and taking cheap shots, until somebody gets mad and goes to swingin'. But not Uncle Melvin, he couldn't hurt a fly. I'm glad for Uncle Melvin and you can bet Mr. Ellis is too, the red faced white man from our old neighborhood. He visits wherever we live. Mr. Ellis is retired. He leaves his wife at home and takes up time on weekends watching the New York Mets get whooped. Today is a double header against the Cincinnati Reds playing out on a small black and white TV, hooked up in the backyard to a long extension cord. Aunt Bea and Mr. Ellis sit around, sipping tea and screaming at the tiny picture on the screen. Aunt Trudy – she comes, now and again, and sometimes Aunt Tess. I can't say that I blame the rest. Watching my Daddy wring a dishcloth through the middle and draw the ends tight around my sister Minnie's neck makes me shiver. Her head swells to twice the size and her eyes run water. Then he laughs straight out loud.

Suddenly I think about that homemade ice-cream. We churn it ourselves in a wooden bucket and fight over whose turn it is to crank the handle. My big sister Celia, she's the oldest. Minnie is the second oldest, then Alfreda and Nadine. Next, come Ernestine, then Cedric and finally, Rhonda and Giselle.

Having four older sisters, three younger and one brother younger, makes me the middle child. It's ten of us kids, when I count cousin Toby; he's Aunt Bea's boy. Having Cousin Toby is just like having one more brother and I like that 'cause he's the same age as me.

"Move."

"No – it's my turn."

"No it ain't."

"Yes it is."

"Move."

When my turn is through and after sitting in the blazing sun and sipping Kool-Aid half the day, I rush inside to use the toilet. The door slams. I lick my lips, "hmm" – and do my business, thinking about homemade ice cream. Then – flush-shh-shh, I'm done. The door knob turns, and the big door opens. When I go back into the hallway, I see Mr. Ellis. He ain't watchin' no more ball game. He watchin' me. He hushes me with a finger over his mouth. And with the same pale, curled finger he tells me to come. I step close and he takes hold to my hand. Quiet as can be. He guides me to a nearby room and lifts me on a quilted bed. Mr. Ellis licks spit on his fingers, then, slides his hand between my knees. In a little while he lifts me on my feet and smoothes my clothes. Mr. Ellis smiles. He nods his head and puts a quarter in my hand. "Shh" He makes the sound, so I don't tell.

Before, when I seen my sister Minnie go behind that same door, Mr. Ellis gave her two quarters. Minnie – she don't never tell. But now Minnie got a secret, the same like me.

Aunt Bea forgot to take us to the fireworks. It's already dark, when I hear a big crash. It sounds like thunder coming through the trees. "Ooh!" We scream at all the pretty colors. And when it is through, ain't nothin' left to do, just watch my Daddy pop dummy shots from a fire spittin' gun. A shadow falls over a banister.

"Nigga', you thought you was dead, didn't ya." My Daddy laughs so hard, tears run down his face.

My mouth stretches to yawn. I think I will have some more of that homemade ice-cream. "Nah," I think I'll go to bed.

First comes summer, then comes winter. Then comes summer, and again comes winter. Tomorrow is Christmas and it feels like electricity rushing from my head to my toes. I'm hoping for a baby doll, but I don't 'spect I'll get one of my own. Me and my sisters got four baby dolls to share between us. But, half of 'em don't have no hair. It all got pulled out from

too much combing, except just a patch or two. One of 'em is missing its eyeballs and the other got two eyeballs, but they pushed way back inside its head. The big baby-doll hasn't got no head and the other one's face is cracked. I want a colored baby doll. Never had one of 'dem before. I only had blue-eyed babies with missing arms and legs.

"Look! A toy soldier!"

"Ooh! Can I hang it?" Cedric squeals. He don't care. He just ripped it from my sister Ernestine.

"Gim-me!"

"Celia! Cedric's snatchin' agin!" Cedric takes off. But Ernestine is fast on his heels, grabbing for the tail of his shirt waving behind. Whoa! He slams square into Celia. Celia snatches him in his collar, while Ernestine slaps him in the back of his head. Cedric crinkles his nose and gives Ernestine his middle finger.

"Brat!"

"Cut it out!" Celia yells, yanking the toy soldier from Cedric's dirty little hands. "Can't yawl do nothin' without fightin? Here Ernestine."

Ernestine slides herself and sprawls clear across the floor, twirling the shiny decoration between her fingers. She twirls it round and round. Cedric giggles, then creeps and squats behind her. Just when he is sure that Ernestine won't look around, his tickly little fingers walk straight up the back of her neck. Ernestine jumps up and starts to hollering. Cedric rolls on his belly, giggling so hard I think he will bust. Celia slaps him – clean upside his bald-shaved head.

"So … it didn't hurt!" Cedric thinks everything is funny. "Ahh-hahh, didn't even hurt!"

"Ya better go-on boy!" Celia warns, "'fore I knock ya little head off."

Another year is gone and ain't much changed since the Christmas before. Rhonda and Giselle do belly flops all over the living room rug. Nadine tries to strike Boogie Woogie on our old piano. Me? I sit beside her plucking high notes out of key. Celia is tacking Christmas cards all around the doorway, and she strung colored balls all over our naked, skinny tree. I think when I look at it, some of its branches maybe fell off. But, it only cost two dollars. Daddy says six dollars is too much to pay for a fresh cut tree.

The front door hinge squeaks and Minnie walks in to take a warming, after shoveling the snow. Fresh flakes lay like a collar on her shoulders, outlining her not-so-slender frame. She slips out of her soggy mittens and blows her warm breath into her icy hands. She eases out of her coat. Tosses it over the banister and vanishes up the stairs. Celia and Minnie are in charge, while Mommy works, cleaning house for some white people, a well-to-do Jewish lady and her lawyer husband. Aunt Bea took cousin Toby shopping. They live with us, though Aunt Bea ain't ask none of us to go. Cousin Toby is an only kid and Aunt Bea spoils him rotten. Alfreda, she's just twelve years old and she should be having fun, right along with me. But she's on punishment in the bathroom sitting on the floor crying her eyes out. I know 'cause the door was wide open and I could see her.

"What's the matter, Alfreda?" I keep asking her. But, she don't answer me back. "Alfreda, do your stomach hurt?"

She stays doubled over, grabbing hold to her belly like she got a bellyache. She don't say nothin', but her tears don't stop, just keep rolling down the sides of her face. I run into the bathroom, then back in the living room and sit next to Nadine. Soon again, I run to the bathroom. Then, back in the living room and sit next to Nadine. Running back and forth to take a peek. I think I hear her holler; but it's hard to tell when Nadine keeps banging on the piano so hard. I slide off the bench and race to the sound. But, Alfreda ain't sittin' on the floor no more. She just squattin' over the toilet stool, drawers dropped 'round her feet. Her cheeks are wet with tears. Big veins pop from the sides of her neck. Her eyes stretched so wide, it looks like her eyeballs gonna pop. And she don't stop hollering.

"My kidneys are fallin' out! My kidneys are fallin' out!" When I see her, I just start screaming, jumping and screaming! WAILING – to the tops of my lungs.

"Alfreda's kidneys are fallin' out!" Then I hear my big sister Celia calling back.

"Edwina, what's the matter? What's goin' on!" My hands slap my ears and my mouth pops open.

"Alfreda's kidneys are falling out!" is all my mouth can say. Same words over and over – feet glued to the spot.

Now, Minnie runs down the L-shaped staircase. She sweeps the banister with her hand and leaps over the whole bottom flight. She and Celia run into each other when they rush from opposite ends of the house. They stand beside me in front of the open door. Soon everybody is there, Nadine, Cedric, Rhonda, Giselle, Ernestine – all standing with 'dey eyes stretched. Until Celia shoves our tongue-dropped, dirty faces back into the living room. The bathroom door slams shut and Celia stays stuck behind that door, while Minnie calls my mom at work. Mommy comes in a hurry, then my daddy and next the family doctor. Seems everybody is behind that closed door.

Everybody wanna know what happened. All I know is what I saw, and still I don't know.

CHAPTER 2

RUPERT THURMAN JORDAN

Every holiday seems smeared with trouble. On Easter Sunday He rose from the dead," so the Bible tells it. My daddy rose up shootin' blanks from the barrel of a fire-spittin' pistol. Me and Minnie stooped behind a long dresser, duckin' shots. Today it ain't no holiday and I'm glad for it. The Christmas lights have been safely packed away in their little boxes in the attic, where they will collect dust for another year.

"Br-rr-ding", a little alarm clock sounds a little bell at six-forty-five in the morning. I pull the blankets over my head, wishing for another hour, but soon roll out of bed. School is scheduled to reopen. Alfreda runs barefoot across a cold tiled floor to the bathroom as the thermostat reaches a less than modest peak. Cedric waits. So cold, he's plopped his narrow butt clear across the heater's iron floor vent. His knees draw near his chest and a dingy tee-shirt drapes like a tent. He wraps his feet and traps the heat, slow to rise. Minnie profiles in front of a full-length mirror, doing the do to her hair, while Celia stuffs her too-thick hiney into a straight skirt, two sizes too small. Nadine washes in the basin downstairs and the rest of us wait.

"Woman, ain't you done cooked dem eggs yet?" "What da hell takin' you so long?" Dad yells, when eventually I arrive downstairs to the aroma of bacon frying. Mommy sighs a deep breath. But, soon come the bacon and eggs, fluffed and soft. She flips them from a cast iron fryer. "It took ya' long enough." Daddy complains.

He reaches with his neck when Celia walks into the kitchen. His face frowns as his eyes examine her with a rhythmic flow from head to toe. His stubby nostrils flare at the sight of his daughter's swollen behine' in a tight-tail dress.

"What?" he says, his cheeks are swollen with food and jaws working like a malnourished, underprivileged poster child. "You cain't speak?"

"G'mornin," She murmurs.

"Moanin'." He snaps as Celia takes her seat beside me.

"Gal," (girl) He scowls, "Why 'dat der waist you wearin' so snug?" It looks like a skirt to me.

Nobody calls a skirt a *waist*, except Daddy, and maybe other folk from where he come.

"Annie Belle!" He yells.

Mom is sullen, slamming dishes and making a clatter. You can't much get her to part her lips in his presence. It is the identical, same story every morning. If it ain't the tight skirt, the coffee is too hot, or breakfast too slow coming.

"Ain't no sense in no young gal' goin' out lookin' like … lookin' like"… He stutters. "Look rhat (right) whorish to me. Ain't 'dat der youngin' got nuttin' better she kin' put on her triflin' behine'?"

"Girl, go-on upstairs and find something else to put on!" Mom shouts. She pacifies him instead of telling him what she really feels.

Celia disappears and Minnie arrives. She whispers "G'mornin'," then scoots low in her seat. She bobs her head, says her grace and digs in with an oversized spoon. Daddy watches bitterly.

"When 'dem 'der other triflin'-ass, good-fo'-nothin' youngins' gonna brang dey behines down heah?"

Again, it is just another situation to complain about. Mommy hastens to the bottom of the stairs. "You'll git your behines down here! RIGHT-NOW! LET'S GO!" she shouts the command. Suddenly Daddy's attention is drawn to the dulling wall behind the kitchen table.

"Minnie!" He calls her name twice more, "Minnie! Minnie!" He demands and points annoyingly. "Git' 'dat der cocker' roach climbin' up d'-wall der." Minnie's eyes stretch wide, while pulling a big spoon from her dropped mouth. Swallowing really hard, she turns her head slowly to have a look. "Rhat' der, rhat' der," Daddy yells. "STUPID ASS!"

STUPID-ASS is a proper noun. I think it must be Minnie's middle name. Her name, my name, Mom's name, he calls us all STUPID-ASS. Daddy has no patience. It must have fallen out in his diaper, or in the womb. To say he loses his temper is an understatement. He gets angrier by the second and goes from cold to hot without measure. He pounces, suddenly grabbing a greasy work cap by its snapped visor and hanged over the post of his chair. He lunges! All the while reaching clear across Minnie's breakfast bowl. The cockroach falls to the table and paddles upright next to the sugar bowl. Daddy lunges again, this time shoving the table off center. The chair flips. He swats! With a yank he drops the slime to the floor, then lifts his fork and starts back eating.

Minnie gags and a momentary hush falls over the room. Suddenly…

"Why dey ain't no shuga in 'de' shuga-bowl?" His temper climbs at the notice of it. "Dogonnit!"

Mommy slams a five-pound paper sack on the table before me. Then swings her back to Daddy and continues dousing dishes in a dishpan full with soapy water. When his eyes meet mine my head lowers.

"Gal, fill 'dat der bowl," he says. "Triflin' ass niggas' ain't good fo' nothin'. Won't much as put shuga in the bowl when dey sees it's empty. "Annibelle" he calls. Where's da coffee I ask ya 'fer? Ya ain't forgot I asks 'fer a cup o'coffee, is ya?

"For Christ's sake, Rupert!" she yells angrily, "I only got two hands!" Daddy don't say nothin' and there is an upset, a fog of hostility settling in the air.

I lift the bag of sugar, trembling nervously for the grains that scatter the table with the flow.

"What 'da hell ya wastin' it fer? DUMMY! His thick knuckles flail in a backhanded motion, just missing my face. "I oughta … "His words trail off into cold silence, then quickly he shouts, "STUPID-BEHINE'!" Suddenly he notices Celia is back and wearing a sack-dress, as he would say. Kind of like a pillowcase or the paper sack the sugar is in, which pleases him. I am certain Celia is not impressed. She is a sixteen-year-old junior in high school and would much rather dress like others her age. Just when Minnie shovels in the last of her cereal, Alfreda hurries into the kitchen to sit in Minnie's emptied seat.

"G'mornin', she says softly. Daddy doesn't notice, just turns to look at the big wall clock. "Well ah guess ah betta be gittin' on to wuk." he says. until, Giselle eases into the little bathroom set next to the kitchen and the light flashes on.

"Annibelle! Who 'dat in the bafroom 'der, wastin' lectwicity (electricity)? Dad hollers.

"Giselle, turn 'dat light off" Mom yells.

"Hell, whatcha' thinks I got shares in the power company? Don't pays no bills 'round heah."

Mommy sets a hot cup on the table before him.

"Darn! Woman," he says, "took ya so long, I just 'bout forgot I ask."

Mom's eyes roll inside her head. Dad's nose crinkles when he grins a soured grin. He lifts the steamy cup by its handle. His head swings back and he swallows boiling coffee, hot enough to blow holes in his belly. His head jolts and the cup slams the table.

"What da hell you tryin' to do, Woman!" Daddy's eyes flash like fire, "scald me to death?"

"Hell" she says, "you oughta' known it was hot."

"Oh — you is one a dem smart mouth Negroes." He winces sarcastically. "Come on ova' heah and let me thump you upside your head," he says, shoving the cup and wasting hot coffee over the sides. "Heah, you kin have 'dat." He tells her, then tosses his hat onto his balding head and goes out the door.

Celia and Alfreda finish up. Cedric, Toby, Ernestine, Nadine, Rhonda and Giselle eat. Soon we gather our books, hop into our coats, then out to school we go.

Every day Ernestine runs so fast, she gets to school before me. Soon I lace my shoes, grab my lunch and say goodbye.

I run my fastest. "I did it. I did it! Ah hah!" I tease my sister Ernestine. "I got to school before you." But Ernestine ain't so happy 'bout 'dat. She hauls off and hits me square in my face.

At the close of the school day a dinner of leftover split pea soup has been warmed over. It don't matter that somebody forgot to set the pot in the fridge overnight.

"Should I give it to the dogs?" I ask earnestly.

"Give it to the dogs? What you tryin' to be a wise mouth? What you mean, give it to the dogs?" He scolds. My nose turns up. My hand waves briskly, fanning the vapors of an awful whiff.

"What you fanning your nose fer?" He says. "It ain't nuttin' wrong wit' 'dat soup."

The soup is sour. It will be served, anyway. Gobs of greasy fatback float to the top of a huge pot and the taste is worse than the smell. My belly retches and I gag with every mouthful. The fatback hides beneath my tongue. Then when nobody is watchin', I spew it into the toilet bowl. Just in time, before I barf.

With dinner out of the way and the dishes washed, dark falls early. Minnie, Celia and Alfreda hurry to their rooms, having wit enough to stay out of Daddy's sight. The younger bunch, we swarm playfully between the kitchen and the dining rooms. Creating the typical back and forth mayhem stirred between kids. Squealing little girls expend lots of giggling, exhausting idle energy left over at the day's end.

And now comes Cedric, my misfit brother to kick his foot square up my rear. I shriek! He snickers with pleasure and muffles his toothless mouth with his mischievous little hands.

"Ma!" I scream, flying into the kitchen and rubbing my backside – just in time to see Rupert Thurman Jordan, my daddy, RISE FROM A PIT OF HELL. The heat of blood rushes to his face. His mouth wads like a closed fist. Barely do I escape his grasp before sinking my already aching bottom inside a big-armed chair.

He roars like thunder! "Damn it! Yawl sit yawl monkey asses down somewhere. 'Dis heah ain't no jungle!" Now, Mommy is screaming.

"You kids sit your behines down somewhere, before I make you go to bed early."

"Annie Belle!" He yells. His wrath is evidenced in the flicker of his eyelids. They flash open then shut. Flickering fast like blinking lights.

Playful giggles are shut-up behind hushed walls and tender mouths gape. "Cain't you control 'dem der youngins, Annie Belle? He hovers over me. "Dey acts like a bunch of wild heathens! You hoodlums – set yawl's ignant' behines down somewhere. Pick up a book! Write! Read! Do somethin' constructive for a change!" His chest heaves and eyes flutter, until finally he goes back to his seat.

Night has been shut down and the moment silenced. Eight o'clock and already it is time to prepare for bed. But not before Daddy sends me to his room for his chocolate covered pecans. Katydids, expensive treats, two dollars and fifty cents a can. Calmer now, he says.

"Edwina, go on upstairs in my dresser and brang 'dat can of Katydids."

"Katydids?" I ask softly. I'd never heard of Katydids.

"Candy! – Candy," he stutters, -"S-T-U-P-I-D!" He calls me by my other name.

And why should I know that Katydids are chocolate-coated pecans and caramel? He keeps them stashed away in his drawer.

"Go on up der and look. Dey is settin' right in my dresser, second drawer from the top, on the right. Ya cain't miss 'em. And don't open the can fer ya gets back down here neither," he remarks with a snarl.

I retrieve the tin can just where instructed; in the right-hand side of the second dresser drawer, directly between his .45-automatic-pistol and a box of unspent caps. I return with goods in hand.

"You ain't open the can and take none, 'fer ya brangs 'em, did ya?" My eyes stretch wide, my head shakes "no", as I place the can before him. He leans forward mysteriously, palming his thick knuckles flat over the lid of the container. He shields its view as if inside there lay a million dollars. Daddy peers with intensity, deliberate and methodical.

"Who 'dat got sticky fingas? Which one of ya, huh?" In the stillness of the moment his eyes search the room. He waits for our reply. We say nothing. "Ain't nobody got nuttin' to say?" he asks. "Let me put it to you 'dis way", he says slowly. Who 'dat been in my room, stealing my candy?"

We chime. "Not me!" In unison, "Not me!"

"Not me" he mimics with a soured smirk. "Somebody been stealin' my candy. Which one of ya is it? It ain't take up legs and walk." Then he asks. "Who da liar?" He smirks a crafty grin. "Da one who lying, tell da other one to hush." It is a twisted attempt to trap us with his words. With the coldness of heart and a devious smile, Daddy lets another somber moment follow. Suddenly he releases his grip over the lid. He removes the top and offers up the can before our drooling faces.

"Have some," he says with contempt.

"Yes, thank you." We receive in our hand, with dulled excitement and genuine gratitude, one piece each. He reseals the lid and shoves the container to the table's center.

"It's two things I hates," Daddy tells us, "and I don't know which one I hates more," he says; "and, 'dats a LIAR and a THIEF." We watch in fear as we nibble on the tiny morsel of caramel-coated pecans covered with chocolate. His head swings back and he pops a Katydid of his own. His mouth grinds repetitiously and I hear the crackle of crunching nuts. Daddy's words are frigid. Quickly he tosses another Katydid. "I bet if I puts rat poison in dis heah can," he grins skillfully, "bet I finds out which of you little niggas been stealin' my candy."

Suddenly, "You'll go on upstairs and get some rest," Mommy says. "It's time to get ready for bed."

"Ma, can we watch TV before we go to sleep?"

"One program," she admonishes, "then you'll turn that TV off and take your butts to sleep, you gotta' get up for school in the morning."

"YAY!" Everybody squeals with delight, trampling for the stairs, like wild stallions.

"Walk!" She yells the command. The clatter of little feet slows to a gentle patter. "What you waitin' for? Do you think you get special privilege?" Mom asks, looking at me. "Go on upstairs, like everybody else."

"I don't feel good," I whine. "I got a headache."

"I didn't know wood ache." Dad's full of sarcasm.

"Girl, every night, you got some kinda complaint. You're just sleepy. I can see it in your eyes. Go on upstairs and go to bed." With that, I say goodnight.

⁂

I hug the comfort of a woolen blanket on a full-sized bed. One I fondly share with my big sister Minnie. I don't mind shoving my back to the wall to make room for my little cousin Nathaniel. He's staying over and he's sleeping next to me. Minnie sits at the edge of the bed under a dim light, finishing up her studies. But I am sleepy. My eyelids fall.

"One, two, three ..." Mommy says counting sheep brings sleep in a hurry. One behind the other I visualize them leaping over a long wooden fence. I hug my pillow, my rest is snug and sweet dreams come easy. Quickly I drift away. Then Minnie begins to rock me to and fro.

"Wake up! Edwina!"

"What? Leave me alone," I roll over with a groan, then fall back to sleep.

"Edwina, wake up", she whispers impatiently. "You woke, huh, you woke?"

"Um woke, Um woke?" I look at my big sister with one eye open. "What?" and listen to her with half an ear.

"Edwina, Daddy said he's coming in our room tonight. He said I better sleep in something where he can get to me easy." I don't know what Minnie is talkin' 'bout. And I'm too sleepy to care. "When he comes in I'm gonna wake you up, okay?" My eyelids flutter. "Do you hear me, Edwina?" She pinches me.

"Oww! What you doin'? Why you pinchin' me?" I growl.

"Edwina! WAKE UP!" Trust me, I'm woke. But, if Minnie's got something to say, she better say it fast. I wanna go back to sleep.

"I want you to start squirming, alright? When he comes in here I'm gonna pinch you." Minnie you must be out of your tree – fool! I don't tell her that, but I'm thinking it. How could I not start squirming? That hurts. "That will make him leave the room. "Okay, Edwina? Okay?" she shouts.

"Okay, yeah! Okay!"

Having heard every word, I go back to sleep. My body surrenders and sinks into the coziness of a comfortable mattress. In seconds flat I am out cold, as the night sends forty winks to greet me. I can bet the walls are holding to the ceilings for balance as the rumble of my snoring surmounts. The clock strikes twice, maybe three times, until, I feel a stiff pinch against my thigh.

"Stop it!" I say. When – My Jesus, I am fully awakened in the darkness of my room. Barely can I make sense of the form, thrusting and rocking in the bed beside me. Like a hazy image through a zoom lens, a silhouette peaks into view. It is him! Stripped naked on top of my sister and straddling her plain like day. It is him, bucking his daughter, just like Minnie told it. I gurgle deep inside my throat, like a sleep sound, fidgeting side to side. I kick the covers all over the place. Suddenly – he jumps clear off her and runs his bare bottom straight out the room. The room remains dark as Minnie springs to her feet and quickly smoothes her flimsy gown.

"Get up!" She orders me on my feet and snatches Nathaniel in her arms. She stands him upright beside her. Little Nathaniel starts to cry, conveniently working into the scheme of Minnie's plan. She takes hold of his tiny hand and guides the two of us cautiously through the space of a blackened hallway. We pass the stairwell, where the bathroom door sets parted on its hinge. Minnie hesitates for a moment, then, gives it a shove. There appears a shadow as the door flings forth. Again, it is him. Having stood watch from his vantage point in the darkness and prepared to strike. He wanders slowly past us, Minnie, little Nathaniel, and me. With a tiptoe step, he disappears behind a door and slides back into his bed next to mom.

CHAPTER 3

YOU'RE A BIG GIRL NOW

"Giselle and Rhonda, git on up 'dem stairs and change your clothes. Toby, take the trash out." Aunt Tess yells. She's come to stay awhile, with my sisters gone and all. "Edwina and Ernestine – if you'll got homework you better git it done before your father gits in." Auntie's expression turns sour when Cedric races through the kitchen. Nadine runs behind.

"Black Nigger!" Nadine screams.

"Now, don't let your father catch you talkin' like that." Auntie yells. "Nadine, you know Rupert don't play. "And Cedric what I tell you 'bout all 'dat runnin?"

"Fat turd." Cedric laughs loud and runs faster.

"What's wrong with you Edwina?" Aunt Tess asks when she looks at me. "What you doin' walking around with your face all tore-up?"

First, Celia and Minnie and now Alfreda hurried away in some ol' State Patrol car. What is wrong with me? I wish I could know.

"Go on up the stairs and get the brush so I can brush your hair." Aunt Tess tells me.

I pull my behine' up from my seat, slow and lazy.

"Girl git the lead out your ass. Move like you got some life in ya."

Then I mosey on and do as I'm told.

"I don't know what's wrong with you kids. Act like you're as old as Methuselah."

Now, I don't know who Methuselah is, but he must be pretty old.

"Sit down here." She yells. "And don't take all day!"

Aunt Tess is feisty and energetic and she don't mince her words when disciplining me. She sits in a chair, and I take a squat between her parted knees.

"Ouch!" She smacks the brush flat against my scalp. "Ouch!" I pull one way and Auntie Tess yanks another.

"Keep your head still."

"Aunt Tess, 'dat hurts."

"Chile I can't help that your head is nappy." She giggles. "Now, keep still." Soon she finishes. Hands me the brush and orders me to place it back where it belongs, on the dresser in the room where she sleeps. I drag myself up, then, mosey cross the room.

"What I tell you 'bout dragging your behine', Edwina? What's wrong with you, anyway?"

I don't say nothin'.

"What's wrong with you chile?"

"My teacher said my socks was dirty."

"What?" she scolds. "You're eleven years old, Edwina, and, big enough to wash your own socks." Soon she smiles and sighs with relief. "My God!" Aunt Tess is tickled. "I thought something was wrong. Take them socks off girl and go on up 'dem stairs." She moves me along with a shove in my back that trips me forward. "Your mother works every day, she ain't got time to be washin' clothes for all you kids." Aunt Tess guides me into the bathroom to stand before the sink. "Turn that water on." I give the faucet a spin. "Not cold water, what's wrong with you?" she yells. "Put some hot water in there." I watch as the water trickles into the basin. Aunt Tess hands me a bar of soap.

"You're too big to walk 'round stinkin', Edwina." Aunt Tess don't never stop scolding, giggling and fussing all the while.

The outer door slams at the lower landing.

"Mommy's home!" Everybody squeals.

"Rhonda," Mom hollers loud and over all the commotion, "go upstairs and get my slippers outa my room." Rhonda runs past the open doorway to grab Mom's slippers.

"Have you got clean drawls?" Aunt Tess asks me. She brings me fresh ones from her room. "Now, you should be able to fit these. Your behine' ain't that tiny," she laughs. Rhonda runs back through the hallway. Now, Ernestine hurries through. "You kids stop all 'dat runnin'." Auntie yells. She shoves a bunch of safety pins onto the bathroom sink. "If they're too big, put some pins in em." Do you hear me Edwina?" Auntie's voice rumbles like gentle thunder.

"Yes"

"Now don't wear 'dem drawls till they fall off you. Take 'em off and wash 'em. Hang 'em over the shower bar. That way you'll have a clean pair for the next day." Auntie turns and walks away.

When the dishes are back on the shelf and supper is through, Mommy pours a drink and Auntie sips the bubbles on a frosty beer. But when Auntie drinks, she talks too loud.

"'Dat ain't no tumor", Bea can tell 'dat lie to somebody else. She looks more like she's pregnant to me."

"Giselle and Cedric, Rhonda, Ernestine, and you too Edwina, you'll go on in the other room, don't you see me and your Auntie are talkin'."

The rescue squad came early this mornin'. Aunt Bea was crying with a bellyache. Sure as the days are long, Aunt Bea gave birth to a newborn baby boy and somebody say he's my daddy's baby. And now, cousin-Toby got a little brother and somehow, so do we.

Following a few days' stay in the hospital, Aunt Bea comes back home, "tumor" in arms. And when Aunt Bea comes home, Dad gets rushed in. The doctors say my daddy got a big blood clot on his brain and he'll be a vegetable, if he makes it. And they tell my mom don't be expecting for him to live too long.

The days pass and I watch you Mommy. Deep lines fold the thick skin between the corners of your eyes and tiny teardrops make their stay. Silver hairs announce their presence with each new day.

I can't imagine what you must be feeling, between Aunt Bea's new baby and Daddy's stroke. You probably don't know whether to pray for him or pull the plug. "Statue… statutory rape or somethin' like 'dat, I heard you say 'it. And somehow I don't imagine Celia and 'dem is never comin' home.

After three days he wakes up and I go with you to see him. He's got tubes coming out of everywhere and he sounds like a drunk man when he talks. I feel sorry for him. And Daddy, despite the hurtful things you bring, still I don't wish for you to die.

"Do you want to feed him?" you ask.

You proved 'dem doctors wrong, Daddy, from the day you came home. You're gettin' stronger. You squeeze a rubber ball and it squishes in your hand. When the other kids are playing, you call upon me, to close a button or fix a collar. Sometimes I even put a knot in your crumpled tie. Day turns to night, while I clip fungus-filled toenails, or pluck ingrown hairs from your stubby chin. I don't mind all that much, trimming your hair, or giving a shave if you need one. But asking me to snatch hairs from your nose is not a thing I smile about.

The grass is turning green beneath the snow. We hurry home at lunchtime and there you are propped against the stove, with a dead leg dragging behind. You scramble eggs, cheese and scrap ends of meat collected from the corner deli. It's nice of the butcher to set them aside for us.

"You know what, dad?"

"Was 'dat?" you say.

""Dis is good."

"What?" you ask playfully. "Ya thought I couldn't cook?" I smile when you tell me, "I taught ya mutha to cook."

Yeah, Dad, you are getting stronger. And just like you used to, we find you in the backyard, fixing on old cars and piling up junk. It wasn't long ago when Minnie and the others had to clean 'dem greasy pistons you like to collect. Well, if it puts food on the table, guess somebody's gotta do it. I just hate those tiny cuts in my hands; they hurt when they bleed. I hope the scrap man pays you well for all our hard work. Oh, and don't forget to trade those newspapers in the cellar we've been saving.

Oh, and Dad, 'bout those shoes you bought me from the Salvation Army Store – I know you can't afford to buy me new ones. But, they are ugly and the toes on them are so round and big. This ain't the turn of the century; its nine-teen-hundred and sixty six. Remember I told you I lost them? Well, actually I burned them. Well, not both shoes, only one. Figured if there was only one shoe, you couldn't make me wear the other. I thank God for better days, and pray to God you never find out.

When summer comes, you are driving! The doctors said you would never; but you do. Remember Palisades Park? With nothin' but time on your hands and too many free coupons, we road the Ferris Wheel, and oh yeah, the Caterpillar – all afternoon in the blazing sun. The tickets weren't good for nothin' else. The Caterpillar was cloth covered, like a green umbrella and it opened and shut like a convertible car. First we were in the light, then we were in the dark, then we were in the light, and then we were in the dark. It was enough to make me nauseous. But no Dad, really, I'm not ungrateful. With everything that has happened I don't hate you. I could never hate you. And only God gets the credit for that.

Sure I sometimes get tired, being cooped inside and seeing the other kids ride their bikes, while I listen to you talkin' 'bout 'dis or fussin' 'bout 'dat. But at the day's end, more often than not, the revelation of "mother-wit" spurts from that mangled skull of yours.

"Hold ya head up high," you tell me. "You kin' do anything you tries, if ya' puts' your mind to it. And, "Don't be like some of 'dem other good-fer-nothin'-niggas, who don't want nuttin' outta life."

"Daddy, did you finish school?" I ask.

"No. Never finished – never finished. I was promoted to the fifth grade, but I never did go."

"How come, Daddy?"

"I was nine years old and my Daddy died," he says. I left grade school to hep my mutha wuk the fields."

"How old are you now?" I ask.

"You sure do axe a lot of questions!" He winces with impatience. "I were born in nineteen-o-nine! Nineteen-o-nine." He says it twice, always repeating.

My daddy's old, I think, after doing the arithmetic in my head. Quickly, Daddy shifts to a different subject.

"Mary! Mary!" he says. Mary McLeod Bethune Cookman!" He almost yells it. "Ain't you never heerd' the name befo'e?"

"No." I answer.

"Ain't dey learn it to you in school?"

"No."

"Well, I knowed huh. I knowed huh well," he says. "She da woman what started Mary McLeod Bethune-Cookman College, named afta huh. Started to teachin' in a one-room schoolhouse, right down in South Carolina. Daddy grins. "As quiet as its kept" he says, "Ms. Mary had two daughtas she were tryin' to pawn off on me."

"Huh?"

"She were tryin' ta' pawn em', get rid of em' and put em' off on me," he says loudly. She wanted me to marry one or the other and it didn't matter which." Daddy sits quiet for a second, then he continues. "One of the two stepped over me, like stepping over a broomstick."

"Huh?"

"Superstition has it 'dat when a woman step over you 'dat way, she got her mark on ya and will soon be your wife." But Daddy's face frowns like he swallowed something sour when he tells me. "I didn't find no attraction to neither one of 'dem womens."

"Why not?" I ask. He sniggers and his face stays twisted.

"I weren't lookin' to be tied down wit 'dem der womens." He laughs. "'Dem were some UUGGLY womens." He laughs so hard his shoulders shake, cackling 'til water runs from his eyes. Suddenly, I'm giggling.

"How old was you, Daddy?" I ask, while he fingers the tears from the corners of his eyes.

"I were just a boy comin' into manhood," he recalls.

"Do you have any sisters and brothers?" His expression turns somber and his tone softens.

"I had just one brother. Flames caught hold to his gown, while he were warming his hands, tryin' to keep warm over the fire."

Daddy's gets quiet and his eyelids fall, until quickly I ask another question, so he don't have to think no more about his brother and that fire.

"Daddy, are you from South Carolina?" He looks at me with a smirk on his face and a twitch in his eye.

"Why you axe so many questions?"

Suddenly Daddy smiles a rare smile. There's talk of a juke-joint, and I imagine my Daddy dressed in a loose fit suit and a soft-knot tie. The same like the fading photo that sets atop Mom's dresser.

"As quiet as it's kept," he says with a grin, "I were quite a jitterbug back in my day, and a pretty good lookin' young feller' der too." He shines a shifty glance. "Ask ya mutha, sometime," he says snidely. "Annie Belle know." I smile softly as slowly his eyes drift. "Now 'dis heah is a true story," he says. As now his memory begins.

Negroes dally, a graveled lot, before spilling through a stingy, paint-chipped entryway. Inside, some twirl on stools and others grin their teeth. Others tip their hats to a never-ending influx of elevated cleavage. Wine and high spirits bring a frolicking crowd, flowing in inferior fabrics, soft like silk and with the shimmer of satin. Hips slap walls, and seamed stockings kick high in the air. People straggle clear across a wooden floor. Unlike diamonds, cut glass lacks the glitz of extravagance under a dingy light. But the lack thereof is replaced with rich laughter, smiles and warm embrace.

Rupert Thurman Jordan appears to float on the sharp of his heels as he struts amidst the regulars frequenting the Muddy Water Juke Joint. He steps soft, not to kick up too much dust on his newly spit-shined shoes. He can just about see his broad-toothed-grill in the reflection.

He gives a wink for a bashful lady, twirling a candy striped straw inside a half filled glass. Quickly he orders drinks for two and slips into a chair beside her. Just as the icy glasses arrive, he leans back in his chair and frames his puckered mouth between his thumb and forefingers.

"Ah's Rupert Jordan," he says, "Rupert Thurman Jordan. And whatcha say ya name is?"

"Olivia," she smiles. Rupert nods.

"Well ah do say, Miss Olivia, is ya husband married?"

The crowd is wild with applause, "Go on gal, do 'dat stuff!", as a female entertainer wails into her second solo. People are everywhere. Some sit, and others grab for a partner to take to the floor. Just a couple of feet from Rupert, is an unpolished spectacle. His fingers pop and hips grind slow and low.

"Man, take your drunken-ass and go-on 'bout ya business." Rupert examines the man, then, scowls. "Don't-cha sees me sittin' heah?" The intruder flashes a toothless smile.

"What-da hell is wrong witcha, NIGGA!" Rupert roars. "I axe you to take ya drunken ass and sit down somewhere." Rupert's fist slams square and the table collapses as ice and cold liquid wash the shiny uppers on the shoes of a man whose table is squeezed close by.

"Man, what you doin'? You done lost your damned mind?" retorts the hostile bystander.

"Mind ya damned business!" Rupert returns the snap.

"This is my business, mutha' fucka'! You don't buy my damned shoes!"

A chorus of oohs and aahs escapes the crowd as the derelict who initiated the affair slips away. The two men collide. Their legs coil and they dance. Rupert lands with his back against the ground. His throat is strapped and a grinding knee burns inside his chest. His tongue hangs and a hushed gasp whispers inside his throat. His eyeballs split their sockets. His skull pounds the planks, when suddenly Rupert grabs the man's head, palming it around his ears. Slowly, he drags him face-to-face, eye-to-eye, and lip-to-lip, then bites down with his oversized teeth.

"Ahhh!" There comes a sharp howl from this man who nearly whooped him dead. Rupert Thurman Jordan rolls his head to one side and spits; speckling the floor with droplets of blood and gritty flesh. He stands, eyeballing a stupefied crowd. "You wants some?" he taunts. "Who wants some? Huh!" he yells. He dusts his crumpled suit and walks away.

Outside and near the exit Rupert sees two men, one markedly older than the other. Their voices carry loosely into the night.

"Oh, shit!" exclaims the younger. "Look" he says, while zipping his fly, still trickling water after piddling aside the opened door on a paint-chipped truck. "Ain't 'dat der think he pretty nigga', one who you been tryin' to see?"

"What nigga'?"

"Rhat der, 'dat nigga'!" His wet lips part hold on a nearly emptied bottle of moonshine. "Da nigga' what got your daughta pregnant."

"Well I'll be damned!" cries the elder. His pants heist high at the crotch and pulled tight with wide suspenders. "I'll kill 'dat nigga'!" he utters loud.

Rupert sees the butt of a shotgun laid inside the truck in plain view. He quickly grabs hold on a baseball bat thrown on the ground and hurries to strike the one with his back turned. The other smashes his moonshine bottle against a tree. Rupert wields that bat, like a blade of grass in a wind storm. The broken bottle crashes to the ground, and the thunder of running feet take off in the night.

Now I expect you know my Daddy ain't tell it to me in all 'dem fancy words. But, if the truth be told, my Daddy ain't 'spect the old man would die, neither, but he did.

"I killed a man," he says somberly.

"He died?" My eyes stretch wide.

"Well, if I ain't kill him, he were gonna kill me. It weren't my intention to kill em." His eyes search mine, then, his eyelids fall. "Now, don't go 'round repeatin' everything you hears. Ya understand? You keeps 'dat between me, you and the gatepost."

Suddenly, Daddy cries out. "Lawd have mercy on poe' me." when a pain rips through his shoulders. "Go on in der and run some hot wata' in 'dat 'der tub."

I draw a hot bath and sprinkle a little Tide and a lot of Epson salts. Daddy slides onto his knees to pray.

———※———

The roads into the city are far reaching. I knew this day would come. A curved dome appears on an old gray stone building in the distance. It peaks high above all the surrounding structures. Inside the courthouse the walls stand to kiss the ceilings in silk-smooth, ceramic artistry. Carved patterns are the polished works of a skilled craftsman.

A big man wearing a long black robe walks into the room. We all stand up. Then, as soon as we stand up, he tells everybody to sit down. There are twelve chairs lined along a side wall, and each one taken. Sitting next to my dad is Mr. Eisner. Mr. Eisner is Daddy's lawyer. Night after night before the trial, we sat inside Mr. Eisner's office preparing for this day. I sat in a wood-framed chair next to a tall shelf filled with books. Nadine, Cedric and me reciting like it was the coming of Easter Sunday.

"The State would like to call Edwina Jordan to the witness stand." Daddy stares into my eyes from across the room. "Place your right hand on the Bible, and repeat after me. I, Edwina Jordan ..."

"I Edwina Jordan"

"do solemnly swear ..."

"... so help me God."

"I do."

It's been a very long time since I saw my sisters. There are many rows of shiny benches and here they sit, in front of me.

"State your name for the record."

"Edwina Jordan"

"How old are you Edwina?"

"Eleven."

"Do you attend school?" the prosecutor asks.

"Yes" My throat is dry as I sit in this leather-backed seat, so vast it swallows my rump.

"Speak up Edwina."

"Yes"

"Did your father ever beat you?" the prosecutor asks.

My mind trips back to the day and I can hear Alfreda screaming, "My kidneys are falling out". Then I see him on top of Minnie, plain like day. It was the same for Celia. And just when I think my sisters are coming home to stay …

"SURPRIZE!" We scream. But when the door swings back – HOMECOMING! It really is – it really is. But not the kind we hoped would be. My heart gagged at the sight of him; my daddy, Rupert Thurman Jordan dragging himself across the doorsill masked beneath a matted beard of facial hairs and looking worse than something the cat dragged in. I'd been a liar to say I'd missed him, when I never knew he'd gone.

"Edwina, answer the question."

"No, I answer slowly, he chastised me. He only chastised me, but he never beat me.

Suddenly it feels like Easter Sunday Mornin' when Aunt Trudy gives us a verse to remember. "Chastise" … it rings inside my head. I know it ain't Easter Sunday, but I know I won't forget.

For many hours, first one and then another takes a seat in that big ol' chair. But after many days and many weeks …

"The jury has reached its verdict."

Every breathing thing in the courtroom stands. On three counts of statutory rape, we find the defendant, Rupert T. Jordan, NOT GUILTY!"

Quietly, the courtroom empties. I look down to my feet, hop-scotching between the old wooden benches and proud to show off my shiny red shoes. I look up and see Minnie. She's watchin' me and calls my name. Then with one foot, I step toward her. Suddenly, Dad is watchin' me. I look down to my red shiny shoes, and I run away.

CHAPTER 4

DAMAGED GOODS

Many weeks after the trial and when Uncle Melvin comes to stay I'm glad for it. Aunt Tess cooks and I help out, peeling potatoes and stuff. Uncle Melvin don't like Aunt Tess' cooking. He just only likes center cut chops.

"Get three of 'em," he says, when he sends me over to the butcher shop, one block away. ""Edwina", he'll say, just as I am about to run out the door, "get one for yourself, too. "And don't forget to pick up a can of spaghetti." I cook pork chops for Uncle Melvin and he looks at Superman and chuckles out loud at the TV screen.

Ring-a-ling

"Hello" Mom has arrived home. "Yes", she says. "Uh-huh" she listens. Her casual expression turns sour. "She what!" she answers and looks straight at me.

She crashes the receiver onto its cradle.

"I know you did it," she snarls. "'Cause don't nobody in this house draw – but you."

She says that I am the artist of the family, but really, I ain't looking for no commendation.

"I'm gonna whoop your ass!" She screams. "I'm gonna tear your ass up!" She puts it to me one more time, IN OTHER WORDS.

The phone call was Barbara-Ann's mom. It was about the picture drawing, the one I passed around in class today. The kids in school had a pretty good time looking at it. It was a pretty nasty picture; the male and the female private parts inside one another, the same like I seen Daddy on top of my sister Minnie.

"Get your ass up them steps!" she waves me with the flow of a long extension cord coiled three times with a loop. She cracks it. Aunt Bea, Aunt Tess and even Uncle Melvin are so tickled, since I'm just gettin' my lesson taught.

"Ow –Wow -Wow-Wow!" I reach to stop the blow.

Ding-dong. Its Johnny's Liquors with a couple six packs and a fifth of "Canadian Club Whiskey".

"Ooh that tired me out, whoopin' that child's behine'." Mommy motions to the tall bottle, hidden out of sight beneath the kitchen table.

"Melvin" she laughs, "pour me a drink!"

Uncle Melvin chuckles hoarsely then grabs the bottle next to his leg. Aunt Bea and Aunt Tessie burst out laughin'.

It is late when Dad gets in. I take a fall against a wall, next to a room where Uncle Melvin sleeps. Aunt Tess and Mom sit somberly; the emptied cans and whiskey bottle have been tossed away. There is laughter coming out of the attic. It is the volume from Aunt Bea's TV. I tumble into the corner of a dimmed space, my mouth swells, my nose drips and somehow I gotta' pee.

***

"Somebody oughta tell 'em 'bout the Lord," Aunt Trudy always said that. If you don't know Him, Aunt Trudy is sure to introduce you. Today is Sunday morning and Aunt Trudy will have her way. She is on a lifelong mission for the Lord, not to mention the Superintendent of the Sunday School. "Let us pray," she says and afterward, all the little kids start to singing, "Yes Jesus Loves Me."

Somebody loves me? I think. I am tickled from my head to the bottoms of my feet, with joy bubbling over. I just only wish that my Sunday joy would last me through Monday morn. But, "good fruit can't grow up from a bad seed", Aunt Trudy taught me that. And somehow it always leaves me feeling like a thorn bush among the morning glories.

After Sunday School we stay for Morning Service. Nadine, Ernestine and me sing in the choir. The church folk get to dancing and hollering, after they get all filled up on that Holy Ghost. Later, we say good-bye to my aunties; Aunt Trudy and Aunt Mildred, wearing her winter coat in the summertime. Aunt Mae ain't here no more. She went home to be with her brother Bodine.

"Now, go on." Aunt Trudy yells. "Get yourselves some ice-cream."

She pours a bunch of pennies in our hands. Then she gives us a shove that sends us stumbling through the parted stained glass doors.

"And go right home, so you don't get yourselves in no trouble." Aunt Mildred yells.

"Aunt Tess," I utter, "Why does he" … "Why does he …?" I sigh and catch my breath. Tears stream my cheeks and Aunt Tess wipes the welts streaming my back and arms with Witch Hazel. We stopped to buy an ice cream, then we set on our way. He was waiting. Rupert Thurman Jordan, my daddy, herded us like a pack of wild animals. He beat us for every unmade bed and for every unswept floor. He beat us for the dust his finger peeled from between the rungs on the banister. It cracked! Dad's thick wooden walking-stick broke, like the skin off my back.

"Why … Aunt Tess?"

Aunt Tess' head nods slow. She answers me in a whisper. "I don't know, baby. "I don't know." She don't wanna stay no more. She hops inside Daddy's truck and he drives away.

With a fryer full of bubbling chicken sizzling on a hot stove, Mom unzips her pocketbook and removes a bottle from a long brown paper bag. She unscrews the cap, tilts her head and swallows.

"Edwina," she says. "Look after that chicken, 'til I come back. I'm goin' upstairs and get me a quick nap, before your father gits back.

And as soon I hear Daddy's truck bumping into the drive, I hurry up the stairs.

"Ma, git up! Daddy is home." A quick swipe with the back of my hand removes a bit of slobber from her dribbling mouth. I comb my fingers through her matted hair. The back door slams. I hear him moving closer, until suddenly, he stands in full view.

"Git' your drunken' ass up 'fer I … "

Without another word, and as if his anger is too great even for himself, his fist draws back. One foot drags behind the other, as he turns and walks away. `

"Sometimes I wish I could just go to sleep and never wake up" she says. "I don't have nothin' to live for. I might as well be dead."

"I care mommy." I whisper in her ear, "I care."

Monday evening, I ride along with Dad to drive her home from her housekeeping chores at the Steinberg's. When we get there the button-activated doublewide garage roll up. Mrs. Steinberg steps out and two brand new shiny Cadillacs appear. Mrs. Steinberg makes her way down the long driveway to greet us.

"Hello, Mr. Jordan." She smiles cordially. "Annie Belle isn't feeling very well. Maybe you'd like to come in to help her."

Mrs. Steinberg is a wonderful friend. A woman Mom confides in. She is a Jewish lady and a lawyer with a big heart. She has offered Mom with all of us kids a brand new beginning when she relocates to sunny Florida, just as soon as she and her lawyer husband retire. Mom can't fathom the peace in leaving Daddy. Peace would be an unfamiliar place for her to be.

"Go on in der and hep ya mutha."

Dad gives me a shove to nudge me out of the car. I swiftly follow Mrs. Steinberg through the garage. We pass through her den and elegant adjoining kitchen, where she graciously offers me to eat.

"No, thank you." I answer in my most mannerly way.

Just three short steps up and away from the kitchen is a bedroom. I see mom, tucked comfortably under a fluffy colorful blanket in the Steinberg's fabulous guest room. She sits up in the bed the second I call her name. Soon, I take my mom and bid Mrs. Steinberg a goodnight.

Dad speeds recklessly out of the driveway. He punches Mom with one hand, while zigzagging across the roadway. Soon we are home. Mom convulses. Her eyeballs don't stay still, just float inside their sockets and disappear. She falls out of the chair, splits her head and spatters blood all over. A red light flashes and the paramedics shove her in the back of the ambulance. Every now and then that drinking just takes its toll. She is sick when she drinks, and sicker when she can't get a hold to it. Likely, she's got a concussion from all that pounding. She is huddled beneath a heap of blankets, freezing cold. Now she is kicking covers and fussing about being too hot. I'm afraid one day she may take her last ride in that speeding automobile.

Beep, beep. She waves with a smile, tapping the horn on a rusted automobile. Ever since that day in the courthouse, I have been warned not to talk to her.

"Edwina!"

"Minnie!" I shriek, as she rolls to the curbside.

Minnie is half the size she used to be. A scar marks her face at the jaw line and Minnie's mouth is wired shut. She talks through the meshed wiring to tell me how a tractor-trailer truck hit their car months ago, when her driver fell asleep. Thank God she survived. The driver wasn't so lucky. We talk a little before another car drives through. It passes slowly and I know that it is Aunt Bea.

"You'd better go on," Minnie says, "so you don't get in trouble." We give each other a hug. I wave goodbye, then drop my head as the ol' rusted Desoto putts away.

LETTER TO AUNT BEA

Why'd ya tell him Aunt Bea? What if my head busted wide open — or even worse — when he swung that hammer that day? Why do you protect him? Is it to protect the demented daddy of your babies? He is your man too, ain't he, Aunt Bea?

I remember, the phone rang? Rupert Thurman Jordan, my daddy slammed the receiver so hard that it went clean through the wall. Was it another man ... huh, Aunt Bea? He whooped you and when Little Toby jumped to defend you, he stuck his big fingers clear down your baby's little throat. Little Toby gagged. What is going on inside your head when you defend a man this way? Maybe there was a time that you liked him chasing after you, but has he gotten' too brutal, even for you Aunt Bea? You are a single woman and this cock-blocker don't so much as allow you to have your own love affair. Instead of defending him, you should be defending me.

I wouldn't say that "time heals all wounds". But it has been a couple years and in the early days of summer, Daddy agrees with Mom to let Minnie visit, since he can't keep her away.

"Hi mom" she says, with a big 'ol grin.

"Minnie!" We yell excitedly. Minnie's eyes look straight into Dad's then, her eyes roll away. Daddy's face lowers. He grabs his hat and drags himself away.

Minnie talks with Mommy. Then, with Mom's permission we head to the park for a good game of baseball to lighten our day.

In swerves a curve from the pitcher's mound, too high to swing.

"Strike one!" Then another slides low to the ground. Rhonda wraps her body forward and swings.

"Strike two."

"Gosh, Rhonda, you'll swing at anything." We laugh. Now, a third ball and SLAM! Rhonda hits a fly, straight to center field. Toby takes off running toward the sun. His head is raised, his eyes meet the sky. Smack! It's Toby's head, bashed against a tree.

S-T-R-I-K-E … HE'S O-U-T. So ends another game of baseball.

<hr />

"What 'da hell is wrong witcha? Stupid ass!" A two by four inch wooden slat waves in his hand. "Push the damn thing. Push it." He yells and she screams. I wish Minnie were here now. Daddy swings the big stick flat across the back of Rhonda's shoulders. A white patrolman cruises by pretending not to see. "Push it, push it – STUPID ASS!"

Rhonda can't handle that big ol' lawn mower.

Summer nights! I am glad for 'em. Watermelon? I'm glad for it, too. We go behind the house to have a slice. We whisper softly and make our plan to run away.

"Minnie said we gotta run and just keep on goin'."

"Are you'll comin'?"

Nadine won't partner in our affairs. She's preoccupied with plucking dead notes on an old piano out of key. Giselle is too little, Cedric and Toby are scared. Ernestine, Rhonda and me run the course to Minnie's girlfriend's place, eight, nine blocks away. Minnie gets called from work. She'll meet us at Headquarters, 'fore somebody wakes up dead.

We tremble before a miserably tall, oblong counter opposite a nonchalant front desk Sergeant and the details unfold.

"He beat me with a board, across the back of my neck." Rhonda pleads and uncovers the bruises for the Sergeant to see. He breathes an impatient sigh and soon let's go a quiet chuckle.

"What do you want from me?" he jeers.

Just then, Minnie arrives. She steers attention to documents of past abuse, already stashed away in some old file cabinet. Soon, from an inner hallway comes another officer; a burly, heavy-footed man, who sways side to side when he walks. He stares silently over the desk Sergeant's shoulder as together they smirk. They take turns shrugging their shoulders. The fat officer reaches into his pocket to squeeze out a handkerchief, then blows his nose like a marching band. One spins the dial on an old black telephone with big numbers and an even bigger receiver. More silence. Then it becomes painfully apparent that the Sergeant has called our home. Five minutes go by, until Dad drives up and is seen through the big glass window. Rupert Thurman Jordan is a cowardly man. He sits his gutless ass inside the car. He cowers over the steering wheel, while Mommy struts inside. The gray, steel doors push open. A gruesome gash from a can opener is concealed and the truth hides beneath her bangs.

"Let's go," she commands her little army. It is Sergeant Jordan who commands the control panel, the control panel inside her head. These jerk-officers don't ask any questions. Just tell my mom to take her kids and go away.

She scouts us through the door to slide our narrow bottoms across the vinyl seat of a green station wagon with wood side panels. We sit, staring at the back of the big-headed Sergeant Jordan, who mans the wheel. Whoosh! Over and out! We disappear, like ghosts – gone --- leaving Minnie gasping, before the desk of two counterfeit Sergeants at City Police Headquarters. I see now, it's Jordan who's really in charge.

Daddy is "disabled." Well, that's what the doctors say. He walks with a limp. But I don't see much else wrong with him, just puffed-up and arrogant is all. He's got a faded, paint-chipped tow truck purchased from his disability money. With a pretty good-sized piece of change under his pillow, he hires Mr. Jenkins, an ol' dusty, blue-black fellow from Georgia. Jenkins' carpentry falls far short of professional grade and his craftsmanship is damned right tacky. Why Daddy sees fit to hire him, I can't figure.

"Yes suh, Mr. Jordan. No suh, Mr. Jordan. How's ya doin' suh." Nodding his head, always in agreement, like one of them house niggas I see on black and white TV. He's built like 'em too, tall and strong. Just now, someone knocks at the door.

"Who 'dat poundin' at da doe' dis errly in da moanin'?" Dad exclaims. He belches and instructs me to get it. I find it to be old man Jenkins come to call.

"Good moanin' Miss Edwina." Jenkins smiles with bogus respect. I answer him, "good mornin'", then roll my eyes when Daddy ain't watchin'. "Good moanin' Mista Jordan, suh.'" Jenkins drags his words and stretches the syllables, making them sound really long.

Peering upward from a nearly emptied plate, Dad glances snidely. He lifts his fork, then replies. "Jenkins, what brangs ya heah so errly in da moanin'? I's just having breakfast. Have some wit me, won't ya suh?"

"Honey-hush," Jenkins twangs. Grinning and showing all of his pearly white teeth. His tar-black skin shines and his eyes jut forward.

"Ah sho thanks yuh suh. Jenkins feigns surprise. I sho' kin use a bite ta eat!"

"Edwina, fix dis man heah' somethin' ta' eat."

"How's you doin' 'dis moanin', Miss Edwina?" he says, flashing a devious wide-toothed smile. Jenkins skillfully seats himself at the kitchen table, intentionally cocking his chair, just enough that I might step over his outstretched leg, each time I pass through the narrow pathway. Obvious and deliberate, he slaps his hand across his broad lap ever so often, then slides his hand back and forth, suggestively rubbing his thigh. He watches carefully as I move about in my subservient skin. This big grown man makes me nervous, sneaking wicked glances at me from the corners of his winking eye.

"Ya kers fo' a cup o' coffee?" Dad offers, with no notice to the tension that I feel.

"Don't mind if ah do," Jenkins calls back, stealing a grin and a glance when he looks my way.

Turning quickly, I lift the heavy, spurting kettle, whistling hot, as once again I step across his gapped legs. I feel his eyes searching. But, my eyes stay focused on the trickling water pouring into his cup. I would have liked to pour it in his crotch. But, da good Lord ain't build me so hateful as that. I turn away to wash the dirty dishes that have accumulated in the sink. The hands on the clock tick slowly and not a moment too soon, before Jenkins finishes his meal. With fixin' to do around the house, Jenkins retreats to the yard.

Dad guzzles the last of his coffee, then he looks toward the staircase. He bites the last half of a slice of dry burnt toast and notices the eight o'clock hour ticking two minutes away.

"Where dem youngins'? He mutters. Toby! Cedric! Get yawl's trifling, good 'fer nothin' asses up!" Without warning, Rupert Thurman Jordan throws from his chair and stumbles heavy-footed to the stairwell. "'Dem der nappy headed niggas thinks dey is gonna sleep all day."

Up the L-shaped staircase he hobbles, dragging his lame foot. I hear a thumping against the underside of every step and a bumping thud each time he loses his balance. A haunting, evil sound, heard always, before the identical beating that follows. The foyer, once quiet, fills with moaning, sometimes broken by a blow that sends Toby and Cedric crashing to the floor or against a wall. Dad expects we rise early, seven days a week. Property – that is what we are – precious commodities that help bring in money. He brutally owns us, every tender limb. "Shut up! Shut yo' mouth nigga!" He hushes them to silence, while beating the light of day from their sight. The sweet taste of life sours with every impact. Thereafter, he thunders clumsily, returning to the kitchen and the boys soon follow. There is work to do. The old, faded tow truck speeds out of the driveway.

Nadine, Ernestine, and I have tackled our chores for the day. By ten in the morning the dishes have been washed, dried and placed back in the cabinet. The floors are swept clean, kitchen mopped and the beds made as we roll out of them. It is one o'clock and time for the three of us to head to church for our weekly choir rehearsal. It is one of the few occasions we get to goof off with our friends. I especially like Mrs. Jones, our pianist, who lets us laugh out loud without telling us to "quit acting' stupid."

Following rehearsal and two hours later, I climb to the attic, where, I unexpectedly find Jenkins' big black exterior towers over me. Jenkins lifts his heavy foot and slides it between my legs. His parted knees block my way. Staring over my head, his thick hand shoves my back and bends me forward. Jenkins yanks my skirt, snatches my crotch and pushes deep inside of me.

LETTER TO MOMMY

Mommy,

It's been two months now, since I began my period, and mommy, didn't even know. Even I didn't know. I did what I could to take care of me. I was too scared, too shamed and I thought it was something happening, because of what Jenkins done to me. I'm afraid, Mommy. Jenkins been sneaking in my room at night, doing things to me after I'm asleep. I've seen Daddy take a hold to his rifle and aim it on you. What am I supposed to do, when you are just as 'fraid as me?

CHAPTER 5

LOCK-DOWN

The school bell rings signaling the last period of the day. The cleats on my pointed-toed shoes click repetitiously. They sound nearly unheard over the boisterous chatter in a narrow corridor, rushed by rowdy students and crashing lockers. I rotate the metallic wheel on a combination lock, first to the left, then to the right and now to the left again, before snatching my coat from the hook. With books piled on one arm and raised to my chest, I slam the door and I get along my way. Clickety-click, my cleats and me are off to meet Nadine for the walk home. Where Nadine goes – I go. It's a droning order from Sergeant Jordan, like we're Siamese twins or something.

I see Nadine in the crowd and she giggles, chatting with a classmate. She glows when she smiles. She fixes her hair in grown folks' styles and laughs a lot. No doubt, attracting lots of attention from the boys in our school and more from full-grown men. She's so outgoing now, since she lost all those extra pounds. And although she's always been pretty, Nadine could never seem to recognize it for herself. No more fat girl, she is more like Slender Ella.

Nadine is a junior and me, just a sophomore. She introduces me as her younger sister to her new friend Sheila. I smile and say hello. Sheila is a hefty senior, a deep-complexioned Southern gal, with big hips and other things. She acts like full-fledged woman and rolls her stuff when she walks. Soon, Nadine unloads her books and the three of us leave the school for the long stroll home.

I lag behind and out of step, not to interfere in Sheila and Nadine's grown-up business. Sheila is blabbing about some guy in his twenties who wants to meet Nadine. I listen and offer a smile, whenever they look my way. There is a party tonight and Sheila invites Nadine to come along. We say bye to Sheila and get on our way.

When Nadine asks to go to the party, Mommy says, "You better ask your Dad." Daddy says, "See what your mutha' has to say."

I'll bet he'll tell her she kin go. Nadine has always been his favorite girl and he's the one with the final say.

When Nadine was little, Daddy bragged that she won a Beauty Contest. Now he brags that she's smart and gets top grades. He brags about Nadine her hair and says its long and wavy, just like his mother; though most times he just frowns when he looks at me.

"Who 'dis you goin' wit'?" He asks, and "where 'dis party at? What time is it ova'?"

He says yes, but he makes Nadine take me along. I am glad, since I'd never get to go on my own. Mommy drops us off, and I'll bet she has no idea of the rubbing and grinding that goes on under the blue lights in the basement. She'll be back to pick us up at eleven-thirty, sharp. Nadine and I split paths as soon as we arrive.

It is here that I meet Cleophus Witherspoon, a country boy from school, born in the back woods of Mississippi or somewhere similar, where they grow them black and strong. I suck in the scent of his silky woolen Alpaca sweater. I move close in his grip under the spell of his winding torso. Eddie Holman, is singing "Lonely Girl," a self descriptive ballad, while Cleophus and I do the two-step, with a dip and a grind. We exchange sweat, making my Afro hair draw back from my forehead and lay dead.

When the record is over, another 45 rpm drops from the spindle, and another and another. By the time The Dells sing "Stay in My Corner," Cleophus and me are slapped against a dark wall in a corner—when suddenly I hear Mom calling. I make a dash, far from Cleophus, and hear the snicker of my classmates mocking me.

"Edwina, your mother's calling you."

I hurry to meet her and Nadine outside at the car.

On the following Friday, I need no reminder that today is the official beginning of Christmas Recess. School will be closed for the next ten consecutive days. On the walk home, Sheila asks Nadine to join her family down South for the weekend. Dad may be color-struck, but he ain't no fool.

"You should come?' Sheila coaxes. "I got cousins down there who want to meet you."

I expect Nadine will tell her no, but Nadine says. "Yeah, I'll go, when you'll leavin'?"

Later in the evening when Mommy arrives from work, Nadine asks without a flinch.

"Mom, can I go down South with my friend Sheila and her Aunt for the Christmas holiday?" Mommy kind of looks at her with her eyebrow cocked sideways. I don't think she fully comprehends such fool talk. But, Nadine ain't 'fraid to ask, ain't got no speech impediment and surely ain't stutter.

"Go where?" Mom hollers.

"I want to go down South with my friend Sheila and her Aunt for Christmas."

"Girl, you done lost your mind! You know your father ain't going for that!"

Now since Nadine lost all 'dem pounds, she is more brazen, than even Mommy could know.

"Why not?" She demands, with a gutsy attitude and a deliberate tongue.

"Cause I said, you're not! And, that's final!"

"I'm goin' anyway!" Nadine screams, before storming up the steps.

"What you say! What you say!"

Mom's ears don't comprehend rebellion from nothin' that dropped from her womb.

"You ain't goin' nowhere, and I mean it!"

Mom screams to the top of her lungs as the patter of Nadine's feet dissipate at the upper level of the house. Distracted by a house forever in confusion, Mom sends Giselle to get her house slippers, so she can rest her feet. Forty -five minutes later, she stirs a big pot, set afire on the kitchen stove, when a pricking thought comes to mind.

"Where's Nadine?" she yells.

"She left," Ernestine calls.

"She WHAT?"

"She left," Ernestine repeats a little louder. "I saw her come down the steps with her coat on."

"Oh shit!" Mom shrieks. "Rupert is gonna throw a fit. Who is this girl she left with? Where does she live? What's her phone number?" Mom asks. Then, with quick dialing fingers, she calls 411 for a telephone number. But it's too late, Nadine has already left.

"What the hell ya let huh' go 'fer?" He is home and all of hell is loosed. Dad screams blaming Mommy for Nadine's defiance.

"I told her not to go, she left on her own!" Mom yells, visually alarmed. Fear rocks her words, permeating the dingy kitchen.

"What ya mean ya told huh not to go, STUPID ASS? I should slap you 'fer not whoopin' huh ass. You shoulda' make huh keep huh' grown behine' in 'dis heah house. What good are ya woman, when ya cain't control 'dem der good for nothin' youngins?"

Ernestine and I duck the path of anger and listen from the upper hall.

"I oughta' take my gun and blow all you triflin' niggas' brains out." He roars.

I'm afraid to stay.

"Hell! What good are ya?"

But, I'm more afraid to go.

"Bunch a good for nothin', stupid ass, youngins.' And you, wit' yer simple ass ..." he scowls. I hear the commotion of heavy handed pounding and Mommy's moaning. "You ain't no damned good."

"Let's go!" I whisper to Ernestine. "You go first. I'll run behind you."

"What da hell is all 'dat der racket?" Dad's roars when he hears us ripping through the stairwell. But – HE CAIN'T RUN! He's crippled. I'm so glad my Daddy CAIN"T run!

"Go get 'em Toby! Go get 'em!" He yells the command.

SLAM! The outer door crashes shut. I've flipped the latch behind me. The couple seconds it takes for Toby to unlock the night latch, may just be the seconds we need to stay ahead. I don't look back. Not for a solitary second. My knees thrust to my chest. I take an icy slide at the street corner's edge. Clackety-clack, sound Toby's feet, clapping hard and steady as he runs fast behind me. I don't slow down for anything or for anyone. Not for icy buildups on the walkways, not even for speeding cars at the intersections. Suddenly, I don't hear him anymore. I don't hear Toby's feet pounding the pavement. Still, I don't stop. Not until Ernestine and I get to Minnie's apartment in the next town over, about a mile and a half away.

There is no light showing from her apartment. The windows are pitch-dark. Leaning against an outer rail, I reach high to tap against a covered pane. There is no answer. I tap a second time, a little harder. The shade rolls back bringing Minnie into view. In seconds the door flies open. As the weekend ends, Rhonda forewarns Nadine from an open window. Lucky for her, she didn't go inside that house.

Forty-five rpm's stack the box. *The Temptations, The Dells, Aretha Franklin* and *The Jackson Five;* slap one atop the other as the plastic discs eject and tumble onto a felt-lined rotating turntable. Tickling guitar chords reverberate with a heavy bass. *Michael Jackson's* virgin soprano sings. *"Ooh-ooh, — let me tell ya girl, - ooh, ooh"*. You know the rest. It's one of the hottest, if not "THE HOTTEST" songs of the times. Music or dancing, I don't know which I love more. Giggling and laughing, I like that too. It comes real natural nowadays. Suddenly, comes a thumping at the apartment door. It is a forceful pounding that overrides the splitting volume from huge speakers parked in opposite corners of Minnie's small living room floor.

"Who is it?" Minnie calls.

"Police"

"Who?" She calls again.

"Police! Open the door!"

Reluctantly, she lowers the tone on the box. The neighbors are likely complaining that the music is too loud. She parts the door to reveal two flat-footed, pale and stone faced officers standing on the other side. There is an exchange of conversation through the open space. Suddenly, something more is realized. Minnie is expressionless. Already I know what she doesn't say.

"We're only following a court order ma'am. If you don't allow us to take them, we'll have to arrest you." Minnie's eyes fill with tears.

"He'll beat us," we cry.

"They can't go back! They don't want to go back." Minnie pleads.

"We don't have nothin' to do with that, M'am."

"But ..."

"I can't help ya. There is a court order and we have to pick them up. They can't stay here. If they don't go home we can take them to the Correctional Facility, until you all can work something out. Can't stay here." The officer repeats.

He handcuffs us one to the other. Minnie gives a tearful embrace and her promise to visit soon.

Winding through the mountainous backwoods in an old state car on a narrow path, the road climbs onward. My thoughts are bitter with the knowledge that we will soon become temporary "wards of the state." A dense concentration of obstructive trees overtakes the view. Then finally, the vehicle veers slowly to rest along a curved driveway shaped like a U. The automobile stops to park. We enter the secluded building and the outer door locks shut. With few words, we are given over to another officer.

She is a rigid woman; a frumpy, bleached-blond with short-cropped wiry hair that spirals from the crown of her head. She has obviously anticipated our arrival and her orders are harsh.

"Empty your pockets, remove all jewelry, and if you've got any hairpins, take them out." We drop them into a small manila envelope she holds in her hand. "Now follow me." Without a word we follow solemnly down a long corridor. I glare upward at towering ceilings as we move along in single file to an exposed shower area. There we strip naked one beside the other and bathe in open stalls. The steamy shower streams forcefully and the female officer waits with a watchful eye.

We have completed our check-in and already it is 9:00 p.m. She leads us to a huge open room. The only light showing is from an outer hallway, the area is dark. Bunk beds are stacked in replica along the walls. It looks like an Army barracks, although I have never seen a real one before. The lights flash out. There is silence. For a spell, I stare into the blackness. But with warm covers and peace of mind, I say a little prayer and snuggle into an awaited rest.

At six o'clock a.m. morning arrives too early to embrace. While daylight is still sleeping, we are ordered to rise, feet flat on the floor. Then line up for a fresh outerwear and a change of pillow covers and sheets. We make our beds and tuck the sheets with square corners, a special fold to keep the covers neat. After collection of the dirty laundry, our shower is hurried, before we dress in clean sweatshirts and jeans. Finally, another uniformed lady escorts us in single file to a large kitchen. There, we remove chairs, one by one from a stack along a wall. We set up tables and retrieve huge canisters of cooked food from an elevator chute along the floor. As the morning order unfolds I am hungry and ready to eat. Now, another line is formed, where I receive my breakfast plate. Following breakfast is kitchen clean-up. We collect and wash dirty dishes, re-fold the collapsible tables, stack the chairs and mop the floors. When we are done, there is dusting and wiping to do, always by the clock with no playing in between.

Finally, the big doors slam shut. Out come the board games from the closets, the television turns on and playing cards get to shuffling. Some girls lounge or read a book. Others straighten their hair with a hot frying comb, grease sizzling on the backs of their necks.

Three weeks go by, when Minnie arrives for a Sunday afternoon visitation. With her comes the good news.

"We are scheduled to be in court on Monday morning." She says.

The ride is quiet, but going down the fierce, steep mountain range lends a lot more ease than climbing up. Finally, a circular dome shows high on an old gray stone building. Inside and seated on a smooth pine bench, Rupert Thurman Jordan's shifty brown eyes stare away from me.

My mind plays back to when I was that little girl in the shiny red shoes. It was a prearranged fiasco, a methodical scheme. An orchestrated plan to exonerate a man from the punitive action he deserved for the many offenses he did commit.

"All rise." It is the call from the bailiff.

⁕⁙⁕

We arise for school at the same time each morning. We cook, we clean, and do nearly all of the things we've been accustomed to from youth, including going to Sunday School. On Saturday afternoons I work, washing floors and cleaning toilets for a Jewish lady. Minnie could use the help. Me? I could use a new pair of shoes. Saturday nights, my back-woods buddy, Cleophus Witherspoon and me, spin around at the local nightspot downtown. It's a club for teens where Cleophus and I dance 'till they throw us out at midnight-closing.

"You gotta put a little spin in yer' toes," he tells me. I laugh so hard I ache.

Ever since that car accident Minnie stays in and out of sickness, and she's been sick a lot lately. Tonight, when I leave my party-mate, I find her propped in her bed. Her eyes are unfocused and Minnie doesn't know I am here. She dangles ashes to the filter on a lighted cigarette dropped from her lips. I slip the burning tobacco stick from her mouth. Later into the night she wakes up crying, because her head hurts so bad. I follow her from room to room, wiping up the floor. It's "that time of the month", but Minnie don't know she's dripping blood.

NEW CHAPTER 6

"BLIND-SIGHTED"

Food fights in the school cafeteria and open unrest in the classrooms and hallways mark the beginning of a revolution. It's been several years since the 1966 riots changed the face of this miniscule New Jersey community. It was an explosive renaissance that rocked the country from Newark, New Jersey, all the way to Detroit, Michigan. Out of this more than subtle uprising, came flower power, big Afros and peace signs. It was the kick-off for *More power to the people, The Black Panther Movement*, funky music, platform shoes and promiscuity. These events epitomized the early seventies and the free-styled spirit of those who wore the low hipped, bell-bottom jeans, hanged low to the ground. Tie-dyed shirts and rainbow colored glasses brings my senior year of high school to a near finish and I am happier than ever.

He laughs a lot and I like that. For Delbert, giggling is a birthright. It comes naturally. He is nonchalant and nothing seems to matter. If the sky cracks and a bit of heaven begins to fall, Delbert would probably grin. I like that about him. I want to ask him to the Prom. But I'm afraid he will just say no.

I glimpse this slender boy with long stretched legs and seated one row over from me. His skin is chestnut, deep like the earth and smooth like clay. With history class near finish, I pass him a note; then, *ding,* the bell rings. Next day, he still don't say nothin', so I decide to strike a little conversation of my own.

Would somebody tell me why Marcy Jones keeps looking at me funny? And why other girls too, keep asking me if I go with Delbert? A filmed image is projected onto a large screen inside a dimmed Theater Arts classroom, when outside an open doorway I see them three girls. They have been following me. One is a tall skinny kid with a lopsided Afro hairdo. She looks more like a man, is always in a fight and has the battle scars to prove it. Then there is the big-boned one, with big arms and big everything. She's got muscles on top of her muscles. And Marcy, she is fat and round, like a jelly-bear. I tremble at the thought of them pulling me from my seat and causing a ruckus in this classroom. I spare myself the embarrassment and go to meet them in the hall.

"Do you go with Delbert?" They rush me. "Do you go with Delbert?" They keep asking me the same doggone thing, over and over again. I keep telling them, "NO, Delbert and me are friends, just friends."

In my heart, I wish that I were going with Delbert, but, the truth is NO. And right now I am glad for it. Marcy claims that she goes with Delbert, and these girls are backing her up on that. Suddenly, and right on time the fire bell rings and the girls hurry away before they are seen by the administrators. How convenient to see Delbert rushing the stairwell with his class group.

I ask him, "Do you go with Marcy? Hey, I didn't know that you already had a girlfriend. Least, you never mentioned one to me".

Whenever I ask Delbert if he goes with Marcy, he says that he don't even like Marcy. I don't know who I believe. But I choose to believe Delbert, because he is cute, you understand. I start to wonder if maybe, he likes ME.

Next day at school, Marcy and her little clique tail me from my classroom to my locker, making snide remarks and trippin' me on the backs of my heels. When I reach my locker, Marcy stands so close I can feel her breath on the back of my neck, so close I can't turn around.

"I will kick your ASS!" She cusses and screams; mother fucker 'dis and mother fucker 'dat.

My temperature climbs.

"Marcy, ya' betta' git outa my way!"

Suddenly, she grabs my hair and don't let go. I kind of lose my vision. My body twists around really fast and I slam her square in her jelly-belly. I'm swingin', just can't see her anymore. Before it is through, all three girls poke their shot at me. Then I see Ernestine standing in the crowd.

"Why didn't you help me?" I ask.

"You seemed to be doing okay by yourself." She laughs.

———

Finally school lets out. Mom and Aunt Trudy proudly attend my Graduation Ceremony. She orders dinner at a fine restaurant and to compliment the occasion she gifts me with a watch face on a gold chain. The ticker is discreetly encased in the underside of a gold trimmed sphere. Thank you Aunt Trudy. You inspire me.

Everybody is looking forward to me going off to college. The local newspaper did a little feature article on me too, including a snapshot. Mr. Winters and his wife got me a scholarship grant. I am honored. But why didn't somebody discuss it with me? Mr. Winters is the Day Camp Director where Ernestine and I work, boarding a bus twice a week and splashing in our bikinis. We goof off, more than we work. And they've got a couple of cute and playful boys working here, too. I love it when they dunk me in the water and naturally I allow them to rescue me after the plunge. Tuesday nights, Mr. Winters chaperones the group to New York City. Teen girls escort teen boys from the local *Job Corps*. It's a bumpy ride aboard a cheese-colored school bus, jammed with timid girls and bashful boys, who smell a bit rancid. The voluntary excursion gets a little intense with timid girls on one side and shy boys on the other.

But the summer's lilacs' pinks and purple depart far too soon for my liking. It is all exchanged for the bleeding hues of late September's reds and gold. Already, today marks three weeks of institutionalized academics in an unfamiliar setting. College – it is another confine not much different from home. I bustle with a rustle, shuffling through a small pile of leaves before I head off campus. But first I remove an overtime parking ticket tucked on my windshield by the Campus Traffic Safety Patrol. Then barrel away from the school campus for the very LAST time.

When I reach his house, I pull to the curbside. Aunt Trudy peaks from her window. Auntie lives across the street from Delbert, and thinks I have completely lost my mind.

"What you doing over here?" She is always scolding. "Why ain't you in school?"

I just wish that Aunt Trudy and everybody else would mind their business and let mine alone.

"Which one of them Gilliam boys you seeing?"

There are five boys in the family and it's no wonder Aunt Trudy stays confused. Delbert's got five sisters too. They are the biggest family of "smilers" I have ever known.

"Has he got a job? You know better, Edwina."

Daddy says I'm stupid.

"Edwina, that's about a silly young man, if I must say so," he tells me. "Why da hell he grin so much, when ain't nothin' funny?" Dad will be swollen with disappointment when he learns that I've dropped out of college. Oh well.

I leave Aunt Trudy fussing, then bounce up the stairs to the front door and press the bell. Certainly, no one can hear me over the hum of a blaring saxophone. I knock a couple of more times. The door swings back. A long-legged woman in a tight skirt lets me in. It is apparent that she is Neil's girlfriend. She takes her seat on his lap, while Neil, through weighty eyes, gives a nod, and offers me a toke from a passing joint.

Dwight, the eldest of the Gilliam boys, is the saxophonist. He is a phenomenal musician, who hasn't had any formal training. Just the same, he never achieves the kudos he deserves. The younger of Delbert's siblings are off to school. And there sits Delbert in a cloud of smoke. He tips a bottle and guzzles *Boones Farm Apple Wine,* straight from the bottle. A small group of neighborhood musicians gather for a jazz gig, plop in the small seams of the dining room floor. I take my seat beside Delbert, where we exchange a couple of whispered words. Then take off to the room he shares with Dwight on the upper floor. A certain baby's picture catches my attention. It is pinned between huge colorful posters and scotch-taped to a black painted wall.

"That's my cousin's baby." The shades are drawn. The room goes dark. Together, we flow beneath the glow of neon signs and florescent lights.

Wailing echoes flee the wide-angled end on a brass and brazen saxophone. Then, sounds the stinging of the strings on the long neck of an upright bass. A keyboardist plucks the ivory on the keyboard. I pluck a toothpick, jerking spent corn kernels caught between my teeth. Big cars, little ones, new cars and old, line the street from end to bend, extending the entire block and far around a corner. Old folk talk trash with no shame. Young folk carry on with new game. Kinfolk, neighbors and friends sliding hip to hip in a welcomed celebration of good time and shared cheer. September is a time for merriment. Especially on this day, it is Mrs. Gilliam's birthday. I love this place of high spirits, and I LOVE a festive family of folk who know how to make you comfortable. And doggonnit they sure as hell know how to have FUN! I laugh and shimmy my way to a huge plastic bowl of homemade potato-salad. Suddenly, Delbert grabs me by the hand. He spins me around and together we kick a little dirt from beneath our heels.

"Yeah baby!" He roars with delight. Oblivious to everything except the music and a fresh poured glass of rum splashing gently over the outer rim of a half-filled plastic cup he holds in his hand. Delbert turns it to his mouth and swallows. He pivots suavely, with methodical timing. Then sets the glass on a table, without ever breaking his step. Cutting up and acting a fool. Cussin', drinkin', smokin' and roarin' with laughter. "No fool, no fun," Daddy used to say. "Bottoms up."

Night falls as an Autumn-rain drives a never-ending barrage of houseguests inside. They gather around a table. The hub of which covers nearly the entire floor in an under-sized dining area. The small front room and kitchen receive the overflow of traffic as the outer door consistently swings open and then shuts. A tall bottle of rum sits where most folk situate a vase or other décor. Always there are hugs and laughter, lighted with wide toothed smiles and a steady thunder of feet to pound the steps. A glass is set before me. The bottle tilts. I borrow one of Mrs. Gilliam's extra long Kool cigarettes, tip my glass and make myself no stranger.

Later into the night Delbert and I leave for Minnie's. The sight of Nadine, after all those worrisome months, brings added joy. She just left one day and never came home. Seeing her man nodding all over the place, makes me wonder what's worse? What Nadine ran from or what she ran to? I sure hope she's smart enough to drop that baby she is carrying, if she wants to keep getting high the way she do.

Speaking of babies, Alfreda is here. The last time I saw her she was screaming her head off and being carried off in a patrol car. She's all grown up now and got a brand new baby. Celia moved to Detroit, Michigan and Ernestine is meaner than ever. Cedric is doin' time and Toby is doin' heroin. Rhonda and Giselle are cuttin' school and itchin' to be grown. Minnie? She's engaged to a guy named Frank. So – I guess everybody's happy.

With time to share, we bury our cares.

Minnie starts the rotating count – "One."

"Two," Alfreda shouts loud and deliberate.

"Three," chimes Cedric.

"Four," That's Delbert.

Suddenly, except for giggling, the smoke-filled room gets silent; although, silence is never golden and far from serious in this stupid game we play. I stare back among our circle of family and friends. Their snickering focus stays on me.

"Five ..." I say "five!" Everybody's face cracks – LOUD with laughter. Tears in the eye-laughter, so hard it hurts. Even I have become momentarily filled with laughter. I join the comical roaring from my end of the kitchen round table. Number five and all denominations thereof, do not exist in this silly game we play.

"*OOPS!*" I pluck my clouded forehead. "Was I supposed to say *fizz?*"

Cheap wine and marijuana inside a multi-nozzle water-pipe – that is my consequence. Or maybe I will have to take a gulp from a tall green translucent bottle with the *Thunderbird* label on its side. Bottoms up! I part my lips. Frown my face and take a cautious swig. A few more screw-ups and I will be under the round table, as the count begins again.

One, two, three, four – *fizz!* Six, seven, eight, nine – *buzz.* Oh, ten doesn't exist either, that's buzz. And anytime you say a *fizz* or a *buzz* the count reverses. The count rotates again in the opposite direction. This time it is Cedric who will fade beneath a facade called fun.

Suddenly and while we are under the influence of ignorance and stupidity, there comes a rapping at the door. It is a pounding thump, distorted by the earsplitting psychedelic-guitar-fusion of "Jimmy Hendrix. It is a haunting sound. One that is enhanced by personified audio perception, expressly transmitted through the telepathic inner powers of a euphoric state of mind.

Maybe – just maybe – someone wants to come in. How intriguing. Still, nobody has the guts to answer the door. Realistically, it could be the police. After all there are some really illicit indulgences in operation here. Like marijuana all over the table, a huge water pipe exchanging hand-to-hand. Minors under the influence and who knows what hallucinogenic or strange article of paraphernalia may likely be stuck in the pockets of our delusional guests. My sweaty palmed-hand drifts slowly from the side of my resting face. My eyelids battle to stay open. We are stupefied. Our eyes stare at a clamped wooden door.

Suddenly, some courageous soul takes the initiative to holler.

"Who is it?" And the call returns from the other side.

"Breeze. It's me, Breeze."

"It's Breeze! Yeah Breeze! Let him in. Open the door!"

Echoes resound and bring relief to the posse at the get-high table. Booming laughter resonates with broad-toothed smiles. Marijuana cigarettes light again. The stereo volume echoes, while our man Breeze drops off two whole pounds. Damn, this party is just getting started.

The depths of night plays out, hot and long, to a psychedelic tune by Parliament-Funkadellic. The screech of a single word repeating itself on a scratched record, ironically entitled "Eulogy" alerts us to another room where a lost cigarette smolders in the crevice of the couch. No panic. A little water and the situation is put to rest. Hours later most of our sleep-deprived guests have decided to leave for home. No longer able to stay the distance, I head straight for my room.

Come daylight, the last of the six records is still spinning. The album revolves around and around and the needle wavers silently over the center label. Cedric snores, asleep in a chair. His one remaining friend finally awakens and heads out the door. As the quiet of morning creeps through, I sip a cup of coffee and toke a "morning" joint. Then squirt a drop of Visine in each eye to psyche myself for my scheduled interview as a teller at the local bank. Suddenly, there comes a knocking at the door.

"Who is it?" This time our fears are realized.

"Police."

"Police?" We reply.

"Just a minute", Minnie calls. We fan our hands to clear the smoke. Then look curiously dumfounded at one another. The "joint" gets flushed. The door stays shut.

"Open the door!" they demand.

She opens it, leaving the chained lock in place.

"We have a warrant for Cedric Jordan." Cedric springs to his feet.

"He's not here!" Minnie snarls. Cedric softly hurries to exit the room. The chain-latch on the door is still in place.

"Open the door. We have a search warrant ma'am."

"He's not here!"

"Well we need to take a look around." The officer insists.

"He is NOT HERE!" Minnie shouts impatiently.

"Look Miss, if we have to break the door in, WE WILL."

We hold our breath. Minnie slides aside and two more uniformed officers push in. Cops are everywhere. They give particular notice to the bedrooms, the closets and under the beds. But, the search ends cold and the officers leave without my brother. I don't get to see much of Cedric anymore, and I wish he didn't have to be on the run. Stealing and robbing folk has gotten him in a world of trouble. More than he can bail himself out.

***

Daddy don't believe I'll ever make anything of myself. Sure I like to blow a joint now and again. But it ain't the only thing I do. He says I oughta' be in college. But I'm fixin' my sights on a radio career in New York City. I got the idea while listening to a smooth D.J. on a big time radio show, just last night. I am trading my unemployment check, now after getting fired at the bank.

The bus drops me and Delbert at the terminal and just fifteen minutes away from my big career. I am greeted by a receptionist who instructs me along with forty or fifty other people to a big room. Inside the instructor is one of New York's big-time radio announcers with a very deep voice. After an hour of orientation an accordion door folds shut and the recording light flashes. An overhead audio speaker sounds outside the audition booth for everyone to hear.

"Th-th f-f-forecast for tt-tt-ttoday calls for sunny skk-k-ies and ..."

The young man in front of me reads just three short paragraphs. It is the instruction given to all. Moments later the rigid fellow exits. He stands nervously awaiting his fate.

"You made it."

"Y-y-yeah! he shouts. Th-thank-you!" He says extending his hand.

"You can leave your payment at the desk. I'll see you next week." The engineer looks at me and smiles. "You're next.

"The forecast for today calls for cloudy skies and a chance for showers. Tomorrow looks much the same with a seventy percent chance for rain. Good evening. My name is Edwina Jordan ..." Without a warning the red recording light goes dim. That was easy. I may not have perfect English, but give me a script and I can read it.

"Congratulations, Edwina. You can step to the side so the next person can enter the booth. Follow the arrows through the hallway. My receptionist will take your payment there."

It's all about the dollar. Any babbling idiot can get in. He shakes my hand. "I will see you next week." he giggles.

"Delbert, please come."

"NO! I ain't going to New York with you."

I'm aiming to get myself a job in radio, now since I finished up my six weeks in broadcasting class.

"Edwina, they ain't gonna hire you just like that." Delbert tells me. "You don't have no experience."

But, I don't listen to Delbert.

"I'll go by myself." I tell him.

"Go ahead and be stupid," he yells. "can't tell your ass nothin'. See what you say when somebody grabs your dumb ass."

I know nothing about New York, except the dangers that everybody keeps telling me. It is a scary place, but not when Delbert is by my side. I've been good at getting the bus to and from school for the past several weeks. And sometimes Delbert and me come to the city to catch an afternoon movie or hang out in the park, smoking reefer and wasting the day away. He always scolds me.

"Hurry up, hurry up!"

But his legs are much longer than mine. I grab hold to his hand, when he lets me. But most times he just hurries away.

The winds are icy and my ears are blistery cold. My woolen hat is pressed inside my pocket. And that is where it will stay. I hate that stupid hat. I'll never get hired wearing it. It sheds too much focus on my chubby cheeks and makes me look like a baby. It's bad enough that I only stand four feet eleven inches. I really want this job.

I take a window seat at the rear of the bus, prepared for the hour ride. As I peer through a large tinted window, thoughts of the interview process, vast acceptance and immediate success rush me. Then I see him, a hefty gentleman waving from the curbside. The whirling wheels hiss and the transit bus comes to an abrupt stop. The doors open wide. "New York City!" he calls out, while the driver makes change of a twenty-dollar bill. Again, the engine turns and takes us down a busy road leading to a major expressway. He rocks side to side between the double-row seating. I slide a bit closer to the window, to give plenty of room to this oversized stranger who takes his chair beside me.

"Say, what you got there?" he flatters me, taking notice of the huge manila envelope set upon my knee.

"It's my demo-tape. I'm going to apply for a job as a radio announcer."

Then a juvenile thought comes to mind. I must be lookin' the part, attracting the attentions of this full-fledged man. A smile leaps inside my belly, but my face don't give in. We talk and he tells me that he has no plans. He just wants to hang out in the big city and waste the afternoon away. I welcome the conversation and his company for the duration of the short trip ahead.

The clock ticks swiftly as we roll into the terminal. I hurry down a couple of escalators then onto the swarming streets of a bustling metropolis, only to catch myself in a harried mob. They ride the backs of my heels in over-drive. This is New York City, with its humongous skyscrapers poking fun at the clouds.

It is New York City, a place where frosty stares lack focus and distant smiles melt like snowflakes before they hit the ground. It is "The Big Apple"; bearing bitter fruit and a lot scarier than its catchy nickname. Mindless automobiles drive mass mobs onto the seams of the roadways, while it is clear to me that no one is getting anywhere fast. Idling engines cut my breath. Sounding horns override my speech. My heart stammers as I wave my new friend goodbye.

Standing amidst a crowd of frenzied folk rushing precariously, I unfold in my hand a wrinkled page of directions. I read the scribbled note. Just two steps behind and over my shoulder, he watches me. It is the gentleman in business attire. He's been watching all the while. He offers to hail a taxi. My numbed fingers peel through the holes in my pockets and press against a frayed inner lining. I look down to my feet and see my worn-over spiked heeled shoes. I agree.

Several blocks and many traffic signals later, together we arrive to the hottest station in town. No fancy lights or big signs distinguish it from either building it sets between. (I had expected a limo parked at the curbside and a red carpet leading the way.) Inside is worse, where I meet a dim, dark booth. I slide my envelope along with some black and white photos under a plate-glass window. The clerk shoves the pictures back.

"You keep those. We don't need them," she says.

Disappointment meets with me in an outer corridor.

What? Does she think I'm just a dumb kid from Jersey, with a big envelope in my hand? No interview, not even a relative word of hire, and already it is time for me to go. My new friend insists I join him for an early dinner. I say yes to the burly gentleman, when the only cash I have is two dollars and fifty cents; enough to get me home from where I started, not HOME from where I am.

Soon, inside the Dinner Club, he requests the menu. I am anything but hungry. There is nothing I wish, except to go home. He orders for himself a full course meal and a couple mixed drinks for two.

"Really, I have got to go home."

"Just relax. Enjoy yourself. I'll see to it that you get home."

A string on an upright bass, strikes a final chord as a small group of patrons lends a generous applause. He blots his mouth with expensive napkins. I "click my heels three times" with a wish to go home. I wet my mouth on the lip of my glass, pretending to drink. My stomach fills with marbles, and if I don't get out of here, 'um gonna be sick.

"Please, can we go?" "I gotta go home."

The big man's chair slides back with the screech of deep scraping that marks the floor. When he stands, my eyes meet his belt line. When I gaze up, he snatches me by the hand, leaving behind a half-eaten meal on a frilly table. He drags me back to the street and lifts me under my armpits. My feet leave the ground and come to rest on a waiting stoop.

"What is wrong with you?" He says harshly. He scolds me for my girlish whining, and his finger shakes loosely in my face. I scream out to passers-by, in hopes that someone will recognize my distress. He grabs me by my shoulders with his swollen hands and shakes.

"Please, just take me home." I cry.

He yanks my arm at the wrist for the mention of it.

Against a darkened sky, dressed for snow, the sun don't shine no more. Following a taxi ride, it is another smoked filled room and two hours later. We have a seat in a crowded bar. He orders a double and I order a rum and coke. I don't want to anger this big stranger, who don't take kindly to the little girl inside of me. While we wait for our drinks, he slides off his stool and to the men's room to take a piss

There sets the Port Authority Bus Terminal –RIGHT ACROSS THE STREET, 'der! I've got enough change from here to get me home. Make room O.J., um' comin' straight through 'dem 'der double-doors. I'm buckin' straight across Eighth Avenue. Darn it! I forgot my photos. He can have the damned things, cause 'um already mixing with the crowd. My legs fly high and I think my knees gon' slap my chest.

"Did you sleep with the guy?"

"No! I didn't sleep with the guy!"

"I told your stupid behine' not to go. I told you. I knew it. I knew they weren't going to hire you just like that. I told you, didn't I?"

Shut-up Delbert!" That's what I wish to say. Instead, I just sit looking stupid.

Our feet patter side by side along the wet and rainy pavement. The whizzing early rush hour traffic spatters my stockings. The dampness chills my legs. It is my first time back to New York City since that day. This time Delbert is by my side. We board a bus together. Not to catch an afternoon flick and not to dawdle the day away. We have talked many times of marriage and of babies. We have agreed on marriage and more babies. Together we walk inside a dim brick building, where the furniture is old and paint on the stained walls chips away. Delbert waits for several hours. When I return, I am cold and weak. My body folds and my belly aches with cramping. His arms fold around me as the bus pulls away. Baby or none, Delbert means EVERYTHING to me. And no matter what NOBODY thinks. NOT EVEN MINNIE, he will always stay the love of my life.

Not for a split second, do I believe that nonsense; Minnie accusing Delbert of stealing a quarter pound of pot from Frank. Just a couple days gone and we don't start out heading to Delbert's mama's house. It's just where we end up after walking around the block, all day. Frank told Delbert to "get out!" And, where Delbert goes, I'm there behind him. It doesn't matter that Delbert don't have "a pot to piss in, or a window to throw it out of" as Daddy would say. And Minnie, she don't want me to leave, but she sure don't argue for me to stay. She wishes me well and shuts the door behind us when we leave out on our way.

CHAPTER 7

JUMPIN' THE BROOM

Delbert's sister is married to the son of a minister. He will perform the ceremony at Katrina's house. There is the Italian baker, the same who'd saved for us day-old bread. He delivers a three-tier wedding cake, with deep chocolate and butter-cream frosting; his special gift just for me. Fried chicken and potato salad are the main course, as tonight I wed Delbert Gilliam.

Mom dazzles in the lilac gown she wore to my high school graduation. Dad is clad in a pinstriped suit and has left his frown behind. There is quite a spillover, as some listen from the back bedrooms inside this little abode. A swelling crowd fills an undersized living room to witness me and Delbert say our vows.

Mommy says that a bride should wear something old. My shoes are old with new cloth sewn over the uppers. Something new is my gown. I sewed it myself, out of white fabric. Something borrowed is my smile and suddenly, I'm feeling so blue.

Delbert staggers in, teetering side to side. A hush falls over the room. A snicker and a whisper grow in the crowd, before the pastor brings all to quiet.

"We are gathered here together on this twenty-third day of November 1974, to bring together Delbert Gilliam and Edwina Jordan."

"Edwina, do you take this man …?"

"I do."

Delbert is silent and the room stands still.

Delbert, do you take this woman, Edwina Jordan to be you lawfully wedded wife, for better or worse, for richer or poorer, in sickness and in health, from this day forward?"

To everybody's amazement, Delbert explodes with laughter, rousing a roomful of family and guests. His hand flies to cover his cackling mouth.

"Could you repeat that?" He giggles. Weaving forward and swaying back.

Following the ceremony and to formally captivate this most blissful occasion, we eat cake. Then return to Minnie's, where we will share our honeymoon night. Tick-tock, tick tock, before the clock strikes twelve Delbert passes out and falls clear across my little bed. I slide beside my husband, for tomorrow will be a better day.

It is the perfect day for a picture-taking affair at Cedargrove Park. The air is crisp and the sun shines bright. Frank is anxious to shoot a few rolls, snapshots for our wedding album. November is beautiful and so am I, standing in my husband's arms. The 35mm zooms in to capture the sight. Click-click, the camera lens smiles with reflection. We huddle close to the stillness of a rippling pond for a picture inside the handsome brick construction of the nearby gazebo. Fondly, I watch as a school of proud geese glide along the water's edge. From the biggest to the smallest, they stretch their necks and stride with honor, the same like me. Then, Minnie prompts Delbert to move in closer. He steps his foot on a pedal to activate a stream of water, flowing into the metallic basin. I bend, as if swallowing a drink. The camera snaps, again. Clickety-click-click! This is my day and I am the happiest I have ever known. "I done jumped the broom."

Delbert,
What does he mean to me?
Delbert
More than the eye can see.
Delbert,
My husband, my brother,
my friend, my lover.
My heart sings a song for Delbert.
Even when he's not around,
he touches me.

Just weeks into our marriage and I am pregnant! Yes! Again! And – my wonderful husband is no longer unemployed. A pharmaceutical company has hired him. But that's not all. We are moving into Delbert's sister's place. Katrina is moving out, and Delbert hasn't even collected his first paycheck. We will explain it all to the landlord later.

The two-bedroom dwelling is so adorable and perfect for newlyweds. I am so excited! I am carrying Delbert's baby, I've got a house. Best of all, I just love being Delbert's wife. I welcome the cooking. I welcome the cleaning. And I can't wait until I hold our newborn baby in my arms.

Hanging plants and window-length curtains threaded with a bamboo stick add a finishing touch to the living room. The bathroom shower sparkles, following a good scrub. A bedroom set, old but sturdy is given by Frank and Minnie. Now that they are engaged, they won't be using it when they move into their new home. Colorful accessories brighten the kitchen and a thorough cleaning on my hands and knees brings new life to the floor. Antiquated cabinets, aged with layers of paint are refaced with a three-dollar roll of contact paper.

"Bleach is good for removing the yellowing and for brightening kitchen sinks," Minnie says. Frankly, I don't give a care. I don't need household hints from *Helpful Hannah.*" If I could afford a brand new countertop, like Frank and Minnie, I'd buy one. I wish Minnie would quit telling me how to clean my house. I don't need advice from nobody, except maybe, Dr. Joy Brown.

Ever since I moved out of Minnie's and married Delbert, it upsets me to see her. First, I'm happy then I'm angry. But I'm never as happy as Minnie seems to be. It shames me that my poor sister doesn't even know that I feel this way. She dropped by yesterday and I didn't even bother to open the door. I'm just not in the mood for her self-importance. Always carrying on about Frank and what he does for her. Gibber, gibber, gibber, always bragging about the rock she's got on her finger – and the new house. All Delbert and I have is a rental. I stay on my knees trying to scrub it clean. Already, I am tired of rubbing with 'dis heah toothbrush and trying to make something new from something old that somebody else already done used up. I can't tolerate her good fortune. I love my sister, but I love Delbert too. If she can't accept him she won't be seeing me.

With all that said, I wanna see her. I miss her terribly. Truth be told, I love her more than anything. She is always there, offering nothing short of never-ending love and care. It is my own inadequacies that have visited disharmony between us, while Delbert sits waiting to co-sign my foolishness. He hates when I visit Minnie. He says there are too many men visiting Frank's house. He's jealous. That husband of mine is just insecure.

But oh, when I see her lying flat on her back. Her eyes are so weak and they stare afar. Today is not a good day to share with Minnie that I am pregnant. I sit softly beside her. I kiss her cheek and say softly. "I love you."

Monday morning, Delbert rises early for work. With fried sausages bubbling in a skillet, I help him to gather a couple of cold cut sandwiches for his lunch. Two large eggs are beaten to a fluff and thrown onto a hot fryer. He eats, then his ride skirts round the bend and zips him off to work. I go back to bed for a couple more hours of uninterrupted rest.

Ding-dong, ding-dong. Ding-dong, ding-dong. I rise quickly to my feet. Then pull the curtain and take a peek. Ding-dong, ding-dong. Ding-dong.

For crying out loud, I heard it the first time. I hurry barefoot across a chilly floor, dragging the long tail on my night gown behind. The instant I twist the knob the door parts. It jolts forward with the force of Mom leaning into the other side. Ernestine hurries in and with her the blustery March winds snap square across my bare arms.

"Get dressed!" Nearly breathless, Mom tells me, "Minnie has taken a turn for the worst."

"Huh? Turn for the worst?" My hands slap my gaping mouth. "I didn't know she was in the hospital."

"Frank rushed her to the hospital last night."

"What?"

"Hurry up," Mom insists. I snap into motion. Hurry, I do.

We arrive at the hospital's Intensive Care Unit, Mom, Ernestine, and me. Inside a scant and dingy lobby we seat ourselves on a short black plastic sofa. Spitting nervous chatter and wringing our hands. We wait. I watch the long black appendages on a humongous big-face clock scan the way around its diameter. Two wide double doors spread open, then again spring shut against the gowns of hospital whites and green. Within the silence, the unrelenting ticking clock has consumed a whole quarter hour. Fifteen minutes escape, until I see a cloak of black and a hint of white. These are the colors worn by a priest, the same who'd swept by us moments before.

"I'm sorry," he exclaims in a whisper.

He drops his head and his palms fall to his sides. The door to her room remains parted and I see Minnie, still as can be. She wears her bed-clothes. Not a hospital gown, just the green sleeper she wore to bed at home every night, when she'd sleep in her own bed and dream her own dreams. Instantly, I am angry. Why didn't they let me see her before the blood stopped running through her veins? Why? My trembling forefingers stroke her face, and I find it still warm. I think how I used to stand over her bedside, watching to see her breasts rise and fall. But her bosom doesn't heave. Not once, not up, nor down, and her ears no longer hear. Still I whisper and tell her I love you. Then brush her parted eyelids shut, forever.

I find my way down the stairs to meet with Frank as he pulls to the curbside. There is no recall for the short drive to the funeral home. Nor is there any reflection of the walk down the long carpeted trail leading to the open white coffin. The tension in my palms relax, just enough for me to caress her hair. It is coarse and hard, brittle like an inexpensive baby doll. My trembling fingers scan her cheek and it only serves as confirmation. There's no cause to lean into to her to validate the soft warm breath blowing out of her broad round nostrils. Cold, like wet cement and hard as stone, Minnie is no more. My feet don't move. My stomach wrenches. I am nudged away from the metallic, satin lined cubicle to leave behind the remnants of a once vibrant, beautiful, witty intelligent young woman, who was once my very special Minnie.

<hr />

The old timers say that just before a woman goes into labor she gets a burst of energy. I guess I spurted last night. If I had my way I'd choose the scrubbing and scouring, because having this baby will be the harder job between the two. My labor is coming every fifteen minutes. The pain is unbearable, when I am wheeled into the hospital. Some excruciating hours later, my healthy, beautiful baby boy arrives. I will call him Keonis.

Three days later I carry him home to his proud Daddy, who steals him from my arms to show to all of the neighbors. In a moment alone, my marriage to Delbert feels like a fairytale. My worn and fuzzy slippers, parked in a corner of the room are the first sure sign that this is not a dream. Yet, I wonder what it might be like, me and Delbert growing old together; Delbert with prickly gray hairs, testing his youth, and I, with a silver crown and curved spine. Silly me, I'm in love with the essence of the words "love and marriage," not to mention, diaper changing, midnight feedings and kissing little damp tears away.

On an early afternoon and in the weeks ahead, the doorbell sounds. I answer to a man clad in suit and tie. He paces casually on my doorsill.

"Hi. Are you Edwina Gilliam?" he asks.

"Yes, I am Edwina."

"I am here from the Furniture Warehouse. I have come to collect on some furniture you purchased."

"Have you come to carry it away?"

"No!" he exclaims. "I would like to pick up the payment. There has been nothing paid on the balance in months."

I look at the sofa, as does he. It is well used with dense body imprints from long wear and tear. Two end tables and a glass top set in plain view. I don't expect Delbert will pay for them. Our refrigerator, we've had it three months and Delbert hasn't paid a dime. And then there are my baby's pictures. I'll never see them, because Delbert never pays for anything.

"Well, I will be honest with you, I don't have the money. If you want to take the stuff with you, help yourself."

We go back and forth. Frustrated, he turns to walk away.

Soon thereafter a second stranger appears. He identifies himself as the hospital photographer. Anxious to see my baby's photographs, I invite him in. Unfortunately, he hasn't brought the pictures along. He explains the cost and further invites me to browse a huge catalogue from one of two attaché cases he carries in his hand. Scrolling the pages he reveals several items, one that I am particularly excited to see. It is *Baby's First Book*, a simple chronicle to keep track of Keonis' growing years. Then there is *The Family Tree*, a keepsake to pass along one day to my grandchildren. It would give them a sense of where they come from. Unlike me, who knows very little of how I came to be.

"How much?" I ask, while flipping the pages on the oversized catalogue as if I have the money in a locked safe. Not to my surprise, the figures are no match for an empty pocket book. The telephone was disconnected last week.

"We can't afford this stuff," I tell him.

The salesman watches me closely, then, removes a different catalogue from the opened case at his feet. Together we thumb the pages. There are brightly colored picture frames, some shaped like building blocks and others to be imprinted with Keonis' name. It is a varied collection and a magnificent keepsake that he now offers to sell as a package and for a discount price.

Still it is impossible for me. There is no money to be had.

Just then, he has the ideal proposition. A little touching of unseen places to cover the entire expense. A lucky quarter or a package of baby photos, isn't it all the same? No! No! No! I nearly respond with favor. As this is precisely the way things were always handled, as I recall. I will have to live without my baby's pictures.

"It is time for you to leave." I say.

To have entertained such an unthinkable act sets off immediate anger inside myself. I order him out. I am disgraceful, disgusting and accurately the whore that Delbert has always said of me.

To my amazement, some few weeks later, my unlocked screened door pushes open. It alarms me to see the intruder pushing his way across my living room floor. I am petrified to see his drawn face, when following his previous visit I learned through a conversation at the hospital that this stranger has no business with them at all. He pushes through uninvited. Suddenly, I grasp a dense carved wooden stick. It is an African piece, placed for decoration and propped against my wall.

"GET OUT!" I scream. "I know who you are. The police know about you too. My phone is disconnected, but only I know that. Now, GET OUT, before I call the cops!" I say.

Suddenly, he hurries out of the front door. I run behind him, screaming to the top of my lungs. He dashes across the front lawn. Grabs hold to his license plate and rips it forward, bending it out of view. He jumps into his car and presses the metal to the floor.

Just now, Kevin, Delbert's kid brother hurries along the walkway. Just in time to witness the tail end of this God-forsaken calamity, as he heads home from school.

"What's the matter, Edwina? Is everything all right?" He watches in amazement to see the car shooting backwards down the narrow road.

I must tell Delbert. It would be better for him to hear it from me, than his kid-brother. I confess to him, the whole truth.

"You whore! You bitch! I hate you! You probably fucked him. I know you did!" He opens his fly. His pants fall to his feet. Then, Delbert punishes me in a way that no woman should ever know. I gag. Delbert stands up.

"Payback is a bitch." My heart is splitting. "And revenge is a mutha' fucker" he says, then turns to walk away.

***

I have prepared a warm bubbly bath of scented water and parked his house slippers conveniently in his grasp. There, draped across a bathroom stool lay a soft fluffy bed-coat made of flowing fabric. It is my handmade gift just for him. Two embroidered hearts on the hip pocket overlay one another as a sign of my love. In the bedroom, freshly washed towels smell of incense, perfumed with coconut. An old Billy Holiday tune, "My Man," cries of affection, confusion and twisted love.

Lady Day,
Eleanora Fagan,
singing the songs I love so much.
As if I were there,
hearing more than I hear,
feeling more than I feel,
"Lady Day" you were so real.

Them There Eyes,
Good Morning Heartache;
Giving all you could give,
taking all you could take,

makes my heart break.
My lips smile.
Billy love,
you sure had style,
class,
and sass.
It came to pass
When you went away.

A car sweeps to the curbside and the passenger door opens. I rise, wearing black and frilly lingerie. I reach for my Delbert at the door.

"Happy Birthday," I whisper.

His hands motion toward me, but it is merely a gesture to shove me aside. Quickly, he peels out of his coat and unzips his fly. All at once, Delbert runs fast into the bathroom, where he goes to take a piss. Surely, he will notice his bathrobe and house-shoes conveniently set outside the bathtub. The door bangs hard behind him and I wait. He returns in haste as if I am not there. He slides swiftly from room to room. Then he grabs his jacket, wraps himself in it and dashes toward the outer door.

"Delbert," I call to him.

"What!" With bitterness, he calls back.

"I was hoping that ..." I speak softly, wishing not to antagonize him.

"I'll be back." He harshly calls.

"But, Delbert I cooked and ..."

"I said I'll be back." He is without temperance.

"Delbert, please ... I have a card for you."

The card stands propped against a table lamp in plain sight. "Would you at least read it before you go?" It has been sealed with a kiss, the pinked stain of my lipstick imprint on its face.

"I'll read it when I come back."

"Where are you going, Delbert? Please don't leave."

To read it may give him a change of heart.

"I would like to spend some time with you," I plead. "I made dinner for your birthday." I plead again, "Just, read the card before you go."

He fidgets with impatience, then snatches the envelope and rips it apart. He flashes a quick grin. As his first observation is the enclosed marijuana joint. Completely distracted he sparks it.

"Read the card." I nudge him.

Delbert's eyes scan the page with careless concern. He tosses it back to the table, next to where I sit. He inhales. I talk, while he takes in smoke, nearly to finish.

"I am sorry, Delbert. Really, I am. I love you."

In this single stolen moment, I express to him how much I want things to change.

"I love you with all of my heart."

I apologize to my husband for the error of my ways.

"I can make it up to you."

Delbert interrupts.

"I'll be back."

"Where are you going?"

"What did I tell you?" He raises his tone. "Didn't I tell you – I'll be back."

Slam! The door crashes and the room falls hush.

"Payback really is a bitch," isn't it Delbert? His words rip my gut in his absence. "And revenge is a mutha' fucker." He means every filthy word. Delbert, revenge would only come back to bite you in the ass. Don't you realize it'd be better for you to forgive? Really it would. Tears well in my eyes and stream my cheeks. You come home drunk every chance you get. How dare you? We have a baby together. Don't do this Delbert. A wave of heated emotion sends me crashing to my face and across the sofa. I roll into a ball, with my knees to my chin. I cry aloud. "I can't fix this thing by myself."

Irreconcilable differences are evident in a single exhausted candle at the table's center. Myself and I have agreed to store the meal instead of allowing it to spoil. Ultimately, Keonis has been bedded and I hold my pillow in my arms, where Delbert ought to be. It's been several hours, and I miss him.

Suddenly, a key clicks inside the lock. It is followed by a tottering of footsteps across the living room floor. Then there is a voice. It is the feminine tone of a woman. Her voice carries softly through the hollow hallway and into the room where I rest. Tonya makes her presence known. He's got a lot of damned nerve! — bringing his bitch into our home, nearly into my bedroom for God sake. I'd like to piss on both their heads.

Tonya smiles cunningly and charms with superficial conversation as my husband, Delbert stands at her side.

"She just stopped in to see the baby," he says.

At midnight? I should be hysterical, when my thoughts keep silent. My husband escorts Tonya to our sleeping baby's crib. I hear the both of them in his darkened room, cooing over him. Too often, I look and there she is. A few more moments of fussing over little Keonis and Delbert shows his hussy to the door. Then quickly returns in an attempt to redeem himself.

"Tonya is just like family. She's Uncle Johnny's niece."

"What! She's no kin to you! Uncle Johnny ain't no kin to you, neither. Uncle Johnny is married to your mother's sister. But Uncle Johnny ain't NO KIN TO YOU! And there sure ain't no bloodline connecting you to Tonya." The boldness in my tone is nothing Delbert has ever heard before. His eyes look at me, wide opened, like a little kid trying to convince his mommy that he didn't steal the red lollypop.

"Are you screwing Tonya or what? What's going on? I want to know the truth?"

"No, honest, she just stopped across the street to see her Uncle Johnny. When she saw me, she asked to see the baby!" A juvenile mischievousness in his tone makes me think, liar, liar, liar!

"And you just happened to be there, huh?"

"That's my mother's sister … Aunt Dora is my mother's sister. You know that. You know that I always visit Aunt Dora."

"How convenient"

"I don't know why you think that I'm sleeping with that tramp. Tonya ain't nothin' but a whore. I don't want Tonya." He yells emphatically. "I can have her anytime I want. But, I don't want her! She ain't nothin' but a tramp." Continuing to ingest this wad of malarkey is making me sick to my stomach. I've got to know.

"Are you sleeping with her? Huh! Are you, Delbert, are you?" Deliberately, I hammer him. Figuring, I'd better strike while the iron is hot. If he will ever be honest with me, it would be now.

He confesses. "Yeah, I slept with her. But that was a long time ago, before you and me. But I ain't sleeping with her NOW, honest. Remember that baby picture, you asked me about on my wall? When we first met?"

"Yeah"

"And, I told you that it was my nephew. Well, that was Tonya's baby. Tonya runs around telling everybody the kid is my son. But, that kid ain't mine. She's just a slut and it ain't no telling who the father is." Delbert has got me listening to him now. "As a matter of fact, Tonya is married."

"Married? I can't tell!" I cut into him. "How do you know so much about her?"

"Because, I just know"

"How?" I press him.

"I've known Tonya since junior high school, when Aunt Dora married Tonya's Uncle. We used to mess around then, but it wasn't nothin' to it. She only wanted me to screw her. Tonya has always liked me. But I am telling you, she ain't nothin' but a 'ho." Delbert tries vehemently to redeem himself, but seems only to cosign his own indictment. "As a matter of fact, on the same night that she got married, she wanted me to screw her," he blurts with passion. "She invited me over!" This all sounds so bizarre, nearly too bizarre for fiction. "Then she answered the door for me and she was butt-naked."

"Where was Tonya's husband during all of this?"

"He was there!"

"He was there?"

I can't grasp what I am hearing.

"Yeah, he was there, but he was drunk in another room, asleep."

"Did you do it Delbert? Did you screw her that night?" I ask.

"Hell, fuckin' NO!"

"Do you expect me to believe that? Why not screw her, Delbert! You screwed her before."

"Yeah, but that was when we were younger. But now – I wouldn't screw that slut. I wouldn't screw that bitch with my Daddy's dick."

"I don't believe you." I tell him. I want to trust his word, but "for a man who don't want her," I scream, "you sure as hell know a whole lot about her."

Surely, Delbert, you have an explanation for everything. But what will you say when I tell you, while cleaning this afternoon, I found a termination letter from your job. It was a notice that was issued a couple of weeks ago? And – where do you spend your days? Thinking about it makes my head throb and my world is turned upside down. I reach for a long Kool cigarette. I strike a light and inhale. Even worse – I have crabs! I spend my hours at home, ALONE, Delbert – for Christ sake!

And then there is Minnie, who is never around when I need her. It's been eight months, since she went away. Only God could know how much I need her. Twenty-six lousy years she spent on this earth. I'd have thought the Lord would've given us more. We used to talk about everything. Alfreda, I miss her too. Ever since she took off to New York City, I don't see nothin' of her. I imagine that she has a pretty bad habit, spending time in the shootin' galleries, or so I've been told. The truth is I worry about all my sisters. Nadine included, with that *monkey* on her back. I guess Celia done the right thing by gettin' the hell up out of here and moving to Detroit, Michigan. I don't' see Rhonda and Giselle, both of 'em are running wild. Then, there is my brother Cedric, who done gone from robbing parking meters to bigger hustles in crime. Ernestine is 'bout the only one who I do see from time to time. But judging by some of the crazy things she do, with no presence of mind, maybe its best she stay away.

My drifting thoughts are redirected in an instant, when comes an unsettling noise outside my door. Next comes the pounding of footsteps and Cedric peeling across my living room floor. His tee-shirt is sopping wet and sweat trickles from his forehead, straight down the length of his nose. He presses toward me.

"Here!" He says, abruptly, pushing something into my hand.

It is a man's black leather wallet. Panic consumes me. There are several bills poking from the inside fold. "Take it," he demands and thrusts the object into my chest. It is a coin slot. A familiar kind affixed on the city bus.

"Where'd you get this?" He pushes it toward me. I shove it back. I struggle. Brother's weight wrestles nervously against mine. "I DON'T WANT IT – Cedric!" I shout. The device falls to the floor. He swiftly picks it up. And with a shifting glance through the parted curtain on an exposed bay window he sees her. Katrina walks fiercely and leads a pack of officers to my door. "I don't want this stuff!" Cedric runs off. I hurry behind him, nearly tripping on his heels. "Take it Cedric! Get it out of here! CEDRIC - - CEDRIC!" I scream.

All of a sudden, he throws the bathroom window. The cops plow behind him, trampling like a herd of wild horses. Cedric's feet toss awkwardly over the sill. It's over for my brother. With one cop on each side and a tall and sturdy fence blocking the way, Cedric ain't headed nowhere, 'cept back to jail. And this time it won't be a visit to the boys' home, or a youth correctional center. Cedric you are a full-fledged man – and Cedric – NOW I will be missing you.

That was yesterday. I am so thankful that today is a better day. The weeks unravel in view of a roped clothesline pegged with diapers, tiny undershirts, sleepers and such. All washed by hand and wrung over a kitchen sink. They are strung on a line to flutter in the autumn breeze. Like billowed sails on a big boat, the blankets swell with flowing air and propel in the wind. Blowing with equal ease are thoughts of my birth child, who is even sweeter than I could have ever hoped. He greets me, while smiling toothlessly early each morning, then reaches for me to carry him up in my arms. With Daddy away we pass the mornings with breakfast and a little play. Following a gentle bath we set out for our daily stroll to visit my mom. On her kitchen counter, I find a huge four layer chocolate cake.

"Hmm-mmm, can I have a slice?"

"What are you asking me for? It's your cake. You're the one who has a birthday coming." Mom asks with a lot of love and a bit of redundancy. "You can do with it what you like!" She smiles and I laugh.

"Oh Mom!" I give her one of my biggest hugs. It touches me when she does this, especially with all she's going through. She never forgets my birthday. Even when I ran away, Mom was there with a telegram. These things I will never forget. I pour a cup of coffee and offer a cup to Mom. She shakes her head.

"No. No-thanks, I'm okay." She says with a playful smile, while removing from her pocketbook a brown paper-bag. It is a bottle of maple colored liquid, a half-pint liquor bottle hidden deep in her purse. "It calms my nerves," she claims. She unscrews and pours a swig. Her head turns back. She swallows quickly and frowns. Mom exhales and with a smile, before stuffing the package back, inside her purse. It's a strange thing to visit this house and to find its rooms calm with quiet. I like it when Dad is not home. And although I don't enjoy seeing Mom drink, if that's what it takes to keep her nerves from crumbling, I suppose it's what she's got to do.

The hours pass swiftly and already it is nearly time to go. I gotta cook dinner before Delbert gets home. I pop on Keonis' hat, kiss Mom's cheek and say goodbye.

"Mom, I'll see you tomorrow."

"What's your hurry?" she asks, with a slur of disappointment in her voice.

"I gotta go, Mom, Delbert will be home soon."

"Delbert – Delbert – DELBERT—that's all I ever hear! FUCK DELBERT!" she yells.

"Mom!" She never cusses until she gets to drinkin'. Still, she never cusses at me.

"You could stay a little longer if you wanted to." Mom is tired. She's tired of being alone, tired of being without her children. She's tired of being alone with Dad. But I can't stay. I've got a husband, and a family of my own to care for. "Mom, I've got to get going. It'll take me about twenty minutes, to get there in time, if I start walking, now."

"I'll get you there. I'll take you home," Mom says. She's right. I guess I could stay a little longer. Delbert ain't in no hurry to rush home to me. And when my visit is through, Mom sets out to drive me home. But first, there is another swig. This one is for the road.

Mom's not seeing too well. The big car swerves. I slide her into the passenger's seat and drive her safely, BACK HOME. Once there, I remove little Keonis' carriage from the trunk, then set out as I should have at the start, for the ten-block stroll. There'll be just about enough time to prepare dinner for Delbert.

While Keonis naps I cook. The choice is an obvious one. An undernourished chicken is all to be had. I should have asked Mom for food. But she'd tell Dad and it would only serve to make them both angrier with Delbert. I am mindful these days of the provider my Dad is. I think back to when I was a girl. We always had dozens of fresh eggs. Dad would hurry us to eat them, so he could rush back to the farm to buy more. Five-gallon drums lined the floor of the basement, filled with sugar or flour and rice. Most know it as a china closet. But with no window in its wooden frame, for us it was a food cabinet. It set in the cellar, loaded like a pantry with can after can of evaporated milk, canned vegetables and more. Then would come Fridays or "Fish Day", when a little old man in a little old truck sounded a loud, little bell to alert the neighborhood that he is in town. Packed on ice next to a big meat scale was always a new catch to pack in a big deep freezer alongside all the other goods. Another portion was removed and thawed for the evening meal. On Saturdays I enjoyed baking cookies or cake just because I felt like it. All of the ingredients were there, just like on the shelf at a grocery store. I never recognized just how blessed I was. But, as I sprinkle its back and season its belly, I thank God for this scrawny little chicken and for the leftover potatoes to supplement the meal. I shove the bird inside a hot stove. As the oven door slams, the doorbell rings.

Well if it ain't *bruzzin'* Toby. "Come on in," I say, "And make yourself at home." Toby attempts to introduce me to a buddy of his, Nathaniel.

"Nathaniel," Toby says, "this is my cousin Edwina … I mean my sister." But Toby laughs nervously.

"Just call me your *sizzin'*." I poke fun with Toby to break the ice. "Sister, cousin, *sizzin'*, call me what you like. It's all the same to me." It is an inside joke between us. Toby slips a giggle and I slide him the knowing-eye, before showing him and his friend to the kitchen for a seat. "Would you like something to drink?" I ask, handing Toby a glass of water from the fridge. His reaching exposes pockmarks from a hypodermic needle and shooting heroin in the inside fold of his arm. It seems that all these many years Toby has believed Aunt Bea, when she'd tell him that his Daddy died in the war. Well, for Toby it's been difficult learning that the uncle who raised him is really his Dad.

"Remember when… " Toby and I talk and reminisce over our growing up together. He's just six months older than me and we recall our first day at school. It was kindergarten. Toby cried and Aunt Bea came to the rescue and took him back home. Then, there were our high school years. I can't count the times I called Toby from class to get my old car to start. Under the hood he would go, pounding or screwing on something.

"What a car," Toby says, F—O—R—D," he spells it. "FIX OR REPAIR, DAILY." We laugh. The old, brush-painted, green tin box has completed her mission. She has since retired to junk yard heaven. Time passes quickly and Delbert appears, just as he returns from his day's work. I rise to greet him.

"Hey man. How ya doin'?" Toby cordially says hello. "This is a friend of mine, Nathaniel. Nathaniel, this is Delbert, Edwina's husband."

Delbert nods silently, without focus then proceeds into an adjoining room.

"Well, we're gonna go, Toby slides his chair. "Don't want to intrude on your dinner." Toby smiles, gently.

"It was nice meeting you, Nathaniel." I extend my hand. Toby caps his visit with a hug. Respectfully, I see them to the door. Delbert plows out of the bathroom with his pants half-zipped and no sooner than the outer door shuts, he exclaims.

"Who's Nathaniel, one of your little boyfriends?"

"What!" I ask in surprise. He repeats again.

"Is Nathaniel one of your little boyfriends? You been fuckin' him behind my back?"

"Why are you saying that?" I reply in disgust.

"Well, you screw everybody else. You sure you ain't screwing him too? Huh bitch?"

"Why are you acting like this, Delbert? Why? I love you."

"Fuck you whore. I hate you. Don't you know if you were stuck inside a bottle bitch and needed air — I wouldn't pop the cork?"

Sputtering, demented words from the lips of the man I love. He is the father of my baby. My eyes stream with tears as I remove the steaming bird from the oven. I turn the dial to the off position and move to the bedroom to tend to Keonis, who has awakened from his short nap. Delbert pulls a chair and shovels in his evening meal. He finishes quickly and without a single word storms out of the kitchen and leaves through the front door.

Ding-dong, ding-dong, ding-dong, ding-dong! The sounding of the bell, ringing rapid, alarms me. Seeing Ernestine on the other side does little to bring me ease. Her clothes are soiled. Open rips in her denim pants reveal abrasions still bleeding on her knees. She stumbles inside.

"What's the matter, Ernestine? What happened?" I ask, hysterically. "Ernestine, what happened?"

"Daddy charged at me!"

"What!"

"I jumped out of the window on the second floor."

"The second floor?" Suddenly, my mind flashes and images of a mad man rush my mind.

"No! No! You can't go back there." I offer Ernestine a bathrobe. "You don't have to go through this. No! Come into the bathroom and clean yourself up."

We talk awhile, until Ernestine begins to relax. I find no need for further questions. A soft pillow and a blanket will do. When Delbert returns, I explain. Soon we all turn in for a good night's sleep.

Tick-tock, tick-tock, the night is long as little Keonis stirs in his sleep. Quickly, I rise, without the flick of a light. I head first to seat myself on the bathroom stool. Keonis has settled, thank goodness, and the house returns quiet. All that stirs is the trickling of the water inside the toilet bowl. In the foggiest of mind, my business is finished. Suddenly my eyes draw to the shower curtain. It strikes me as odd to find it drawn in the middle of the night. With one good tug I snatch a hold and drag it on its little hooks.

"That's my retarded daughter." Daddy always said that.

"She ain't retarded", I'd always protected her from his snide remarks.

"ERNESTINE – WHAT ARE YOU DOING!' I scream. She cringes in not a single drop of water. Her hands wrap her naked breast and her raw thighs clench. I wonder what I'd say to Daddy, now.

The calendar pages fade into the most frigid days of winter. The electricity is shut off for non-payment. The windows glazed over and the toilet bowl holds a block of ice. When Daddy asks, "Edwina, why is your house so dark?" And, "Where is your husband?" I don't lie to him.

"Edwina, why didn't you tell me you didn't have no food?" I don't lie to Mom, neither. It would only worry them to know the truth. Besides, I'm not about to cosign Dad, when he says, Delbert don't mean me no good. Long hours waiting on Delbert to bring milk for the baby or an evening meal is sufficient burden for me to bear.

Today, no warmth condenses in my spirit to help defrost the chill inside these icy rooms. My breath is white and my fingertips draw tight. January is frostier than I have known. The months accumulate as does the past-due rent on our much loved one hundred and twenty dollar-a-month abode. I thank God for the heat from the gas stove, and for the mattress shoved to the oven. I thank God for quilted sleepers and outer clothing to keep Keonis from catching his death of cold. A for-sale sign pokes from the lawn. Had it not been for the sympathy of a compassionate landlord; although compassion don't pay the bills, we'd have confronted this crossroad many months ago.

"So what time does your flight leave?"

Mom asks as I make final plans to set off to the Georgian countryside for a brand new start. Today is a bitter-sweet visit. The last I will spend with her, until the Good Lord blesses me to make it back home. Delbert, Keonis and I will be takin' off tomorrow to live with Delbert's brother Vernon and his wife. I won't pretend that 'um gonna miss the cold weather. I surely won't miss the bill collectors knocking at my door. But, Mom's pudgy cheeks have fallen with the aging of time and somehow I can't imagine my life without her. Tiny lines trace her forehead. Dim crevices map the underside of her muted brown eyes. Gray hairs frame her temples and her smile is less than bright.

She offers me a cup of coffee, while Ernestine sits with her butt plopped on top a kitchen counter. I wince with discomfort as she reaches into the pocket of her faded denim jeans. Shamelessly she pulls out a pack of *EZ-Wider*. Ernestine tears a sheet from the inset of the package and creases a fold. She reaches again, inside the same pocket. Out pulls a little manila envelope. She loosens the flap and sprinkles the dried green leaf, then reaches for a chilled can of Colt 45, set at her side. Mommy blows a deep sigh of disgust.

"Don't start, Ernestine", she says. Ernestine tips the can again. Mom scowls with displeasure.

"Bitch," she looks at me. "You think your shit don't stink," Ernestine's legs wag, "just because you're moving to Georgia, huh?"

I don't think I'm nothin' in my own eyes. But, sitting high and looking low is the way Ernestine sees me. Living high on the hog in a little white cottage behind a white picket fence. She has no insight for what I'm going through.

"You ain't shit BITCH, just 'cause you are married and got a baby." She says.

I don't know what it is that troubles my sister. Mom's eyes roll inside her head. Suddenly, "Ernestine" she shouts without temperance. "Watch your mouth." Ernestine's eyes stay fixed on me and her feet sway to and fro.

"Mommy, I have a stop-over in Augusta." I restart our conversation to quell the tension. "I will call you when we get there."

"You think you're better. Don't you bitch?" Ernestine screams even louder, "Don't you bitch?" I pretend I don't hear.

"Just ignore her, Edwina," Mom says.

"You think you're better, – just because you're married." I don't answer. "I KNOW YOU HEAR ME — B-I-T-C-H!" She shouts. I can't for the life of me figure what keeps my sister so angry. Then I hear a whisper inside my head. SHE IS JEALOUS.

"I'll take you outside and beat your little ass!"

Insult upon insult. Never has Ernestine allowed me to love her and only God knows her reasons why.

"Come on outside – bitch!" She is calling me. "I'll cut your ass up with this knife!"

Then visions of my sister take hold in my head. Ernestine cringing in my bathtub, NUDE and dry as sand. Suddenly Ernestine's eyes squint as though the evil of hell has come to possess her. And before I can react she moves swiftly behind me and hits me, while my back is turned. Ernestine, I am not your competition. I am your sister. Why can't you get that through your thick head?"

Finally, the police arrive just in time to see Ernestine's back arched beneath the tabletop. Her back stretches high as she raises it up on all fours. She is handcuffed, for lack of a straightjacket, and shoved into the back of a flashing patrol car. Ernestine hollers, LOUD, raspy noises and gurgles from the pit of her throat. Terrifying signs of hatred from a sister I no longer know.

Tomorrow is my birthday and I will be every bit of twenty-two years old. I celebrate with Katrina, tomorrow morning I will be off to the Georgia pines. I am leaving all these bad memories right here in New Jersey. I am ready for a brand new start! I give a toast to new beginnings. Yeah! NEW BEGINNINGS! A toast to NEW STARTS! Uh-huh! And, a toast to a fool whose stomach is churning, like butter. ME! I've got to get to the shower, NOW! Oops, I spit-up – ALL OVER the shower wall and inside the tub. I'd better lie down, yeah, on a flat surface. PLEASE stop spinning, floor! Then, back into the bathroom. Oops, AGAIN! Oh how my head hurts! Finally I sit on the sofa until the floor gets still.

Katrina has gone and left me and now comes Vernon – with MORE LIQUOR. He chuckles at the sight of me then he pours me a drink.

"Oh no, I can't join you. I can't even see you. I've had way too much to drink." Vernon plops down in a chair on the other side of the room. He pours himself a drink.

"What are you doing here all by yourself? Where's Katrina?"

"She went out with a friend." He laughs again.

"I don't mean to offend you, but your husband is a jerk. You know that, don't you?" Vernon smiles gently. I don't know if Vernon asks a question or is he stating a fact. "Has he come back here since this morning?" he asks.

I look to Vernon and nod. The answer is no. Still I'm in no state of mind to discuss the absence of my husband. I just only want my stomach to stop turning. My head falls forward into my lap. I get more nauseous, listening to Vernon's rattling. My stomach gives way, again. "Where do you think he's been going all of these nights?" He jeers, mocking my denial of Delbert's affairs. "Leave me alone Vernon. PLEEESE!" I get up from my chair to return to the revolving floor across the hall.

CHAPTER 8

GOOD FRUIT
DON'T GROW FROM BAD SEED

It is a long trip ahead. By afternoon I'm viewing the world upside down. I could sit in the clouds if I wanted to. Least it looks like it from here; fresh cotton on a blue background. Then, a little turbulence sets my mind back on level ground. I can't wait to land. There is no control up here in this silly piece of machinery. Soon the plane slides in for the two-hour stopover. A call to Mom confirms to her that we are nearly there. Another to Vernon, who flew out before sunrise to plan ahead for our arrival, confirms he will be on time to meet our flight.

It is a meandering drive, where cows, hills, pigs and empty lowlands separate one lonesome shack from the next. Then before me is an incredible sight. "High as a Georgia pine," it reminds me of myself, celebrating with Katrina last night. Georgia pines are tremendous and I never wish to be that tall again in life. All of a sudden, everything gets murky, as we feel our way over winding roads in the absence of streetlights.

Already I miss my mom. Each time I think of her I see her pouting eyes and I nearly start to cry. She is getting older now. Now, when we two, Mom and me, get to a point in life when we can enjoy one another, it is time for me to venture away. Before I left to get the plane she drove me on a few errands in preparation for the trip. I laugh to think how she took her own sweet time, likely hoping I'd miss my flight. My drifting is interrupted as finally we arrive to a small housing complex set adjacent to a wooded area in a remote section of town. We have arrived at Vernon's to find his family already retired for the night. Delbert, Vernon and I opt for a little jazz and a nightcap to help us settle in.

Come morning I meet the family, three small children and Helena, Vernon's wife. This is maybe just my second time being anywhere near Helena, but her chilly greeting already tells me that I wish to limit my stay in her home.

"Oh my goodness," there go a lizard climbing the curtain! But Vernon don't seem to mind. He removes it and carries it outdoors, then warns us of the snakes we'll see. It is not rare to come upon one of the slithery creatures from time to time. He entertains us with the story of the coach-whip, a snake that beats you 'til you're stifled dead. I heave a breath, "hmmph," and shrug my shoulders, 'cause I WON'T be exploring too far from home.

It's a quaint town. The water, gas and light companies, the courthouse, jail, police and fire departments are all housed in one brick structure. It is a place where inmates' clothing drips water in plain sight, while stretched on a pulley drawn clothesline.

"Hey," we hear that phrase time and time again for the next several days. Or "h-ā-ā-y" as it is spoken with a true Georgian twang. It is the customary "down home" welcome of friendly folk, unlike the snooty-faced Northerners, I left back home. And it seems everybody and their mama knows when a new face comes around. Warm and genuine is the impression I get of most of the town folk here. Except for one woman, Regina, who plops on Vernon's sofa whenever Helena's not around. She is a Jehovah's Witness friend of Vernon's and should be out somewhere handing out pamphlets, magazines, saving souls or something. Spreading the word for the Kingdom – wouldn't you think? Vernon's been known to sit home on occasion himself, here lately. He claims something is wrong with his back. He looks okay to me. The weeks sweep clean, while Vernon piddles. Poor Helena grows tired. She's tired of him, tired of us. Eventually she packs up and runs away. With two months accumulated, not one red cent is stashed away and I wonder when we will have a place of our own.

"Mommy, where's my Daddy?" Keonis wants to know as he fidgets in the grasp of weariness. For there has been no sight, nor sound from Delbert. It's been many hours since his day's work ended. Exhausted with questioning, Keonis slowly gives into slumber and his heavy eyelids fall. The apartment is quiet, except for the music of "Killer Joe," a jazz vibe whispers through a couple of stereo speakers. Vernon sits studiously at the dining table with his long legs stretched beneath its length. He gazes through the lenses of a pair of reading glasses and holds a huge Bible with its worn binder cracked. With Keonis asleep on my knee, I rear back and recline the length of a retractable chair.

"I hope Delbert is okay." Vernon peers over the tops of his gold-wired frames. He responds with a chuckle.

"We both KNOW," he exclaims, "that it doesn't take long for Delbert to learn his way around." Straight and forward are the words of a brother-in-law, who knows his brother well. Gently, he removes his glasses and lays them aside. He puts a marker in the page, shuts the cover, then slides the big book to the table's center. Vernon smiles casually. He lifts his glass and takes a sip. "Is he asleep?" he whispers and takes notice to little Keonis still resting on my outstretched knees. "Why don't you go lie him down? He looks so uncomfortable."

"He's okay," I assure my brother-in-law. My legs shift to accommodate the weight.

"You look a little bit tense yourself," Vernon says tenderly, "are you okay?"

"I'm okay."

"Are you sure?" he asks, with undiluted compassion. "Can I get you anything? I can fix you a drink if you'd like."

"No, I'm fine. Really, I am. Thank you."

"You shouldn't ostracize yourself." Vernon draws a broad smile. His high-set, chunky chocolate cheekbones rise when the corners of his mouth turn upward. He exposes a perfect line of pearly-whites. "You know that you are NO stranger." I say nothing. He grins. "You do trust me – *don't you?* I wouldn't do anything to harm you, honest." He laughs. "As a matter of fact I wouldn't do *anything* to you that you didn't *allow* me to do."

Vernon is absolutely the most gentle, most accommodating and confident man that I have ever known. It is just his presence that sometimes unnerves me. I smile timidly, wondering where Delbert could possibly be.

"I'm just teasin'," Vernon says. He gestures with his hand and calms me with a smile. "Relax," he tells me. "Don't be so uptight, – Delbert will be here soon." Then he sniggers, deviously, "unless he's gotten caught up at ol' Regina's house." I look at him sideways. Vernon apologizes. "Forgive me," he says cynically, "I'm just being facetious."

Vernon is always being facetious or so he says. Sometimes, I think he just tells the truth of what he knows then covers it up with a grin. Suddenly straight-faced he walks soft and clever, standing at the foot of the long chair.

"Why don't you go lie the baby down and when you come back I'll fix you a drink." With Keonis tucked in, I return to find a glass set on the table directly in front of me. Vernon pulls a chair and offers me to sit. "Are you okay?"

Vernon never stops asking that question.

"I'm fine."

"One piece of ice or two?" he asks, holding a loaded pair of icy tongs over the rim of my glass.

"One," I answer. I look away from Vernon. "Thanks."

No matter how long I've known my brother-in-law, his gracious mannerism never ceases to amaze me. Yet and still, his congeniality leaves me to ponder. I stir my drink and make conversation to mask my unease.

"You know," I say, "I was admiring your commitment."

"Commitment?"

"Yeah" How long have you been a Jehovah's Witness?" I didn't know 'til now, that Vernon is an Ordained Minister. He studies a lot and it's no wonder he knows that big, black, gold-lettered book, cover to cover, the way he do. Reciting quotes and verses, like he's got 'em scribbled on the back of his hand. Vernon's eyes gleam with tender eagerness before he makes his reply. The corners of his mouth turn softly when he reveals one of the biggest, brightest smiles I have ever seen.

"Actually," he says with unwearied forethought and a glint of confidence, "it was my wife Helena, who got me involved." He inhales patient and long, lending his attentions entirely to me. "BUT" – he adds, with further meditation and a smile growing more passionate. Even broader than the morning sun – "my study doesn't mean that I am not mesmerized by the company of a beautiful woman."

Even the minister talking inside him doesn't stop Vernon from fresh-talking me. Quickly, I am learning that there are no safe moments with Vernon. I shake my head in disgust. As always I do, but Vernon just smiles the more. Still I don't mind taking up time with Vernon, 'cause he's charming and articulate, not tongue-tied like Delbert. I just tell him, NO! A million times over, NO – NO– NO– NO -NO! He don't never get disheartened. Just the same he never quits.

In an instant Vernon's position shifts. His eyes go fetching far inside his forehead. Suddenly, "Second Samuel, Chapter 11, verse 2," he recites it as if he had summoned the heavens. It is the story of Basheba and David, a Biblical king. "It is not uncommon to man to find beauty in a woman who is not his own," he explains. And it never ends – that all-encompassing smile. Devious yes, but tender and warm as Vernon fervently entertains, mixing jazz, conversation and strong drink.

He steps soft across the room's length and his eyes light up. His stubby fingers pop to the baseline tempo of the stereo sound. He paces rhythmically, scatting, "shabba-dibba dit-dah," in a cool vocal expression, executed in a style all of his own. Just like one of those great musicians of the jazz era.

"You like Quincy?" he asks casually.

"I love Quincy – I love jazz," I answer.

His smile is smooth with unspoken confirmation as we get caught up in the flawless chords of a sometimes forgotten musical age. Together, through an open screened door, we experience the coming of nightfall as it catches hold to a summer's breeze. C-R-A-S-H!! sounds the rumbling of thunder.

"I wish Delbert would come in." I utter restlessly. Tipping my cup in full view of Georgia's swaying pines. But the eagle flies on Friday and so does my husband, keeping late hours and marking a path to the bootleg house. The sky turns bright with electricity as the curtains are drawn on a dimming sky. BOOM!! Crashing echoes mark the presence of a pending storm. Suddenly, in plain view we see him. Delbert rushes in like a gust of wind. Staggered and unsteady, he blows in through the unlatched entryway.

"Man – Look at you!! Where have you been?" Vernon asks excitedly. "Pour yourself a drink." With the bottle already in his hand, and even before the invitation is completely rendered, Delbert pours a glass half full of the clear and potent liquid. He colors it with cola soda then quickly turns its bottom up.

"Your wife has been worried about you." Delbert's empty glass startles me as it slams with a CLATTER, hard against the glass tabletop.

"Au-aughhh", he belches. "Fuck that bitch!" he shouts. As if my presence merits no recognition.

"Hey – wait a minute, Man – that's your wife. Don't disrespect her like that."

"Fuck you too Vernon!"

"Hey, that's your wife over there." Vernon humors Delbert's rage to try and make light of a bad situation. "Don't come yelling at me!" He lets go a halfhearted chuckle and apologizes on his brother's behalf. "Edwina, please, forgive my aboriginal brother." But, Delbert only fires back.

"Forgive me? – Forgive me for what? That bitch knows I hate her ass! She's a whore, just like her Daddy!"

"Wait a minute, Man. Don't come with that vulgarity. Show some finesse. You're being petty."

"Go to hell, Vernon." Vernon's head shakes in disgust.

"You are wrong Man!" Vernon says it twice, the second time stronger. "You are wrong!" What makes you think ...?" But, Delbert yells louder, uttering every filthy narrative imaginable.

"You know what Vernon? You can suck my –!" Vernon shrugs his shoulders. He smirks with indifference, mocking Delbert's irrefutable ignorance. Vernon is silent for an instant, but then he speaks is certain to be heard.

"Man – what makes you think that you can talk to your wife that way?" he admonishes. "You're not only seeing Shirley, but you have been sleeping with Tonya too. Man!" Vernon calls Delbert to attention. "I've already told you. I have told you Man." Vernon looks at me and I begin to cry. He turns again to his brother. "You are such a fool." Again, there is silence. Quickly he concludes. "If EVER – if EVER, he says louder – your wife gave me the opportunity – I already told you, Man – I already told you." The tall bottle of rum in Delbert's hand, now half-empty does another turn upward. Delbert swallows quickly and returns his glass to the table with a bang.

"FUCK YOU VERNON!" he hollers. "'YOU CAN HAVE THE BITCH!'"

The outer door to the apartment swings outward with a weighty kick from Delbert's foot. Delbert disappears into the night-felled darkness beneath a rain soaked sky. Visually angry, Vernon gives an apathetic nod to ignorance personified. Even so, he smiles, takes a deep sigh and asks, "How do you tolerate him?"

I say nothing.

"And where does he get off being angry with you? – That's my brother, but he is SUCH A FOOL."

The truth rings inside my head and as many years as I have denied it, it has to be true. Delbert has been sleeping with Tonya all the while we've been married. Why else would Vernon confront his brother in this way? Vernon tries to comfort me, thereby changing the subject. And again it is the story of David and Basheba.

For God's sake Vernon – David slept with another man's wife. I think it's time I say goodnight. "GOODNIGHT Vernon."

I have bathed and coddled with inexpensive scented oil. My head whizzes warmly with mild drink. I settle in for a rest. Tomorrow is another day. Following more than a few empty hours of tossing and turning, I observe his presence near the lower landing. Weighty is his stride, like a man with cylinder-blocks clamped to his ankles. Delbert has ingested more than his portion of the bitter tonic. His climb is laborious. The load of his soles is a burden too heavy to lift and uneasy to carry. The leather toes on his shoes kick the back wall every time he steps. He stammers and stumbles. Delbert tries hard to focus through eyes glazed over. His tongue shines like that of a stray dog come in from the heat. His face is gaunt and long-drawn at the chin. The slime of stayed-saliva oozes white from the corners of his mouth. Seeing the stinging, staggered sight of my husband in yesterday's soiled garments creates a pang in my empty stomach. Silently, I stand in his path, hoping to hear him exonerate himself, while inhaling the muddled stench of bitter body fluids emanating through his open pores. With a crazed grin he totters across the length of this moderately sized room, to catch my gaze. He smirks, then exclaims.

"What the fuck you lookin' at?" Delbert stumbles, jostling my shoulder to make the pass. He trips forward, dumping his spent body clear across the length of the bed.

Somewhere in my consciousness I have arrived at a measure of truth in all deception. To think Delbert has at anytime been in love with me is to say that I am a fool. Delbert doesn't love anybody, because Delbert doesn't love himself. A bitter hurt is swollen in my belly and for every wretched, solitary second that I lie in this bed of thorns beside him, undressed and raw with nakedness; his words mow over inside my head. "You can have the bitch. You can have the bitch."

The bedside becomes warm and wet and just in time I crawl away from this urinating idiot, engorged with anger. I tear for my bathrobe. I stand to my feet, advancing directly and without contemplation. Quiet and deliberate are my bare-footed steps as down a darkened stairwell I climb. Soon I appear in full view, disrobed, discovered and not disowned, before my brother-in-law, Vernon. He rises to greet me without rejection, just only pleasant surprise. The Holy Bible falls from his grasp. The pages press shut and abandoned on the dining table alongside a reading lamp, reading glasses and an unfinished mixed drink. For all the time that he has waited, now he will have, without further deliberation. Suddenly, I feel like a woman, just for now.

Several miles from the housing complex we shared with Vernon are trailer homes. They bear more resemblance to tractor-trailer trucks with windows cut in the sides. Tacky cement blocks mark the entrance to the tin structures. From the premise it is difficult to imagine one of these compartments being big enough to live in. Ours has a miniature kitchen set on one extreme and a bedroom on the other. Two adjacent exits lead to the out. If I stretch my arms really far, I'll bet I could swing both doors at the very same time. Well, maybe not, but it is a stingy space, indeed. It in no way meets the modest standards of the low-income apartment we shared with Vernon, but Vernon has moved back to Jersey. So, here is where we are and here is where I guess we'll stay.

From my window in the quiet of the morning is where I often steal my peace. I watch as the sky turns nearly black, while a tremendous flock of birds fly overhead. Up north we say the birds fly south for the winter. I wonder where they fly now. When in late October Georgia is their home. My eyebrows lift to see barefooted, nappy-headed children, slap flat through chilly mud holes with snot dripping from their noses. I wonder who's raisin' 'dem youngins'. And ain't they supposed to be in school? Keonis sleeps and I close the door, while his Daddy sets out to work. When all seems still, from behind a little hole gnawed inside a wall, mice come into the open to play. Delbert says the rats are so big in the brush that Jeffrey, our neighbor, uses them for target practice. He fires them with a loaded shotgun.

On this side of the creek in the unveiled thickets, everybody knows everybody, somebody is fighting somebody and most folk like gettin' drunk on Friday nights.

"She got a gun!" I was peeking from my window when a man cried out. "She got a gun!" He was hollering 'bout his wife, a convicted killer, who already had done twelve years. The police officer, who'd come to answer the call, asked Ms. Clara.

"Ms. Clara, you got a gun?"

Ms. Clara answered him. "No! Ain't got no gun."

The officer says to Mr. Cleo,

"Mr. Cleo, Ms. Clara say she ain't got no gun. Now go on back inside the house, 'der."

Then, there is a fellow who takes delight in pointing out bullet holes all over his body, six in all. They cover his small frame. He credits his wife and adds, "She even beat me with a tire-iron." Now, that's a crime of idiocy. And if it ain't no crime against ignorance, it might oughta' be when in nineteen hundred and seventy-six, black folk still honor a sign that reads, "NIGGERS ONLY." Do you reckon, they ain't yet heard the news? I declare, it is an unenlightened clan of folk settled in these back woods. Now I know why the coyotes holler, every night the way they do.

Don't get me wrong. There are some good folk here who welcome us with open heart and to whom Delbert makes himself no stranger. Take Jeffrey for instance, down the road apiece. He is the peddler of pot, new records and candy. Everybody loves Jeffrey and his standing invitations to the biggest, everyday, party affairs. A pig on the grill ain't unusual for Jeffery, the-bootlegger. His fish-fries, clam-bakes, marijuana, cocaine and such, provide an outlet to a never-ending influx of hungry lookers and towns-people passing by. I go along with Delbert to visit the happy D.J. and his wife with their never-ending festivities and blaring music, for all of the neighbors to hear. It makes me smile to visit their brightly lit Christmas tree with its glowing ornaments. And best yet, I am grateful for the home cooked meal.

Then, there is a sweet little, eighty-five-year-old widower. Mrs. Boatwright grows fresh vegetables and gives them out straight from her garden and she takes a special liking to my boy. Mrs. Boatwright seats Keonis in a little rocking chair. She rocks next to him, in her well-seasoned chair, three-times-the-size. Keonis rears back, then pushes forward. Just like Mrs. Boatwright, he slaps himself on the knee. Then the two of 'em let it go, deep-down-in-the-belly laughter, while sipping hot chocolate, rocking and wasting the afternoons away.

Back at our trailer home, the darkened face on a little black and white TV is silenced on the countertop. A coat hanger is wedged in the very spot an antenna used to be. The only light in this trailer comes from a battery-powered, nine-volt flashlight. But I am glad the gas stove is still on. Somberly I think of Christmas, already come and gone. There was neither snow nor presents. Had it not been for Jeffrey, wouldn't even had no home cooked meal. Two shriveled potatoes in the refrigerator lay next to a stubbed carrot, nearly concealed by the silk peel of a sprouting onion laid aside. A half bag of beans and a bit of rice come together in a hot pot of bean soup. Keonis is a growing boy and my Delbert has worked all day. There won't be enough for me. Suddenly, three thumps pummel the outer trailer door.

"Who is it?"

"Constable"

"Who?" I answer.

"Constable"

It seems that Claudia Burton and her husband Bo-bo, our neighbor-friends across the way got kicked-out, too. And truthfully, I never thought of them as friends. Well 'til now. With no where else to go, we get our rest in the back seat of their ol' car. Delbert and Claudia's husband Bo-bo get off to work in the daytime. Me and Claudia stay in the car, except to go to the bathroom or to get something to eat. Keonis sleeps over in Claudia's sister's trailer. There just ain't enough space for Delbert and me.

I thank God when the week ends. It is Friday, when Bo-bo finds a property, where the brush grows tall as the house. It is an obvious habitat for slithery and four-legged creatures. The floors are splintering planks that bend and creak. We layer blankets to keep chipped wood from poking our backs, when we lye down at night. Bo-bo and Claudia have extended their kindness and with little consideration, we oblige.

We sit in front an outdated fireplace. I ponder the days past with nowhere to stretch my body's length. Keonis watches the fire next to me and his Dad. Bo-bo fires-up the twisted end of an old newspaper and throws it onto an undersized heap of logs. Suddenly, Keonis' eyelids flutter then close. The fire crackles and Delbert jabbers. Soon, the lights turn out. After all, we don't pay the bills. We are just a couple of peons, blessed to be the guests of a couple of overly caring friends. Bo-bo says goodnight and joins Claudia on the other side of a crumbling wall.

Delbert whispers, "Do you find Bo-bo attractive?"

What kind of question is that? But, coming from Delbert – anything is to be expected. Honestly, I think Bo-bo is a very nice guy. And yes, he is very attractive, well built and all. But, the only personal feelings I have toward Bo-bo are thanks that he and his wife have provided us a place to lay our heads. "Goodnight Delbert." Get your rest.

Come morning, I awaken to find Delbert has stolen off onto a country a path. To where? I don't know. He has no job. He was fired on the very last day of our homeless past. In the bathroom basin, chilled water is all there is. I bathe and Keonis waits his turn. Then the two of us make the mile-and-some, walk to the grocery store.

With just a couple dollar-bills, I take my place in the checkout line. To my delight I discover a twenty-dollar bill nearly under my foot. I lift and position the length of my worn sole to cover it from view. Then bend quickly and sweep it up with my itching hand. A five-pound bag of potatoes, some rice and cabbage, a couple boxes of corned meal-mix, among several other things, line the rim of my tote. It is a couple hefty bags full and out the door we go.

Along the stretch we chat. Keonis' giggling makes the distance easy. Then in the desolate distance I hear a rumble. A hand extends from the downed window on a dusty pick-up truck.

"Hey, ain't you Delbert's wife?"

"Yeah" I say.

"Let me give you a lift. Hop in."

"Oh no, thanks"

"Ya sure?"

"Yeah, I'm sure," I lie. "You go on ahead, we're okay."

"All right, now." The driver yells back before the small truck plows off. It leaves a dark cloud in its path.

Determination carries my load, until my aching back complains to my screaming feet for my tired behine' to sit a minute and allow these ripping arms to rest. For a moment next to a tree is where I lay my load. Soon we walk a while longer. Until, surprisingly, there comes another vehicle. I know that car. But it is too far away to yell. It was Vernon's lady-friend and Delbert is riding the passenger seat. "Darn it!"

Finally, and not a second too soon we return home to discover Delbert waiting. My feet are worn and so is Keonis. That boy of mine is down and out, by the count of three. Delbert sits aloof and peculiarly quiet, combing his fingers through his short-cropped beard. He rears slightly, and now he uses both hands to tug tensely at a stubbed hair growing from the underside of his chin. His foot twitches with nervous rhythmic tapping. He begins to utter, then stops. There is more silence inside the stillness of this dusty wood frame. Empty minutes escape. Suddenly he springs to his feet and asks, "Has my brother Vernon ever come on to you?"

My spine tingles. I've prayed to God and asked His forgiveness, but dealing with Delbert couldn't be the same. I am honest when I answer.

"Yes."

"Have you ever slept with Vernon?"

Dumbfounded, I say,

"Yes," My head lowers and my eyes stare straight into his. The heat of blood rushes his face and the bulbs of his eyes jut forward.

"I knew it," he screams. "I knew it!" He rips a path straight toward me.

I run, but there is nowhere. I hate myself, but not as much as Delbert despises me now. I feel him pounding with his fists – then – everything goes dark. The sight of him disappears. No longer can I see his face or feel his blows. Although I know he is still hitting me. Suddenly, I find myself at the front of the house and in the yard. Delbert is flinging me. I have no remembrance for how I have landed on his back with my arms wrapped around his throat. My short legs flail. He yanks and he throws. Had it not been for Jeffrey, the bootlegger, come rushing from the trailer across the way, I don't know what might have been.

The remainder of this day I plead with apology, but Delbert would much rather serve my head on a rusted platter. He despises me with his every bitter bone and he wants our son to hate me too. Now, a photo clipping rips from a centerfold inside a pornographic magazine. Delbert waves it in his sweating hand. He shakes it before little Keonis, saying, "See what your mommy did with your Uncle Vernon."

His taunting extends deep into the night. Long after Keonis goes to sleep. Long-winded questions, making my head split. My mind peels back to nearly a decade ago and the first time I met this wide eyed kid with the great big smile. I recall his bottle of apple wine. Today it is different drink and the same drunken slump.

"I love you," he says. While holding in his hand a half-filled bottle of rum purchased from Jeffrey the bootlegger on credit. "I'm sorry I hit you, but you make me act like that. You know that, right?" The bottle tilts. He swallows and brings the bottle swiftly from his lips. He frowns and tucks it between his knees. His gaze is cold. "Just answer me one question," I am frazzled and worn, "then I will let you sleep. Do you ever have a fantasy of having two men make love to you at the same time?"

There is absolutely nothing to be gained from this conversation.

"Just be honest," he says, "I promise. I'm not going to hit you again."

When I don't answer, it only makes him more angry.

"Don't sit there looking stupid."

He fumes with anger. The room gets hot, like I'm sittin' with the devil.

"You wasn't quiet when you asked him to fuck you!" The air explodes, "Were you?" He screams. "Were you, bitch? Don't act like you can't hear me bitch. Oops!" He giggles, a demented cackle, "I'm sorry." He laughs sourly. Thoroughly humored he covers his sniggering mouth with his hand. "I'm sorry – that slipped. I didn't mean to call you a bitch." He begins again, "But you wasn't quiet when you asked him to sleep with you, were you? Were you?" Delbert's grin splits to a scowl. "Answer me!" he shrieks.

My lips part to speak, but nothing comes out.

"Speak up mother-fucker!"

"No!" I say – LOUD – with CLARITY.

Remorseful tears, salted and tart, drip steadily into my weeping mouth. My gut shreds with humility. God and I both agree that I am wrong. But why must he torment me and make a mockery of my recklessness. My chin is no longer raised. It hangs low with shame. I am completely and utterly disgraced with no need for blatant insult to add to my gross indiscretion. Just tell me to leave and I will go. Together we have faltered, not me alone.

"Now I am going to ask you again. Do you ever have a fantasy of having two men make love to you at the same time? You can talk to me. I am your husband. Trust me. I'm not going to leave you."

At this moment, I wish you would – LEAVE ME. Oh, you have too many questions ... wicked questions. Fantasies are just that – FANTASIES. I have no need, nor desire to play them out. Suddenly, Bo-bo is suggested into the conversation. He wants me to sleep with Bo-bo or any other man, and with him at the same time. Why? Because it is HIS fantasy, not mine. So deliberately he is tormenting me. I speak with silent prayer and ask God again to forgive me, and for the words with which to answer this impudent fool.

"Everybody has fantasies. It doesn't mean you have to act them out."

He becomes the more impatient and with few hours till dawn, he persists over and over again, while pounding with dark pitted resentment, cursing and threats.

"Answer me bitch! You want to fuck around on me slut? I will fuck you up. You don't know me. I will fuck you up. I will make your life a living hell. I promise you."

Delbert yanks me from the floor and into the shadows of dark. The dry ground scatters under my heels as he drags me kicking and screaming and away from where Keonis sleeps. Beyond the brush is a trailer home. He pounds its door. No one answers. And again …still there is no answer.

"You better be glad, bitch. Because I sure was gonna let them pull a train on you tonight – all five of them. He loosens my arm. You little slut! I hate you!" He yells a deafening scream deliberately into my ear. I cry. Delbert swiftly turns away, leaving me alone to follow in a path of overgrown trees inhabited by snakes.

"Pay-back is a bitch and revenge is a mutha' fucker." His vow has been spoken. I am terrified of his endless bouts of insanity and more afraid to turn away. "You gonna leave me bitch?" I don't answer. He answers himself. "You know I'll find ya. Don't 'cha, slut? You take my son from me, and I will FUCK YOU UP! And you know I will. You filthy whore! I'm gonna make you suffer. What else did you do? Did you sleep witcha Daddy too?" He answers himself. "You probably sucked his d—k, bitch."

A couple of days go by. "Do it for me," he says, when he sneaks a man inside this room. Here where our baby sleeps. "And don't think about taking my son from me, bitch, because I will find you. No court will ever give you custody. And you know that. If I can't have him – neither will you."

CHAPTER 9

BLOOD
IS THICKER THAN THE MUD

A wise old soul once told me "Don't burn your bridges behind you." Well, this here town ain't got enough bridges for all of mine and Delbert's troubles; not when it ain't no place left for us to go. Our life-long accumulation is jammed inside two over-stuffed suitcases. We board a Greyhound headed for a late night and solemn ride. I take an aisle seat and Delbert claims the window with Keonis asleep in his arms. The ceiling lights flash and except for a couple overhead lamps, where people are reading, the coach is dark. I gaze through a dimmed and clouded window and silently bid an unspoken farewell to the fine ol' fashion folk who always extended their hand and hearts. I have no doubt they will stay right here in cow-country, 'til they're as old as the dirt. They ain't leavin' these backwoods and I ain't never comin' back. The big wheels start to spin. So long Wrens, Georgia. Goodbye to all of your desolate wasteland. It has always made me nauseous. I will see you in my dreams, roadside ditches and all you snakes that strike in the brush and dangle in the trees. So long to the dusty, pot-holed trailer parks and stuffy trailer homes with the cinderblock stairs. The sounding engine changes gears. The coach plugs a bit faster, then, finally blows away.

When we got thrown out in Jersey we stayed with Katrina. Now I feel like a burden all over again. Delbert rears his chair and I watch as he twiddles with the hairs in his chin. I shift my weight, trying hard to find a comfortable position. Yet all of this fidgeting does nothing to quell the anxiety of my fears.

After a few hours of riding and rocking side to side, my bladder fills, and I have to pee. I stand and grab a hold to an overhead rail and press my way to the toilet. The flimsy door springs shut and I slide the lock to keep it in place. I take a squat and wonder where all that stuff does go. I know it ain't strewn all along the highway. No way it gets stored beneath the bus, because there's a luggage compartment underneath there. A skinny stream of water trickles onto my hands. I pat them dry, when another question comes to mind. How do all the fat people fit inside this little thing? I guess it really doesn't matter, at least not for me.

I walk the center isle and back to my chair. My body bends, flowing with a curve in the spine on the throughway. I notice Delbert is still fiddling with his beard. If he ain't pluckin' hairs, he's rubbin' his chin and smoothin' the little suckers, except, when he's bitin' his nails. His fingertips are chewed to nubs, already. His mouth is clenched and it is clear that he has absolutely nothin' he'd like to say to me. I close my eyes to try and sleep.

Suddenly, when it seems I have resolved my awkward position and made peace with my seat; Delbert shakes me, just when I am in the middle of a juicy dream. My sleep loses color, like a splash inside a puddle, when the rainbow disappears.

"Leave me alone! Stop botherin' me."

"We're here! Wake up!"

This must be it, Wilmington, North Carolina. Delbert drops a couple coins in the payphone, where we wait next to a newspaper vending machine. It isn't long when Katrina's old Chevy Malibu putters to the curbside. We chug our gear into her trunk and the hood slams shut. Katrina has abandoned

New Jersey living. Her divorce from Fitzgerald, an enlisted U.S Army soldier is final. She has traded him in for affordable housing and a new start with her live-in boyfriend, Sylvester.

Along the drive to Katrina's, already the heavy flow of traffic reminds me of the streets back home. The grounds surrounding the complex are filled with huge palm-plants and meandering paths. The sidewalks are swept clean and there are no ditches to mark the seams in the streets.

In the month of May, the mercury peaks to a stifling eighty-eight degrees. It is hot enough for skinny-dipping. Delbert's eighteen-year-old sister Melinda and her friend Cindy run for the plunge. Keonis, who is now three, gets acquainted with his big cousins, eight-year-old Leslie and five-year-old Dwayne. They do belly flops on the carpet, and a kid-flick shows on color TV. Katrina, Delbert and me, absorb the free flowing breeze of central air conditioning, while catching up on old news. And after the sun goes down, when Katrina's boyfriend Sylvester arrives, we get off to the North Carolinian coast to see the waves of the Atlantic backslap the rocks of the sea.

Sylvester rolls his denim pants all the way up to his knees. He cuts the fool and laughs a lot, while catching crabs with a string and a can. Katrina saunters barefoot. A pair of leather sandals wave casually in her hand. Her hair flies with the apron on her dress, ballooning like a sail on a sailboat. Suddenly the warm winds fold and stand still. Her dress collapses and her swollen tummy parades like a due-season watermelon. In not so many weeks Katrina and Sylvester will celebrate their first child.

Sylvester's family throws an old fashioned southern fish fry, when Sunday comes. We even take in a good ole' fashion game of baseball inside a country park. On Monday Katrina drives Delbert to the city's sewer department to see if he can get himself some work. I'm proud of Delbert. It seems the experience he's gained in Wrens will be put to use. For me, long walks in eighty-ninety degree weather have paid off. I just got hired at Wilson's grocery store. I help out with the cookin' and pile a little extra on my plate.

"Why don't you teach Katrina how to cook?" Sylvester laughs.

He's a true to earth, home grown Carolinian, who is accustomed to a home cooked meal. But, Katrina burns his dinner or undercooks it, and is rather smug at the mention of it. She flashes a self-satisfied grin.

"So damn what if I can't cook." Her nose waves the air.

She is quickly tiring of us. But Sylvester's good nature helps to ease the tension that is no doubt starting to rise.

Katrina slides smoothly from her long chair to sashay into a room, just steps away. In moments, she's changed into a slippery, black gown that sways at her feet. She moves across the floor with a hip-swiveling glide and throws her long legs onto the sofa.

"You'll gotta find a place." Katrina says. She tosses her hair, like the Queen of Egypt in a mansion full of kings.

Katrina doesn't work. Katrina doesn't do much of anything. Except maybe lift a bottle of nail polish to paint her fingertips, while her toenails are drying and while she is waiting for Sylvester to arrive. Early and long before the sun rises she primes her face with a coat of powder and draws greased pencil lines where eyebrows used to be. Then comes the mascara and the lipstick, the eyeliner and ... Me? I would be seated on a throne of thorns, if I sat waiting for Delbert to handle my affairs.

"Sylvester is the only one working."

I bring in groceries, and Delbert gives money. But when we have nothing left for giving, that is when I know Katrina can't be satisfied.

"Sylvester can't ... We've got bills to pay."

WHINE – WHINE – WHINE!

"The electric bill is four hundred and seventy nine dollars."

Katrina, PLEEESE. That bill was made before we got here. What do you spend the money on? It is not me, nor Delbert and Keonis, who sits under the air conditioner, watching television all day. The sooner I can get out of this place of yours and Sylvester's, the better off I will be.

Some weeks into our stay and following a hard day's work, I arrive to find Katrina's apartment door padlocked. The outer hallway is heaped with everything, except the kitchen sink. Laundry bags, boxes, dressers and among the mess are my mismatched frayed and soiled suitcases all piled in the vestibule. Katrina has not paid the rent. With Delbert and Sylvester away at work Melinda, Cindy, Katrina, her kids and my Keonis stand by.

"The kids and I are driving into the country to stay with Sylvester's sister," Katrina says arrogantly. "I'm taking Melinda and Cindy with me."

Her haughtiness trembles my belly.

"I don't know what you and Delbert are going to do."

She looks nonchalantly at Keonis, then at me. Katrina couldn't care if I take up on wings and fly away.

"I will take you around to see if you can find a room somewhere."

I don't have two nickels to slide together, and much less to deposit for a roof over my head. But NOW, Katrina wants to DRIVE me around. Katrina hasn't driven me anywhere, not since the day I moved here. She pointed me to the Boulevard to find my way in the heat. NOW – KATRINA WANTS TO D-R-I-V-E ME AROUND. My three-bucks-an-hour pay is already spent – same day I cashed it – buying groceries for everybody in Katrina's house. I am broke and Katrina knows it.

"When Delbert gets off work," she says, "I will let him know where you and the baby are."

"Ugh, ugh." I can't talk to her. "Ugh" – I think I will choke.

From one "Room for Rent" sign to the next, Katrina brings the blue Malibu to a halt. My baby huddles close beside me. I can't look at him for fear I will cry. Each time the car pulls to another unfamiliar curbside my head hangs closer to my trampling feet. It gets harder, every time I am turned away.

"My husband will gladly pay you on Friday."

I feel like *Whimpey*, the hamburger–begging character from the Popeye cartoons who always wanted a hamburger, and never had a nickel to pay.

I unfold in and out of a hot vinyl back seat, before arriving at a rancid home front with a small sign, handwritten and tucked inside a grimy window. A big heavy-chest woman answers the door. She ponders, then with little forethought replies.

"Sho', you kin stay."

Her slow, long drawn words strike me by surprise. Her burly frame slides side to side, until she returns with a key.

"The apartment is not heah', it is on the next street ova'. It's gonna take a lot of cleanin'. Nobody's lived in it for some time now."

I thank her and I thank the Lord, then load back into the rear seat.

Two blocks away is a dilapidated dwelling with its thickets tremendously high. The house is worn and chipped. I can't imagine Katrina will leave us to stay. In a moment's time she jots the address on a scrap of paper. She retrieves my suitcases and hands me two single dollar bills. Katrina promises to tell Delbert where to find me. The blue *Malibu* blows away.

It is a musky, dank and deplorable abode and the inside is more unsettling than out. The windows are sealed shut with a blackened film of muck. Cobwebs string every ceiling and adjoin the walls. A pile of odoriferous mattresses set at the main entrance and smell of pungent piss. There is nowhere to set my few belongings that won't accumulate spiders or something worse. And in the depth of stillness, "so quiet you can hear a rat piss on cotton", Keonis trembles.

"Mommy, do we have to stay here?" He says in the tiny voice of a bewildered three year old.

"I think so, baby … I think so?" I could answer no more.

The day has gotten along and we have not eaten. I park our baggage amongst the rubbish, then, take hold to my boy. With his little hand in mine, I lead back to the street. Together we begin to walk. We walk and we talk, this little boy and me. Always talking, Keonis and me, he is my son, but also my friend. Too often the only friend I know.

"Where are we going mommy?'"

"I don't know baby, but I have got to find a store."

He talks and I pray. We walk, and then I cry sometimes, until soon I see a residential front. There is a little sign tacked to the wall. It reads – "STORE IN BACK" – and as sure as it is written, away in the back we find it. A little candy store of sorts, set deep in the coolness of somebody's cellar. Only a few varied items line the hand-made shelve. It appears a small-town, illegitimate undertaking with likely no license for such dealings. My accommodations are met with a smile by a gentle elderly fellow, from whose doorstep I depart with a loaf of bread and enough bologna slices for two sandwiches. We would have to salivate to compensate for any lack of condiments.

But I thank God, all the same, as again we walk and all the while I wonder. Where we will sit, not to soil our food? Where we will sleep when night falls? Just as I cross the pathway there comes a calling from a man next door.

"Are you moving into that place?" He asks.

"Yes." I drop my head to conceal my tears.

"Reason I ask … I have a room over here for rent, already furnished."

Quickly, I raise my chin to say,

"My husband will gladly pay you on Friday."

There is a little black and white television on a hard backed chair and a bed with clean linen. When Delbert arrives, I can hardly wait to share the news.

Within the short weeks that follow we get the chance to meet the guests, who frequently call on the gentleman of the house. Honestly, I don't know how to address them; she, he, him or her. SHIMS. That's what they are. Shims. Polite, courteous, overly dainty shims, who wear skirts and makeup so perfectly placed, they'd disgrace any real woman's best effort. I can't deny they are extremely nice gals or guys. And I much admire both, I only wish they'd pull the bathroom door behind themselves and stop throwing up their skirt-tails to pee in front of me.

They truly believe they are women, but really they ain't. It don't matter no how. The rent is overdue and the landlord says we can't stay.

An old man who Delbert has come to know, has a bedroom for rent and our tattered belongings are in tow. The metallic blue Malibu veers a turn down a long curved pathway to a dismal graveled drive before a small decrepit house. This little shack sets aloof from the roadside in a wooded area beside a creek. It is a place where the shrubs grow high and snakes prevail in the bush. Mr. Burton, a dwarfed, ebony fella' pushes himself out from behind a screened porch door to greet us. His back is bent and his gray hair grows wired, like the brush he inhabits. His teeth are broad and discolored, the same as his scowl. His face draws downward from his puckered brow to his crumpled chin. A grimacing tale is etched in his jowl, like a dissected map, charting a grueling journey of his long years tolled. He snarls when he talks and growls with impatience. But a bit of humor escapes his ebony flesh, when he calls my husband, "Black like me."

The house is tempered by long lapses of inattention. And like its owner, it smells of time overdue. In the bathroom, mildewed cylinder blocks overlay dank walls. Fat velvety bugs, striped and spotted, slither along a soggy cement floor. They wade uninhibited in an inch-or so water. From an old wood-burning stove that rests at one end of the front room, heat is drawn. While the light of day hides beneath heavy curtains and a murky film of paned glass.

There is no little black and white for viewing, on a hard backed chair. Not even a radio to distract me from the tick or the tock, as I watch the metallic hands inside the cracked-faced battery-operated-clock on a bedroom night stand. They frolic with a staggered ticker. The sun don't shine so high in the sky and the leaves fade, fall and wither with the onset of autumn.

In the short weeks ahead, I wave an axe high over my head. It crashes with a blow. Again, WHACK! The dense log cracks in its center. Finally with enough for a good fire, I tuck the logs beneath my arms and carry them inside the darkened house.

A long stemmed match sets the potbelly stove ablaze. Then I listen for a sizzle and a pop, from a slow frying chicken in a cast iron frying pan.

I rise to the dawning of countless mornings, when the sun ascends past the ballooning bosom of an awesome cloud form. There is the rustling of bronze and golden leaves beneath my shuffling feet. Free spirited branches wave, with no one to mark the beauty of their disrobing. They flow shamelessly naked in the autumn breeze. Silence sings as I sweep along a fragrant path of fresh thoughts and adoration. Soon my day plunges, like the moon below the horizon. Autumn's colors are hushed, when it begins to rain. Pouring down with the rumble of the old man's rattlin', cussin' and fussin' and stirrin' up woe. I do EVERYTHING I know to keep the old man's place clean and to keep trouble away. Delbert says – sleep with ol' man Burton to cover the past-due rent. I say NO! Delbert says YES!

Soon I'm sitting in the chill of nightfall outside ol' man Burton's doorstep. It didn't matter none, that I'd done my duty. Ol' man Burton's already had his mind made up. I hear the sputtering of the blue Malibu. It rolls along like a chariot, coming for to carry me home.

Katrina is so exhausted with us that she could spit. What Katrina don't know is that I want to be gone – just as much as she wants for me to go away. I have noticed during my foot-long travels that a city bus drives straight through these parts and there is a radio station not too far from here.

"Come on, boy," I tell Keonis. "We've got places to go."

"Do you have any experience?"

"No."

"Well we don't have any openings right now, neither."

Nobody wants to hire me, because I don't have any experience. But how do I get experience if nobody will give me a job? But finally, I make it past the secretary. Eventually I talk to Otis Carter.

"Let me talk to our Operations Manager," he replies informally. "I will get back to you."

Some weeks later, I get a second interview.

"What equipment can you operate?"

"None, but I can learn."

Otis agrees to turn on the tape recorder, I flip the switch and the red light goes on.

There are more meetings and riding the bus. Sometimes Keonis is with me and other times not.

"Good afternoon. It is fifty seven degrees, under cloudy skies. I'm Edwina Jordan with the WMSP News. Atlanta officials are stumped today after recovering a fourth body at a riverfront…"

Although I really wish to be a DJ, playing the hottest music, sliding in back-to-back rotation, I am so excited for this job. It is my honor to report for duty, via the city bus, as Wilmington, North Carolina's new, part time News Announcer. Although I only make three dollars an hour at WMSP, Keonis squeals when he hears my name.

"That's my mommy! That's my mommy on the radio!"

My co-workers adore him. He's a charmer with his Daddy's smile. Today, Douglas, one of the sales-guys put little Keonis to work doing a radio commercial. I can't wait to tell Delbert the good news!

Inside a dimmed cubicle inside the studio at the WMSP Broadcast House, I toil behind a closed door. No one is present, except me and Mike. Mike? Oh, that's my microphone. I press the record button and a red light comes on.

"RECORDING. Testing, one, two; testing, one, two; testing"

Suddenly the room goes black. The reels stop spinning. The microphone is dead silent. I fumble, feeling in the dark and trying to find the big looped handle on the door. The door flies open – pushed inward from the outside. Daylight rushes in, along with my husband, like a Kansas windstorm. He is chokin' me in my collar. Jerkin' and shovin' me straight out of the studio and through a back exit door.

"What? Bitch?" He screams. "You are not going to use my son, so you can fuck one of these mother fuckers who you work with. Where is he?"

"Where's who? Delbert, what are you talking about!"

But Delbert didn't come here to listen. Then, I see her. It is Katrina, sitting in her infamous Malibu Chevrolet and parked head-on in the building's parking lot. My eyes ask why? As she piles her wide hips from under the steering wheel. She bolts in my direction.

"Edwina, uhh," she stutters, "I didn't know."

Sure, Katrina, – you DIDN'T know.

"Delbert asked me to give him a ride. Uhh, I didn't know." She stammers awkwardly.

"Where's Douglas? Where's Douglas?" He hammers.

"He's not here!" I cry.

"Where is he, bitch? If you don't tell me I will fuck you up, right here in this parking lot, in front of all your little friends. And you know I will. Don't you, bitch?"

"I don't know where he is. He's not here!" He shoves again. Until a couple strong armed men hurry over to help me. Katrina and Delbert drive away.

LETTER TO KATRINA

Katrina, it has become all too clear that I am a burden to you. You have always made a mockery of my troubles. Nearly two years have passed since my affair with Vernon. Delbert won't let it go and you Katrina find pleasure in his ridicule. You are devious, Katrina — a double-dealing, instigating damsel, and my heartache has become your contentment. It shows in the rise of your hefty cheekbones, when you try hard to conceal your snickering face.

Delbert is cruel, and his inability to reason, no longer comes as surprise to me. But you, Katrina, leave me baffled. I do not understand your scheme in these matters of difficulty between your brother and me. You err in your silence, giggling and watching, while he commits his offenses against me. You think your brother Delbert is more hilarious than the Sunday Comics. Your faces are two. But your facade has worn thin, like wood-chipped-paint on an old baseboard. I thank God for this crushing revelation. May He always be the adjudicator, who gets to decide the final course.

A full-time position is open at WMSP. I never imagined myself as Gospel Announcer. Yet, I rise early Sunday mornings to flip the switch and welcome a host of God-fearing, Bible believing, hungry church-goers, who can't get enough of me. The WMSP ratings are topping the charts, leading the market with the biggest listening audience ever. This is PHENOMINAL!

With another workday done, I hurry to pick up the grocery, then to get Keonis, before heading home. When I get there I find him suspiciously waiting. One elbow propped, hand holding his chin and sitting in a broad-armed chair. My eyes roll with insult, to see Delbert's face, long drawn and his foot tapping rhythm with the floor. Suddenly, he tosses a pile of sealed envelopes.

"Here's your mail, bitch."

A bundle of utility bills soar to the ground, like paper airplanes.

"Where the fuck you been, out fuckin' around with Douglas?"

"I went to the grocery store."

I'm exhausted with fighting. The heavy bags leave welts in my wrists and slam to the floor. I say nothing of the fact that Delbert should be working; and nothing to the notice that he doesn't offer me a hand. I walk in silence and leave his bitter stare.

"You sure you weren't out sucking that mutha' fucker's dick?"

He follows me. Taunting and itching for a fight.

"What's the matter whore? The cat got you're mutha' fuckin' tongue?"

He burns with anger and trails two inches from my heels.

"I'll bet you talked to that mutha' fucker – and now you ain't got nothin' to say to me? You're wrong bitch. You are wrong. Take your drawers off slut!"

"Leave me alone!"

"You sure they ain't got cum in 'em?"

Delbert slides in close. Then he SCREAMS straight into my ear.

"You gonna give me some bitch? Huh?" He screams LOUDER, then, snatches my skirt and rips it off.

"Leave me alone!"

He pushes. I scream.

"Leave me alone!"

He shoves and lands me back flat across my bed. Hot tears stream my cheeks, when I crawl from under. I leap to my feet and run for the bathroom door. The door SLAMS! It LOCKS, leaving my asinine husband to sit alone with his distress. But, soon he DRUMS the locked door like a winter thunderstorm. My head collapses into the shallow of my parted knees.

"Open the door bitch!"

There is thumping and hammering. My agitated fingers rip through my standing hair. "Open the mutha' fuckin' door!" he screams LOUDER and LOUDER! Until, it crashes. The door swings open! I spring to my feet. He rushes me, like he's lunatic. We go step for step, room to room, and I am more disturbed than before.

"I'm leavin'!"

"What'd you say bitch?"

"I'm not staying here!" I scream.

He strikes. I buckle to my knees.

"Get out, Delbert! GET OUT! Or else I will call the cops!"

"Don't call the cops bitch!" He smirks snidely. "I'll fuckin' leave, WHORE. But, I will be back. You mark my word. You are not going to forget what you did to me," he promises, then steps out of my way.

In the morning I find my tires slashed. Charges have been filed and the phone calls begin. Harassing calls from my dearest husband to my workplace.

"You don't know where I am bitch, and if you hang up on me one more time I will …"

My nerves jangle. I slam the receiver. It rings back. I hang up. Then, twisted letters jam the mailbox, love letters laced with bitter hate and revenge. When the week ends, five-year old Keonis takes time from his busy play. He awakens me with a peanut butter sandwich and hands me a glass of water to wash it away. Today Keonis is mindful of the mommy who usually takes care of him. Today he takes care of me.

There is this really good looking guy at my job. His name is Matthew. Matthew is a DJ and he sure ain't shy 'bout comin' on to me. He invites me and Keonis out for a simple evening meal. I help my boy into his seat, Matthew pulls a chair for me. We check out the menu and Matthew talks.

"I noticed you some time ago," he says. "But Tony (Tony works the drive time shift) "told me you were married."

After seeing Delbert pushing me around at the studio, Matthew suggests I write two lists. One column for all of the reasons I should stay with Delbert, he says. The other for reasons I should go. Well, the *leave* column took up two sheets of paper. But Delbert is my baby's daddy. I don't want to take him from his kid.

Matthew handles the check, then, takes Keonis and me to the Channel 6 television studio, where he works nights, when he's not at WMSP. Cameras stand high and cameras stand low on upper and lower levels. Each one numbered and designated with a special assignment. He guides us close and answers all my countless questions. I am stupefied by the layout and try to picture Matthew carrying out all of his work as a cameraman. Matthew smiles attentively. But even more fascinating than his smile is the encompassing sparkle in his eyes. Our tour soon ends and he walks us back to the car.

Beneath the shadow of the moonlight, my eyes begin to cry.

"Do I detect a tear in your eye?" He smiles.

A few seconds slip away in silence. Then Matthew strikes a conversation about the day Delbert showed up at the studio.

"Do you miss him?" He asks.

"Sure. I miss him," I admit. Matthew and I chat for just a bit longer. But, with a generous embrace, I know it is time to go.

We get together again, the next day after work … and the next day, too – and the day after that.

Thoughts of Delbert pale with Matthew so near. Just today I received a certified order to appear in court on the assault charge I filed. A hearing for child support will be addressed at that time. My days with Delbert are over. In the same postal delivery comes a letter. It is from Delbert, return addressed from Charlotte, North Carolina. It reads:

DEAR EDWINA,

I have to be in court next Monday, but I'm not angry with you. I had some money to send for Keonis. But I got arrested on my job and had to bail myself out. I got fired, because of it, Edwina. Now, I have to come back to Wilmington to appear in court. I can't stay with Katrina. She moved back to New Jersey a week ago. To tell you the truth, I don't even have money to get there, now since I lost my job. But if I don't show up I'm going to get locked up again. Then, I really won't be able to send you anything.

I will call you at work and maybe we can talk. I know that I was wrong, Edwina. I am sorry and I love you. Honest.

Love Delbert

"Good afternoon, WMSP." I pick up on an incoming call at the studio. It is Delbert.

"Why would you need to stay overnight?" I ask. "If you sleep over, Delbert, I know there's gonna to be a problem."

"I'm not gonna start trouble Edwina, honest. I just need a place for the night. That's all."

"I really don't know Delbert. I don't think it's a good idea."

"It's not like I wanna move in, Edwina. It's just that I don't have money for a hotel."

I get quiet. "We will go to court" Delbert says, "and then I'll leave."

Still, I say nothing.

"I promise. I know you can't afford to take care of me, and I know you've got somebody else. But that's okay. You already made it clear that we won't be sleeping in the same bed. I will sleep on the sofa. I just need a place for the night."

"Delbert," I ask, "If you borrow the money to get here, like you say, then how do you expect to get home? I can't pay your way."

"I know you can't," he laughs childishly. "I'm not asking you for anything Edwina. I don't want anything. Trust me, I don't. I just want to see my son. I know you don't want to be with me." Delbert chuckles with emptiness. "And I don't have a problem with that. Even though, I still love you." He giggles with feigned connection. "I won't bother you, I promise. Can't you just do this one little thing for me?"

The living room sofa is prepared, covered with a sheet, blanket and fresh pillow. Accommodations are in order. But just for one night. He arrives aboard a late evening coach to the terminal. I meet Delbert for the drive back to my apartment for the overnight stay. Keonis is breathless and runs a broad jump straight into his Daddy's opened arms. His wordiness, completely overshadows any small talk between Delbert and me.

Later, back at the apartment, Delbert and I share few words, while his pleading for reconciliation falls on deaf ears. Never mind his prodding into my personal affairs; it will not be tolerated.

"Delbert, I think it's time I git some rest. I've got to work tomorrow, when court is through."

"Goodnight Edwina."

"Good night Delbert."

"And Edwina,"

"What Delbert?"

"Thanks for letting me stay."

"Yeah. Goodnight."

Judge Joseph Petrocelli expedites the child support proceeding. He orders Delbert to peel out one hundred dollars a month. Then, quickly moves to the next order of business.

"I'm looking now, at this charge of assault against you Mr. Gilliam."

The Honorable Judge peers with neck forward. His black-framed spectacles encompass Delbert and me in a single sweep. The judge pays particular notice to Keonis clinging to his Daddy's leg.

"You two are married? Is that correct?"

We concede, "We are, Your Honor."

"Are you living together?" He asks curiously, from inside his fluffy robe, high to the neck.

"We are recently separated, Your Honor." I confirm with confidence.

"Let me ask this of you, Mr. Gilliam." he pauses. "How did you get to the courthouse this morning?"

"I spent the night at my wife's apartment last night, and this morning we drove in together."

Judge Petrocelli shakes his head pathetically. Then he smiles. His focus stays on me.

"Don't you want to drop this charge against your husband, Mrs. Gilliam? I mean you both walk in here side by side ..."

The charge of assault is dismissed at the urging of a judge, who laughed at its merit from the beginning. I have consumed enough of my time here and I'm happy it's over. I have a radio shift to do. I will just make it by 10:00 a.m., if I hurry. I offer Delbert the ride to the bus terminal.

"How about if you let me walk Keonis to the babysitter. That way I can spend a few more minutes with him."

I haven't much time for contemplating. It's not a bad idea. I kiss Keonis, say a casual goodbye to Delbert and off to work I go.

"Rick James on your WMSP Radio. It is five minutes now, before the hour of three o'clock on a mid afternoon Friday." My final music selection spins on the turntable and soon I will officially begin my weekend. I can't wait to pick up Keonis at the babysitter. Today would be a perfect day for he and I to spend at the beach. Just then, the telephone rings.

"WMSP, Good afternoon."

"I'm leaving ... and I'm taking Keonis with me." I gasp. "Do you hear me Edwina?" The handset rattles in my hand. Delbert gives the phone over to little Keonis.

"Hi Mommy!"

"Where are you going?" I ask my baby, clumsily.

"I'm going on a bus ... and my Daddy is going to buy me ..."

His tender words end abruptly, when Delbert rips the phone from his ear.

"Give Daddy back the phone, Buddy."

"I gotta go." He exclaims.

"Where are you going?" I ask. "Where are you taking him?"

The handset returns to its cradle. The line goes click.

I barrel out of the parking lot. I can hardly see for the tears fogging my eyes. Red lights, stop signs, nothing can hold me.

"Unfortunately, in this state of North Carolina," my attorney explains,"as the biological father of your child, Mr. Gilliam has every right to take his son wherever he chooses."

It makes no sense. "Mrs. Gilliam, you have no legal charge against him and no recourse to be considered." she says.

"He was kidnapped."

"I'm sorry Mrs. Gilliam, but a judge won't see it that way. Off the record," my astute female attorney says, "I'd pay him a visit if I were you. Go get your kid – snatch him back, same as he'd done to me."

In the coming days I board a Greyhound headed for New Jersey. Many hours later I make a quick stop to see my mother and to let her know that I am in town. I find her lying on an old leather couch, pressed against the dining room wall. I notice a pair of crutches parked at her side. A cast wraps about her ankle and foot.

"Are you alright?" I ask uneasily.

"I'm okay, just got a little fever, dat's all."

I bend low to kiss Mom's cheek, only to discover she is burning hot. Sweat is pouring from her brow. My mind trips back to my visits with her in the hospital, when I was a kid. Either she was huddled beneath a heap of blankets and freezing cold, or kicking covers and fussing about it being too hot.

"Have you been to the doctor?"

"No."

"Why not?"

"I'll be alright."

I am reminded of Dad's complaining. Always moaning about how she cost him in hospital bills. He says she drinks too much, is all. The only way she'd go and see about that fever would be kickin', cussin' and screamin'. I'd have to drag her, and she would fight me every bit of the way. Just to keep from fighting with him.

"What happened to your leg?"

"It's not my leg, it's my foot. I broke my foot."

"How'd you do that?"

"Fell down the stairs." She gives me short answers and no real explanation. Then, quickly changes the subject.

"Why is Keonis here with Delbert, and not you?"

"Mom, I'd like to explain. But now just ain't the time." Then Dad walks in and offers to drive me to Geneva's. I kiss my mom and take the ride.

Dad has questions, too. And he ain't shy 'bout askin'. "Edwina, you is 'dat boy's mutha'. Why in da hell, 'dat man carry 'dat boy of your'ns off in the first place?"

"Because I ... I" ... I stutter. As hurtful as it is, I tell him the truth. "He wants custody, because I slept with his brother." Dad is perplexed and his mouth falls wide open.

"How he find out?" He asks with a frown.

"How did he find out?" I repeat him clumsily. "He found out from me. I told him. I told him the truth."

"Say what?" He gasps. His mouth drops wider than before. "You," he stammers awkwardly and doesn't trust his ears. "You say you told him?"

"Yes, I wanted to be honest with him. I thought it was the right thing to do."

"Edwina," he says, "Don't you realize, some things are better kept unsaid?"

But he always told me that the two things he hates most are a liar and a thief.

"It is not what you do, but how you do it. Don't let the right hand know what the left hand is doin'." Rupert Thurman Jordan, you taught it all to me.

"I cain't for the life of me, figga', what it is you see in that silly behine', ignant' nigga' no ways."

IGNORANT, Daddy, the word is ignorant. Finally is the one instance that he and I agree. The old car parks to the curb outside my mother-in-law's and I am glad for it. And when the passenger door shuts, Daddy rolls away.

Keonis is so happy to see me. I cuddle my boy and assure him I love him. I visit again the next day, but Delbert doesn't give me a moment alone. In just a couple days, my time is through. I kiss Keonis, under Delbert's guarding eye, before I depart on a Greyhound bus.

LETTER TO DELBERT

Dear Delbert,

My appetite for you "Sweetheart" has spoiled, and an unpleasant aftertaste stings my palate. Your mere existence brings with it a bitter tang. One I wished I'd never known. I pray your deafening screams and heartless words fade fast, like descending snowflakes in a winter blizzard, landing softly then disappear. May you become a muddled medley in my mind, distorted by off pitch chords and choruses that never harmonize. And may my spirit for life be freed, like Houdini from a locked box. For everything that you never were, and for all that you could never be, I forgive you. And for all of my sleepless nights, may God be the glory.

Relief and sadness are two irreconcilable emotions. I wrestle with both in the silence of your absence. Any utterance of divorce is cancelled with your promise that I will never see our son again. You contend that I am an unfit mother and that no court in the land would oblige me custody. I am shredding your letters, Dear Delbert, and they will land in the sewer unopened. As for your calls, they too shall go unanswered. Yet still I miss you and may peace guide your way.

Many heartsick days have passed. I press my way and run hurriedly, just in time to catch the bus. The driver takes my bill and puts a quarter in my hand. I take a window seat, facing the center isle. I think of Keonis. He's always had a passion for riding the city bus. I imagine him in my mind, raising himself up from his seat for a better view. I miss him.

Whoosh, sounds the stopping of the big wheels in front of the studio. Just now, I see Mr. Ragland, the Station Manager. His timing seems impeccable. But it is really only by chance that we meet each morning just as my bus rolls in. Shoulder-to-shoulder we meet, greeting one another cordially.

"Good Morning Edwina. How are you doing?" He smiles.

"I'm fine, thanks. And you Mr. Ragland?" I smile back.

"If I were doing any better ... "

It is the same ol' rhetoric everyday, but genuinely spoken. Mr. Ragland is a man of color, a dignified and delightful retired Marine with box shoulders and a distinguished patch of gray. Always he is jovial. He clicks his heels whether it rain or the sky cave in. Mr. Ragland pivots suddenly. Instead of continuing on his course, he steps in stride and next to me. His big hand rests on my shoulder. His tender smile fades.

"Have you talked to anyone from home lately?" It has been some time. I silently think. "Has anyone been sick?" he adds.

"Oh my God!" I think of my mother. And at the same time I reason with myself; she only had a little fever when I saw her last.

Inside Mr. Ragland's small office he tells me to sit.

"I got a call from your sister in Detroit this morning," he says. "Your mother has passed away."

My heart flutters. I move to stand. My knees bow loosely and crash to the floor.

With the coming of night, Matthew waits with me at the station. He carries my bags onto the platform and places them in an overhead carrier. Quickly his lips touch mine, and a tear rolls down my cheek. Without a word he tenderly brushes it. I press my hand against a rain-splashed window to wave him goodbye, until the rumbling coach shoves away.

Inside the Mount Zion Church, a pipe organ plays deep and low, striking chords and stirring a clamor. Aunt Trudy shouts hallelujah. Aunt Tootsie's eyes pour water, and Uncle Buster cries softly, "... my favorite sister."

Tomorrow should be a celebration. It would be Minnie's thirty-second birthday. Instead Ernestine leans into a paint-dipped coffin and moans her name. "Mommy, Mommy". The very woman she showed no regard for in life.

Toby sits near Celia, who flew in from Michigan. Giselle and Rhonda share a pew. Alfreda, Nadine and even Junior, Rupert Thurman Jr., my other brother from Washington, D.C. has come to pay his respects to his daddy's other wife. I was a little bitty thing; still I remember. He came to visit us a time or two. A young military man, who danced about in shiny black boots and army fatigues, the son Daddy gave his name to. Daddy was married to Junior's mother many years before my birth and he is still married to her to this very day. Yeah, Daddy, you are so right. "Some things are better kept unsaid?"

The preacher stands to tell a story of how my mom had recently joined the church and even the choir. But inevitably the lid on the shiny box closes and several men carry it away. Cedric is led away in shackles and cuffs. Two uniformed officers escort him away from the church and drive him back to the Rahway State Prison.

Without the employ of a family car, I seat myself, squeezed tight in the back of a battered Lincoln Continental. A gentleman from the old neighborhood where I grew up taxies the drive. Dad sits front and center, next to the driver. Aunt Bea is pressed to his side. The vehicle swerves behind a long black hearse with tinted windows and my mom's body inside. Dad fidgets to draw a page from his jacket pocket. He hands it to Aunt Bea.

"Bea," he says. "'Dis heah is the deed to my grave."

I shake my head and think solemnly. Aunt Bea is not your wife. But Rupert Thurman Jordan, I am your daughter, full grown and next of kin. I nearly puke with unrest. Couldn't this have waited, until my mother is buried and in the ground?

Later on it feels like an icebox inside this den from hell that I once called home. Daddy used to say, "a man's home is his castle". But this house is not a home without its designated hostess. And this dwelling feels the more uncomfortably spacious without my mom. I have my seat at the kitchen table next to Rhonda, my twenty-three-year-old sister. She is no longer the chubby high school kid that I remember of six years ago. Rhonda is now a full-fledged woman, quiet and somber. I can feel the kinship of our loss. Her face is empty, and her presence of mind flashes in, then out. Rhonda drops her head slow and heavy, until her eyelids flutter and fall. Suddenly she shifts position. She lifts her head quickly and tugs her skirt as it rides up over her thighs. Soon she nods, slowly sliding and slumping low in her seat.

"Rhonda!"

I startle her when I call her name. Her eyelids flash, then open and lock with a penetrating glare from Aunt Bea. Aunt Bea is offhanded. She stands oddly in front of a cold and empty oven in that very special spot where Mom used to be. Aunt Bea's eyes fasten with Rhonda's. No teapot whistles and no aroma swarms, rising from a home cooked meal. Only tension and a bitter chill run the length of my rigid spine. Rhonda gauges the situation bitterly. Arched lines crease Aunt Bea's forehead. Her eyebrows lift with a gaze that pierces Rhonda like chiseled ice.

"What the hell you looking at?" Aunt Bea snaps. She is snide and deliberate, pushing Rhonda to anger. Rhonda pounces from her chair, like a north wind from hell. But quickly, her body folds. She stumbles head first and crashes solid, like a severed log onto the floor. I scream when Rhonda's eyes roll empty inside her head.

"Wooo-woo-woo," a rushing ambulance whines hurriedly, with bright flashing light. It swerves to the curbside. Two-way radios sound coded messages, before the medics strap Rhonda to a stretcher and sweep her away. The gurney is lifted parallel to the opened back doors and shoved in the back, like pushing biscuits in a hot oven.

"We're losing her! We're losing her!"

The bed bounces with a crash as the vehicle makes its way against the potholes in the road. The medics are pounding on Rhonda's chest as the ambulance speeds along its way.

Late into the night Junior drives me back to Geneva's. And though Keonis is inside the house, I cannot bring myself to move toward another confrontation with his loud-mouthed, fighting daddy. Junior parks the car and dims the lights. We talk, this kindred stranger and me, about this and that. And although we have never spoken our hearts before; I know my trust in him is pure, when we share the same blood running through our veins.

After some time, Junior drives away and to a little spot where we find a bite to eat. But again we return, parked in front of Geneva's house. He shuts off the headlamps as another hour ticks away.

"You don't want to go inside, do you?" he asks.

"No," I admit. Brother drives to a little hotel where we talk some more. But soon we decide to double-bunk for the night.

"Where you been all night bitch?" That's what Delbert wants to know when Junior drops me back at Geneva's the next day. "What are you doin'? Sleepin' with him?"

"Leave her alone," Geneva warns, "that's her brother."

It wasn't long before I said goodbye to Junior. I said goodbye to my sisters, too. And to Rhonda and the little girl she no longer is. Goodbye to the chubby little sister I once knew. It didn't matter that I was pleading with her to get a thorough exam at the emergency room. She didn't care none that she'd just suffered a seizure either. It didn't matter that the doctor ordered her to stick around until the testing was complete. Rhonda carried on and cussed everybody, including me. She ripped the hospital identification band from her wrist and strutted through the exit doors and onto some darkened street corner, to wait for another trick in the night.

Memories of my mother take a seat beside me aboard the Greyhound Bus, and my eyes won't stop the tears. I left that place angry. What kind of asinine question was that for Aunt Bea to ask of a young woman who had just buried her mother? I left that place sad. I held little Keonis close to my bosom that day. I felt his little giggle close to my heart. I was glad that I was leaving and sad that I could not stay.

Many exhausting hours later I dragged through a crowd and into a restroom at the terminal to freshen up. I washed my face and quickly moved to the streets to meet a taxi. After dropping my bags at my apartment, I headed back to work at WMSP. There I played a song in Mama's memory. I played it for her. I played it for me.

CHAPTER 10

HOMECOMING

On a canvas pressed against a wall and with a single stroke of a withering brush, I begin to paint. I'd set out to create a wonderful splash of vibrant color. But like the dispersing of a rainbow, all the hues washed down, ran together and faded away. It is a stilled work of art in muddy shades of brown and blue. New life breathes into the face of an innocent child, while distrust takes form in the diluted eyes of the mother who holds him near. It has become a glum depiction of the morbid cynicism taking hold in my own life.

I pass the lonely hours. Sometimes visiting the wife of a co-worker, who is helping me to sort through some of this stuff. Other times another friend drives me to meet her friends, hoping I will relax and hang out together with them for awhile. Matthew comes by, and … What I really want is to pick up and talk things over with my mom or Minnie – that is what I really want.

Boom, boom, boom! The noise startles me and drives me to sit straight up in my bed. Boom, boom! The room is dark. I reach to click the switch on a little lamp set upon my nightstand, when I upset an ashtray filled with butts. I slide my feet on the floor, then stumble over my bedroom slippers, before finally reaching the door. I open it.

"Are you okay?"

"Huh?" My eyes squint, adjusting to the light.

"We got worried about you when you didn't show up to work tonight."

It's Otis and Jay, my co-workers from the station. I agreed to work a fill-in at WMSP, overnight.

"What time is it?" I ask, rubbing my eyes.

"One fifteen."

"Oh my God!" Thinkin' 'bout my Mommy, worryin' 'bout Keonis – it's all getting to be too much. "Let me get dressed." I say.

My hair stands on my head. My eyes are swollen. I wipe my mouth to remove a crust of slobber, dried tight around my lips.

"Go on back to sleep. Get your rest. I got somebody in to cover for you."

"Thanks."

I shut the door and roll the covers over my head.

There goes October and November, and now it is December. The weeks have been nearly impossible without Keonis. I'm just glad for Matthew. His strong arms fold around my belly and my back nestles firmly in the contours of his broad chest. His muscular frame bends forward and clings like connecting puzzle pieces with my form. With Christmas dawning, we caress one another long into the silent night. Already I am missing him. We exchange the heat of warm tears, mixing wet kisses with tender words. Suddenly, night is broken and before the sun comes up, our lips touch one last time. In an instant I step out and into the bleakness of another uncertain day. I will always remember you, Matthew.

"Fill-'er-up."

"Do you mind if I check your tire? I heard something rattling when you came in." The gas station attendant removes the hubcap and another man receives my fare. I wait anxiously to see the gas gage rise. The sooner the tank is filled, the sooner I will be on my way. I can't wait to throw my arms around my boy. I nearly faint with the thought of seeing his little face.

When the attendant finishes looking at the tire, he stands up to show me something in his hand.

"I found this here lug nut rolling 'round inside your hubcap. It's a good thing I had a look at it." He chuckles. "You don't want to lose your wheels." He looks long and hard at the old car and asks, "Where you trying to go to in this thing, anyway?"

"To New Jersey"

He sniggers quietly. He shakes his head in disbelief, then tightens the rusted lug nut back on the wheel. I thank him. I thank God. Then get about my way. From my mirror I see the two men smiling. Waving and hollering, "Good Luck!"

"Luck?" Only ducks are lucky. My wheels are spinning and I'm up to my ankles in slush. Tiny frozen particles bounce about my windshield. After making a wrong turn, my front bumper is slid low in a ditch. I shift the gear in neutral and I begin to pray. Pushing and praying and trying to force this big old car out of this here mud. Soon a truck plows through. The door swings open, and one of two kindly gentlemen steps out. He gleams with laughter and greets me with a hardy hello.

"How'd you get yourself in there?" He asks.

I smile.

"My name's Claude," he says cordially. He extends his hand.

"I'm Edwina, pleased to meet ya.'" We shake.

"Where ya' going?"

"Stay with her," the driver yells through an opened window. His voice rises over the loud rumble of his idling engine. "I'm goin' to get the other truck, be right back." Claude gives a nod as the truck hauls away.

"Where ya' going?" He asks again.

"New Jersey."

"You sure you gonna make it? This weather we having is pretty bad."

With one quick glance at the sky, I know he's right. Freezing rain, sleet or something melts with my body heat and makes my brain freeze. "I'll be all right," I answer him. He grins. His shoulders shake with the cold.

"Just as soon as the driver gets back we'll get you out of there," he says. Then suddenly, "ooh-wee!" he cries, as a big wind carries through. Claude shoves his gloved hands deep inside his pockets. His big shoulders tremble. I'm trembling, too. My teeth chatter and I can't keep them still. "It is some kinda cold out here," he says. "Can we sit inside your car where it is warm?"

I nod my head. Claude runs for the passenger door. I quickly grab the door handle on the other side.

"Here he come now," Claude remarks twenty minutes later. The driver, a big fellow in a red plaid jacket and matching hat, returns driving a different vehicle. It is a big ol' utility truck. I smile to see all the shovels and stuff sticking out of the rear. Claude removes a bag of sand and pours a pile under my tires. Next he clamps a big metal hook to my bumper and the other guy drives the big truck forward. In a couple minutes they are through.

"Do me a favor," I say. "Let me follow you back to the main road."

"Yeah, ain't no problem."

Several miles later and just as I'm reaching the toll station, I get the smell of hot air rising.

"Can you help me?"

"Pull off the road, there," a clerk tells me. "I will be off in a couple minutes. I'll see what I can do." He meets me. A young man who ain't yet old enough to be legally served a beer. He finds me smiling patiently and the engine sputtering steam. "Where ya trying to go?" Now, I think I've been asked that question before.

"New Jersey."

"You can't drive that thing to New Jersey," he jabbers.

"Says who?" I ask.

"You gotta get it fixed. Can't get no parts today, neither. 'Cause today is Christmas Day." As if I need for him to tell me.

"Look, fool," I say to myself. "I know its Christmas." As a matter of fact it's the only reason I'm out here in the first place. After further examination he reminds me, again.

"Can't get no parts. It's Christmas Day. You ain't gonna make it to New Jersey, no how," he adds. "Ain't that where you say you're goin'?"

"New Jersey, yeah, I'm going to New Jersey."

"It won't be nothin' open 'til morning. I don't know," he says, scratching his head, "Except I could offer you to come and stay with me." He flashes a dubious smile. "I go to the University, right over there." He points the way. "You could sleep in the dorm with me and my roomies."

"Oh, no thanks." Who do I look like, Boo Boo the Fool or Stevie Wonder? My car stops steaming. I shift it into gear.

"Wait a minute," he says. I'll be right back."

He returns quickly with a jug of antifreeze. Pours it into the radiator then politely hands to me a ham sandwich. I shovel on my way.

Soon again, the radiator begins to percolate. Steamy vapors are covering the windshield, when just in time I drive upon a huge sign: "OPEN." Today is Christmas, and a lucky one for me. The service station attendant loosens the cap on the heating unit. It explodes. Shooting boiling water into the sky.

"You need a thermostat," he says.

"A thermostat?" I say. "I don't have no money for no thermostat. I've only got money, enough to get me where I'm goin'."

"Well, where's that?"

"New Jersey."

He laughs.

"Well, you can't make it to New Jersey driving it hot like this. You're gonna blow the engine. A thermostat won't cost you much."

"How much?"

"A few dollars. No more than ten."

"I don't have it. I've got toll money and that's all."

"Only other thing I could do, is remove it all together. You won't have no heat, though. And it's sure to get a lot colder driving north as night sets in. But if you want, I can take it off for you. And I won't charge you nothing."

"Take it off, and fill up the gas tank, too. Thank-you. I've got to see my baby."

The front compartment of the car is icy, and the temperatures north are declining by the mile. My hot breath condenses against the windshield, like blowing on a mirror. I swab the frost with my hand. I save a napkin for the rest of the trip. Several hundred miles later, I read: "Last Service Area on the NJ Turnpike." Again, the gas gauge spells EMPTY and I have just six dollars left.

"Will five dollars get me across the turnpike?" I ask.

"I think so," replies the attendant. I hand over my last five and when he turns to walk away, he returns a cheery shout. "I put in six dollars, Merry Christmas, ma'am."

"Thank you Jesus, thank you sir."

One crumpled bill is all I have, a single dollar squeezed in my hand. I drive into the last toll-booth.

"One dollar-ten!" The clerk exclaims. I rattle my purse from side to side. A single coin falls onto the seat. I hold it out to the light, then, thank my God again! It's a dime!

"How'd you get here?" My mother-in-law, Geneva asks, since nobody knew that I was on my way.

"God! God brought me here!" I dump my purse. Three pennies topple to the floor.

Ten long blocks I walked. That stupid car of mine quit on me the day I pulled in front of Geneva's door. I near the old house and see the ol' willow, weeping and swinging in the breeze. With a smile, I reminisce on days stretched on a lawn chair, twice as long as me. I think to myself, that tree sure got posture. I adore its slender branches all fashioned in green. For it weeps in silence, just like me. And for just a moment I can smell the fragrant and colorful flowers. I imagine the vine of morning glories growing through the lattice, beneath the porch. Recalling how the funneled petals doubled over each evening at sunset. But by the crack of dawn, the folds unwrapped and reached like palms, paying homage to the morning sun.

Suddenly, Mother Nature back-slaps me with a cold wind flat across my neck. The grounds are frozen stiff and icicles string the trees. No doubt – it is winter. Remarkably so, I miss the old evergreen that once stood high outside my window. Dad had no appreciation for that tree. It is gone. Cut down like my dreams and all that remains is an unsightly stump. I lower my chin and tug my scarf. My gaze falls upon *bruzzin'* Toby, standing and watching. I smile. I've been a long time from home and the sight of him warms my heart. But Toby's face is twisted. He only turns more sour, when I tell him why I've come his way.

"Get the hell off the property!" he screams. Big veins show in his forehead and neck. Then Toby grabs a big ol' wooden plank and raises it over my head. "You haven't been here. And you don't know what the hell is going on here. Now leave!" His warning is harsh and calculated. Spit flies from his lips to spray my face. I choke to the core of my belly and cannot speak.

Two weeks later and again in the howling face of winter, I make another attempt to visit Daddy. I enter to find the front door opened wide and swaying on its hinge.

"Hello," I call. But my voice returns to me with hollowness. "Hello."

The back door, too, swings open and the only warmth is from the heat of my breath, blowing against my hands. I face the shambles of a once warmed kitchen. It is colder than outdoors. The open entry to the bathroom sends a stench of feces humming from behind a fallen door. I gag. Grab my collar to hide my face, and run outside to catch my breath.

Soon, I climb the silence of the staircase. From the landing I see him. Rupert Thurman Jordan, my daddy, amidst the muck and clutter and seated at the edge of the bed. A collapsible cardboard table sets over his lap and his hands encircle one over the other. He creates a friction from a fluttering flame that glows inside a kerosene lamp. Overspent hairs grow curly and white from his chin to his neck. He is old and worn and his clothing reeks an unpleasant pong. There is a void cast in the dimmed light of his eyes as he struggles to raise his head. The sight of him makes my eyes sore.

"Daddy" I call to him, "Daddy!"

"Where is that woman?" he attempts to speak, "the one what used to bring me food?" He whispers in a wee voice, barely audible. Does he think of his wife, my mother? or does he think of Aunt Bea, I wonder.

"Umm hungry." he says.

I leave briefly to return with a sandwich, then, soon again depart.

LETTER TO MOMMY

Dear Mommy,

The morning air is brutal. But colder still is homecoming to New Jersey, absent of you. Things without you will never be the same, and only God knows how I miss you. My boy, Keonis never had the gift of knowing you, and I wish that I had known you more.

I remember you saying, Dad would be nothing without you. Well, I guess you know his life has turned inside out, since you went away. He's mentally ransacked. Soiling his underclothing, like a kid in training. He wanders around talking to the wind. I think his mind stays set somewhere lost in the day you passed away.

His worth is being stolen by family members and people he entrusts to be his friends. They put a pillow over his face, beat and rob him. Then drain his bank account using a rubber-stamp bearing his name.

144

Everything has been pilfered. Including the silverware he gave to you on Christmas Day. But, that should come as no surprise, when somebody stole your wedding band, while your body cooled in death.

It perplexes me that your house is in foreclosure and that the bills have not been paid. The taxes are past due, the house is gutted and the pipes have been stripped from the walls and sold for scrap. Mom, everything that you and Dad worked so hard to accomplish is gone.

I have filed a motion with the courts to have every last soul evicted. God knows that I refuse to visit Toby with this matter, again. I have sold the house for a mere twelve thousand dollars, all that will be left after the back taxes and other liens on the property have been paid. The gavel has sounded and the decision is final. I only pray you understand why.

"So much for the quality of work-life, Judy," I hear it said, from the mouth of a leg-wagging, female, white employee as she sits atop her desk. I scurry between offices in a corporate high rise dumping garbage pails for a fancy conglomerate. They don't pay me my due. But I got a first chance opportunity at a job and they get their trash buckets dumped. Next, I'm a clerk at the grocery market and a flower arranger at a flower shop. Now I stand beside Aunt Tess at a factory, where we fold curtains all the day. Two years experience is more than adequate for hire at the local radio station. But, no positions are to be had. This job quest in a small town where there is but one little radio station, leaves me exhausted. Until finally, I hear the word, yes.

"But we can only pay you minimum wage."

And that's okay by me.

I'm playing Middle of the Road and Big Bands, two formats that I know absolutely nothing about, over WXLV. *Frank Sinatra, Glenn Miller Tommy Dorsey and Sammy Davis Jr.,* singing *Candy*

Man is about as good as it gets. I tell 'em yes! Three hours on Saturday afternoons. "Yes! Yes! Yes!"

Passing through a lonely corridor inside the commercial building where I work. I see my father. He is two levels off the ground, same as me. He senses nothing of the nearness of my presence in like buildings parted merely by the rushing air of a busy throughway. I imagine his eyes undefined, far-fixed with no conscious bearing. Likely he recalls nothing of his late night ride to this desecrated place in the back of a black and white patrol car. He sits mindless, protected from a rushing spatter of humming tires splashing through a gentle downpour. Never to ponder the chronicle of events, that has delivered his being among queer-faced non-acquaintances, who care absolutely nothing of his disquieting affairs.

But even more somber then he, are my thoughts. Thoughts of brighter days, ... "Brighter days," an over-washed cliché for early times past spent. Childhood memories summon an image of a once vibrant tyrant, who is now nothing more than a homeless man in a homeless shelter, among vagabonds and other abandoned souls, like he is. And silently, a tiny raindrop pronounces itself upon the window. And like the translucence of his frail and decrepit presence, the droplet of dewy moisture falls softly out of view to slide away. Somewhere in the mopping of my tears, the drumming of the rain and the rinsing away, something good has happened for me. I have earned a car, old but sound. And I've got a full time job at the city bank. Maybe soon, I can move out of my mother-in-law's and Dad can live with me.

"This is Edwina Jordan, wishing you a goodnight."

I shut the microphone off and everything goes silent at midnight sign-off time at WXLV. Quickly, I turn off the transmitter, shut down the lights, lock the door and leave. Driving home and speeding through the familiar neighborhood streets, I hear, "EDWINA!!!" My name resounds with an echo.

Quickly, I mash the brakes and peek through the mirror. It's cousin Nathaniel, flailing his arms from a half block away. "EDWINA!!!" he hollers, again. Then he stuffs his fingers between his teeth and whistles a reverberating shrill. This had better be real important, I think sarcastically. I am tired and I've got to get started early in the morning to get to my new position at the bank.

"Edwina!" he says, full of panic. "Have you heard anything 'bout Nadine?"

"Nadine? I haven't heard from Nadine." I answer impatiently. "Nah," I say. "I haven't heard from Nadine, not in a long time."

"No," he says, vigorously. "I mean, have you heard anything about Nadine? How she is doing?"

"Nathaniel, what are you talking about?"

"You know Nadine got shot – don't you?"

"Huh!"

"Yeah! She's in the hospital. Been' there a couple days."

"What! How is she? Has anybody gone to see about her?"

"I don't know. All I know is she was at a bar in Newark. Somebody opened fire and she got shot."

"Has anybody been to see her? I emphatically ask, again.

"I don't think so."

"Thanks Nathaniel." I pull away.

I barrel down the highway and the only exhaust fumes are my own, blowing off steam, violating traffic regulations and pressing the pedal all the way. One half hour later I run straight through the big glass doors. I hop an elevator. All the while asking God not to let me be too late. Finally I see Nadine, lying back flat on a gurney with her eyes clamped tight.

"I love you," I whisper. And she don't even know I'm here. A nurse comes to greet me.

"Are you her sister?"

"Yes" She tells me that Nadine took a slug in the spine. A bullet meant for somebody else. The doctor says she is stable, but with no sign of movement, still it could go either way.

Like my mom always said, "If it ain't one thing it's another." It is beginning to make sense to me now. I wrecked my car on Monday, lost my job at the bank on Tuesday. Now, my mother-in-law thinks I'm pregnant.

"Are you pregnant?" She smiles with a gaze of wisdom.

"Huh?"

"Are you the one who was in my dream last night? I've been having a lot of fish dreams lately."

"Ma, please." I just laugh at the mention of it. "My baby is eight years old. What are you talking about? I need to be pregnant, about as much as I need a hole in my head."

"I had a dream about all these little fish, last night." The old'-timers equate dreams of fish to fertility.

"Oh no, not little fishies." I mock jokingly. But, proof is truth in the old wives tale.

Then there is Dad, who got picked up by the police again, after wandering away from the shelter. I had set him up in a private residence with a live-in nurse. Last week she informed me that she can't care for him anymore. He's now in one of those big old nursing homes in another part of the state. I had a visit with him today.

A tour of his sleeping-quarters reveals a very different picture from the facility's lower lobby, where they roll the red carpet and dangle chandeliers. His bunk smells like piss. And he sits all day. Stooped over and drugged in a hard-back chair. Collection on the closing-sale of the house will meet the expense of furniture, pots and pans and such. A medical supply store will lease the wheelchair, portable potty and a hospital bed. One with side rails to keep Dad from rolling off the edge. Soon, I will bring him home to live with me.

Nothing is more splendid than the tranquility of a winter's snowfall, tip-toeing through the early morn. A trillion droplets of moisture transform inexplicably into a winter wonderland.

Even the great limbs of the grand oak bow dutifully, exhibiting respect for her awesome display. An ol' evergreen tree sweeps low with snow and my eyes trace a trail of footprints, wondering where each will go.

In a path of silence and amidst the spirited February winds, a small team of paramedics appear. They give Daddy's wheelchair a shove along the outer walkway. Then lift him over the snow packed stairs. With a short stroll past the inner entrance and with a medic on each side, Dad's fragile frame is steadied. A couple guys from the facility sit him down in a wide armed-chair. Next, the wheelchair strolls away, as do those who brought it. For today marks another phase of acclimation for Dad and for me. I brush the snow from his woolen hat and softly pull it from his head. A furry U-shape frames his temples and just a couple proud strands remain standing where hair used to be. But Dad always said, "Grass don't grow on a busy street." And busy, he is. Suddenly rising precariously and swaying on the soles of his feet.

"No Daddy!" I say. Then help him back into his chair. "Sit still daddy. I will be right back." Before I can turn around he slips – unbalanced – then plummets safely back onto the arms of the chair. I scold him gently. He is solemn. Discontentment is harbored in his jutting mouth and anger etched in the crevice of his jaw. My eyes discern that any authority, just or unjust, is an abomination before this man. I leave him, and return, strolling with the big blue wheelchair. Cautiously, I lift him. But he loathes my help and snatches recklessly. Rupert Thurman Jordan, falls onto the center of the floor. He winces. I scold. Who is this man who defies the face of meekness? For him, once, the earth quaked with trembling. But now – there's just a brooding murmur from a displeasured foolhardy old man. He is returned to his chair for a sit. His eyes roll with displeasure and his nostrils flare.

My belly heaves and then settles, exhaling upon an opened palm. Spread fingertips massage, making swirling motions over a growing cargo. Already, I am six months and the more my impregnated tummy expands, the harder it becomes to control Daddy's fighting. He lies with his body stretched flat on a couch. I stand at the bottom of that long chair. He throws his feet and I place them back. It is a tug of war and deranged rebellion. And again, thump! Determination is admirable. But this is belligerence, bold and in my face. I lift Dad's heavy feet, when suddenly he hurls them, straight for my belly. I get out of the way in the knick of time. Lately I have had to leave him in that God-forsaken, uncomfortable wheel chair. Until Delbert comes to lift him out. And for more hours than he or I would prefer. After all, Delbert's comings and goings are not set to my watch.

The nights are short, with the days so long. Adjusting to this new and rigorous schedule is a challenge I won't soon forget. Come morning we rise early. Delbert and Keonis take turns getting ready for school and work. After Daddy is fed, shaved and dressed, I do the cleaning, not to mention the laundry that accumulates each day. It stretches far on a clothesline, reaching deep into the yard. I stand on an outer porch, squeezing pins and hanging items in duplicate. Long underwear, shirts and briefs, outer clothing, socks and pants, all hand-scrubbed in a tub of soapy water. I don't forget Daddy's doctor's appointments or the prenatal care appointments of my own.

"Come on Daddy." I nudge his shoulder and tug his arm. But for all of thirty-seconds he just frowns and sits in defiance of me. Daddy, would you please – try and stand up. You've got to help me."

His gaze is withdrawn and he doesn't move an inch. His eyes are cold and pierce like cooling ice.

"Delbert, can you help me? I can't get Daddy out of the tub."

Delbert gets very angry. But Daddy never played favorites. As a matter fact, there are very few folk who Dad really likes. Delbert ain't one of 'em.

"He better get his ass up out the tub," Delbert retorts with hostility. "Look out," he says, ripping hold to Daddy's arm and shoving me out of his way.

"Delbert, take it easy! Don't snatch him that way."

"Tell the mother-fucker to get out of the tub, then." Delbert snatches again. Daddy's eyes cut into Delbert. I wonder sometimes, who is the more intolerable. "I wish you would try somethin'," Delbert snaps angrily, ready to fight.

Delbert is hateful, hateful and angry. And Daddy ... If looks could kill, I would have to bury Delbert tonight.

"Look out Delbert. Never mind. I push him out of the way. Let me do it."

"I got it Edwina. Look out."

"No, Delbert! We go back and forth. "You are being too mean." Rupert Thurman Jordan don't take too kindly to nobody mistreatin' him. I know my daddy. And right now – Delbert is standing in his way.

"Move, Delbert," I demand. I shove him aside with my hip. Suddenly he rips the water stopper from the drain and walks away. When Daddy sits naked and after all of the warm soapy water disappears, Delbert returns to throw the window wide open. In rushes a blast of frigid, howling air.

"Delbert, what is wrong with you?" I scream and make my way around him to slam the window shut.

Delbert laughs and grabs Daddy under his armpit. Finally Daddy climbs out of the tub.

This is not an easy time for Daddy, or me. The hours become days and the days become weeks, when already I count two calendar pages since Daddy came to stay.

"Delbert, um goin' in the hospital soon. What about Daddy? Who's gonna to take care of him?"

"Raymond is gonna do it. I already asked him."

"Raymond? Who is Raymond."

"You know Raymond," he says, defensively. "We went to school with Raymond."

"Not that little gay guy, who picks you up in that yellow convertible."

"Gay guy? Raymond ain't gay."

"He looks gay to me."

"Raymond is not gay." He says, defensively.

"What makes you think he can take care of my father?" I ask.

"He's a certified nurse, that's why. He'll look after him."

I try talking with Daddy to ease the tension. But little does it matter, when he is unfocused, bitter and angry most times.

But I get angry too. Reflecting too much on the past and asking questions.

"Why did you treat Mommy so mean?" Why did you do this – and why did you do that?

"Sometimes ya' gotta let dead dogs lie," is all he'd say. I guess I gotta respect that.

Late into the night, my body doubles over with ten thousand blows. My belly falls into my lap, and the pain pushes me forward. The rescue crew arrives to ask if I have swallowed a watermelon seed. It must be the rising of my belly under this long green robe. They have a hardy ha-ha and a chuckle. My mouth won't grin. It only twitches in between contractions – and only a little on one side. They get me loaded into the back of the truck. The sirens whine, as we go shooting down the open thruway on a bed that's rocking side to side. Suddenly, the vehicle comes to a complete halt, smack in front of the cemetery. I think she's coming. But, we speed away again. Forty-five minutes later, my screaming stops and hers begins.

It is Janiah, the name I have given my wide-mouth, strong-lunged, bouncing bundle of joy. Her nutmeg-cheeks are rounded and a delicate impression is formed between the drawstrings on either side of her little pink hat. Spiral locks frame her jowls. She stares me eyeball to eyeball. Like no newborn I have ever seen.

"What is it you wish to ask me, child?" I think playfully, before I take her home.

I place Janiah safely in a little basket at my bedside, then, tiptoe in to sneak a peek.

"Daddy!" I call to him softly. "Daddy" I call again. He gives no response. "Gosh!" You smell like urine. Oozing sores cover your behine'. Rupert Thurman Jordan, how did I fail you? Emptied and tired, you no longer put up a good fight. You stare into the air, gazing clear through the ceiling, rigid like a pebble in a pond.

It is Easter Sunday morning and I patter about in my bathrobe and slippers. I get Daddy up, bathed and dressed. Then I put him down in the blue wheeled chair. I hold a glass of water to his mouth. He dribbles it like a man with a hole in his chin. He waste away his breakfast, he is too weak to eat.

"Why don't you get dressed and get out of the house for a while?" Delbert tells me.

"I can't."

"Why not?"

"Because, Daddy is here; I can't leave him. No one is here to look after him."

"He'll be all right for a couple of hours. Come on and visit my mother with me. You have been in the house for weeks."

"Maybe I should put him back to bed."

"No. We're only gonna be a couple of hours. He can stay in the chair."

"I don't know, Delbert." Daddy's eyes look far away.

"He is strapped to the wheelchair. He can't fall out. Trust me – he'll be all right."

"Let me try again to see if I can get him to eat."

"Come on, Edwina, let's go. Hurry-up."

Ten days after Janiah arrived, on Easter Sunday in nineteen hundred and eighty four, Rupert Thurman Jordan, my daddy, slipped away.

LETTER TO DADDY

Daddy,

I watched them carry you out in a black body bag. Your funeral was sadly a disgrace. No frills, no lace and no friends to bid you goodbye. Practically no one, except a bunch of confused and tormented offspring with twisted emotions and ambiguous commentary. Daddy, you left a lousy legacy of lethargic rejects longing for answers in a line of dope or a loaded syringe. My heart bleeds for you. But I guess you get back in the same measure that you dish out. You're buried in a double-bunked grave on top of Mom. I sometimes wonder if she gets restless with you so near. Does she fuss and say I told you so? May you rest in peace.

It was Daddy's money that took care of the rent for the last four months and Daddy's money that put food on our table. Now with Daddy gone I carry clothes and pillows to store in somebody else's cellar. Delbert kicks the corners on a metal bed frame. It don't matter none to him that again, we don't have nowhere to stay. The clasp loosens and one side crashes to the floor.

"Just let me start making love to you." A tear rolls down my face every time I think about it. After all the hell I've been through, he says, "Then, Vernon can come in."

I realize now. It didn't mean a thing to Delbert that I slept with Vernon. Only thing bothered him was, he wasn't there to watch.

"Do you need a hand with that?" Vernon laughs to ease the tension.

Hate is a strong word. I try to refrain from using it. Both of them can kiss my …

When the evening comes, I don't wanna eat, don't wanna' talk or nothin'. Just cry inside myself and cradle my screaming baby to my breast. Geneva sits across from me at her dining table. Her head rolls slowly from side to side and her face lowers in her hands.

"I can't take it," she softly complains. "Please, can somebody shut her up!"

But my Janiah don't never stop crying. She screams much of the day. She's not hungry and her diaper is dry. Colic – a gas pain in her little belly, maybe that's what it is? I move her quietly to the sofa in the other room and slap my titty through her face. An hour later she's still crying. Geneva is exhausted. I don't expect she can tolerate all that carrying on. I love Geneva. She would never turn me away. But it sure as hell ain't easy living here in this little three bedroom house. I reckon, with Delbert, the kids and at least a half dozen other grown folk mooching off Geneva, I'm just another stone throwed' in her way.

"Pull the sofa bed out, Edwina," Geneva says gently. "Maybe she wants to lie down."

I don't care that it is early. I lie down too, right beside her. I kiss her pumpkin cheeks. Then wipe the tears from her eyes and mine, with the corner of the blanket, when nobody else can see.

CHAPTER 11

LOVE DON'T LOVE NOBODY

The chilled November rains press cold against my neck. My worn umbrella flips with each blow of a hefty wind. Janiah doesn't like the cold weather. Or maybe it's the bumps in the road. Whatever the reason, that child of mine has been bawling, since the day I pushed her out of my womb. And even more now since I snatched her off my breast. I park her stroller on the porch. Then, carry her up in my arms and inside the house to leave with a neighbor-friend. Soon I take my stand alongside the owner's wife at the dry cleaners, where I work. The proprietor has five daughters. We talk a lot, mostly about our children, while we hustle 'til day's end.

My neighbor has strapped Janiah's bottom inside a mechanical swing. The droning of its squeaking hinge sounds repeatedly. And, "Rockaby-Baby" sings over and over again. Little Janiah screams aloud. Balling her eyes out, the same as when I left her. My elder friend moseys back inside. She sits aloof and throws her backside down on a sofa cushion, after she lets me in.

"What's the matter, Sweetheart?" I drop my purse in a hurry and run to see about my little girl. Her eyes are red and her face swollen with tears.

"She spoiled," my neighbor speaks angrily, "'dat's all is wrong wit' her."

"Are you hungry?" I say sympathetically. "Is your diaper wet?" I poke my finger inside her diaper and recognize that she needs a change.

"Ain't nothin' da matter wit' 'dat chile', cept' you hold her too much. She want me to hold her all day, too – and I ain't doin' it."

On Sunday morning and dragging through the winter's slush, I take a fall, while trying to flag the bus in time to get to my weekend radio shift at WXLV. Delbert refuses to watch the kids. I try not to bother myself with his irrational antics. Melinda has volunteered to stay. When he sees I'm givin' all of myself, I'm hoping he'll change his way.

Then, just in time for the holidays it comes together. Like stumbling blocks, beds, bed-frames, sofa, chairs and tables, boxes stacked to the ceiling and miscellaneous other items, set piled in the floor's center. I carry along a broom, mop, and bucket on just another Sunday, when I'm supposed to be at work. Room by room, I scrub and I tidy for hours. Pushing furniture pieces and unpacking boxes, sorting clothing and giving every item its rightful place. The beds are spread with hand-washed sheets. The floors are swept, dishes washed and set neatly on a cupboard shelf. A small portion of food takes position in the refrigerator. The washed skillet is waitin' for a home cooked meal. Delbert thinks I'm working. But I can't wait to see his face.

"Dinner is ready. Surprise!" I hope he is happy. It ain't no doubt, Keonis is overjoyed. His smile is broad and his teeth glimmer, when he walks inside his very own room. He flops joyfully across the length of his very own bed. Keonis slides his hands to smooth the covers. Still, my work is incomplete until Janiah is received in her wicker basket. Sometimes I believe our little Janiah was sent to test my patience. Patience I have gained and a warp in my spine from bowing over her bassinette before she goes to sleep. It takes a lot of work hushing that child. No sooner than I tip away, Janiah starts all over again. But, tonight we will all sleep in the comfort of our own bed for the very first time.

Christmas sneaks in with nothing more than our recently moved in apartment. I am delighted. There isn't anywhere else that I'd wish to be. Already my three favorite smiling faces surround me. For the first time in many months, Delbert and I laugh together. When the jokester in him struts into our bedroom, decked in Christmas wraps. His naked penis is adorned in holly and a bright, red bow, tied with a knot. I scream with amusement. Then Christmas steals away.

The hubbub of affairs throughout the coming months raises a question. Is there no solution, with a man filled with booze, and no good intent? My joy is fleeting, like my husband, into the crannies of secluded spaces. Rarely do I see him, before the sunsets and long retires into the night.

"Shut that bitch up!" He roars with no tolerance for Janiah's wailing. He quarrels with me late into the morning and accuses that she is not his kin. I peel away the wash rag under her bare behine'. I replace it with one of the disposable diapers that Delbert just carried in. I coddle her in a time when food has become a gratuity. The old lady has no patience for my Janiah's crying. My job has come to an end. Now again, Geneva is dreaming little fishies. After three and a half months into our stay, our belongings line the front of the brownstone building. Set on the corner at a busy intersection. I stand crammed amongst the clutter, with a cantankerous child against my breast. Baby number three is inside my belly and I wait for Delbert to come and help me move this mess. Keonis ponders, knick-knacks, photographs, his toys. Always there is something left behind, locked behind a closed door. If only I could padlock the tears from the premise of his heart.

We are off to stay with Aunt Bea and her family. She's got seven kids now, including my *bruzzins'* Toby and Curtis. Now, there is also, Teresa and Monique. They are always teasing, 'bout us being sister-cousins. It ain't no more secret, when these two big teenagers, look just like me.

Aunt Bea's house is cold and dim. The air sweeps through the walls like an icebox after the sun goes down. The roaches surge in the refrigerator like a waterfall and the rats don't seem to mind. When Aunt Bea fumigates the inside, you need a traffic cop to direct the flow on the outside. The roaches swarm free along the banisters on outer porch and up the walkway. But, I'm so glad its winter. I can put my food on the roof, where it is cold and safe. I just pray the raccoons don't decide to carry it away. As for the lack of heat, I've purchased a kerosene heater. I don't stop hoping. For Delbert has promised. In a little while we will have a place of our own.

But soon the days tally into weeks and the weeks to months. Many months later and already, it is summer. Somehow I know that my delivery time is here. In the middle of the night, my baby boy is born. He is cute and cuddly and doesn't make a fuss. But, when I introduce him to my feisty Janiah, she smacks him clear across his tender face.

"Hello, little brother, I'm Janiah your sixteen-month-old BIG sister. Now let me show you who is in charge!" She seems to say.

"Milk, diapers, and ..." I think aloud, while pushing a - stroller through the isles in the grocery store. Janiah rides the seat and Gerald rides inside a harness strapped to my back. Next, I am off to the city clinic. There they will prick Janiah's finger. Now, she'll really have somethin' to cry for.

It's two weeks now, since I gave birth to Gerald, but already it is time to get back to work. They've got a newly opened slot, seven 'til midnight at WXLV, and they're offering it to me.

"You have been listening to *Frank Sinatra* with, *I Left My Heart in San Francisco*, over 1410 AM, WXLV. It is now twenty minutes past the hour of ten o'clock. Good evening, I'm Edwina Jordan and here is your local forecast with meteorologist Tom Sullivan." With a press of a button a pre-recorded broadcast begins to roll.

"Hi, I'm Tom Sullivan, with your forecast for Central New Jersey. Tonight it will be cloudy with a chance for showers." Soon my good friend George saunters in.

"Edwina, what are you doing here?"

"Working, George, what does it look like?"

"No, Edwina, what are you doing here?"

"Working." I say it again with a smile to my Italian friend, George Torecelli. He is the Operations Manager. He drops by a couple nights a week to make sure the old transmitter is behaving. The station is old and all the equipment is falling apart.

"Edwina." George calls my name a third time. "I am serious. What are you doing here?"

"George, what are you talking about?"

"You are too good to be working in this place. You've got too much talent. What are they paying you ... five – six dollars an hour? I expected by now you would be working over in New York or somewhere, making yourself some real money. They don't pay you enough to stay."

I'm flattered. But time has taken me nowhere. I've sent out resumes, cover letters and demo-tapes, all over the metro area and so far, no go.

"You all right?" George asks. "What's going on?" he says. As if he can read clear through my mind. "Is there anything I can do?" George offers to prepare a letter of referral for me. A reference letter from George, bearing his signature would be very helpful and graciously received. This station was George's only job, too, at one time. But he has since moved on to bigger and better things. I am really happy for him. "Is there anything else I can do?"

"No," I tell him. "I've just been going through a lot, George, if you' know what I mean?"

"Yeah, I do. Talk to me."

"Right now, I'm just trying to focus on getting a place of my own to live." I figure I can talk to George. We always have talked about things in the past.

"What would it take to get you a place?" His generosity astounds me. I am moved to the edge of my seat. But it wouldn't be fair to impose on my dear friend.

"No, George, I can't let you do that."

"Edwina, listen to me. How much? I am Top Operations Manager at WRVN in New York. I bring home two-grand a week. What do you need, a thousand? How much?"

"I don't know."

"Listen. I'll tell you what. Are you working all this week?"

"Yeah"

"You check into it. Find a place and tell me what it costs. I'll write the check when I see you."

"George, no," I insist. "I don't have that kind of money."

"Edwina, don't worry about it. I haven't always been in a position to help. But now I am. You pay me when you can. When you make it big," he says with a smile." George leaves out. The phone rings.

"WXLV, good evening"

"Hello, I would like to speak to Edwina Jordan, please."

"Yes, this is she."

"Hi Edwina. This is Luther Stubbs from WBLJ Radio. How are you?"

My eyes light up. Still I can't for the life of me figure why he'd be calling me. Luther is the Program Director at the Rhythm and Blues and Gospel station. The one I always wanted to work for.

"Edwina, Carla Waters and I were listening to your program over the radio …"

"Carla Waters?" I interrupt. "Who is Carla Waters?"

"Oh, I'm sorry," Mr. Stubbs apologizes. "Carla is the Operations Manager here. Carla asked that I give you a call to set a date and time, when it might be good for you to meet with us. Carla said to get somebody in here who knows what they are doing." He chuckles warmly. I can't believe what I am hearing. There is silence, absolute silence.

"Edwina?" Luther asks. "Are you still there?"

"I am – yes um' here." Actually, I am flattered, ecstatic or dumfounded and all those other adjectives that Webster wrote. It is still local radio, but the pay is a little better than here.

"The Lord is my Shepard" – the pages part on an old and frayed leather-backed Bible –"I shall not want." For good things I give God the glory. A luxurious high rise with two bathrooms and a Sunday shift at WBLJ. ZOOM! sounds my old green Duster flying down the avenue. I bought it myself, with my own green cash.

Suddenly, bzz-bzz, bzzz-zzz. The buzzer sounds early evening and interrupts my thoughts. A young man appears.

"Hello, Edwina." He calls me by my first name. A kid, who's maybe fourteen, enters into our tiny vestibule, announcing himself as no stranger.

"You remember me don't you?" He sounds confident, that I should know his name. "I'm Earl, Tonya's son. Remember me?"

Actually, I don't – remember you. I reflect without saying.

"Who did you come to see, Keonis?" I ask of the young stranger. Perhaps he is a school friend to my boy, although visibly older. I can't imagine any other cause for him to be ringing my bell.

"No," he says, "is Delbert home?"

"Keonis is here. Would you like to visit with him?"

"No," he insists, "I'll wait."

Earl waits, while fidgeting quietly at my dining table for a solid hour. He wrings his hands nervously. He perplexes me, but soon I surmise that his is the face in a baby photograph, pinned to Delbert's bedroom wall, many years earlier. "EARL," the name wallops me. It is Delbert's middle name. I offer the kid to sit. But, when Delbert does not arrive Earl somberly decides to go. Soon after, Delbert comes home.

"Why did Tonya's son come by to visit you?"

"I don't know. He probably wanted to visit Keonis."

"No, he came to see you. He told me so. You told me that he was not your son."

"He's not my son. Tonya got the boy thinking that. He don't know nothin' except what Tonya tells him."

"Are you? – Are you his father?" I scream.

"Fuck you and that bitch! He ain't my kid!"

"Then why don't you tell him so?" I scream again.

Self absorbed and lackadaisical is the man that I have married. Delbert Gilliam is an inebriated empty shell. He moseys about wearing a shaded smile to umbrella his shame. Loving him as I do is impious, like chasing a storm. To catch it would merely endorse my defeat. Why I love him, only God can know. Night after night he wobbles through the door like a duck out of water. Long after the kids have been put down for the night's rest. He turns aside the dinner plate that I set aside for his evening meal. He fumbles with the buttons on his long-sleeved flannel shirt. Delbert sweeps out of his pants and under-shorts in one motion and leaves the garments to stay where they fall. Then he pounces casually onto the bed next to me.

"Where have you been, Delbert?" I ask. He doesn't answer. I ask again. "Delbert, where have you been?" His eyes are overshadowed and I wonder if he hears me at all. Exhausted, I give up.

Quickly, the lights go out. Click – and now he calls back.

"Hey! Can we do somethin'?"

He tugs my gown and slips it over my waist. I snatch back. He climbs atop and shoots his load. Then rolls over like a stranger in a brothel. Tooting an unsettling rumble, as bitter emissions the same as a distillery let go from his breath.

A blanket of moonlight folds back to reveal a ray of sunrise, shined through a cracked shade on a window. Each day mirrors yesterday, with non-distinction. Keonis gets off to school. Delbert moves onto whatever or wherever, when his day begins. For me is a doctor's appointment for little Janiah to attend.

"Ain't you Giselle's sister?" A man prods as I stand awaiting a chair inside a crowded hospital clinic.

"Yes," I reply. Quickly turning to tend to little Gerald, fidgeting in my arms.

"You know," he says. This time he speaks louder and sure to have my listening ear. "It ain't right for your sister to be sleeping around when she knows she's sick."

I turn to look at him. Suddenly, his mouth still motions, but I can't hear. I recall the death of Giselle's husband some years before.

"AIDS – ain't that what her husband died from?"

I hear him again. His prodding comes with no regard that he is an utter stranger, come in off the street.

"You really should talk to her about that. That shit ain't cool. Ya know what I mean?"

Just in time, the doctor calls the name Gilliam. I vanish, without a word.

Giselle has come to stay at our apartment, and it is no wonder she closes herself off in a room to stay. I go to her to have a talk. I gently push the bedroom door and find breakfast cold and untouched. She is still asleep, the same way I'd left her.

In an instant an old frayed pocketbook, one I no longer carry, gets my attention. It dangles by its handle from a ledge on an open closet shelf. I grab the strap to place it back. Giselle is startled by the clatter when it crashes to the floor. She awakens suddenly and sits straight up in the bed. I kneel quickly to gather the mess: lipstick, nail polish and an emptied change wallet, wrinkled Kleenex, a fresh sanitary napkin and … a HYPODERMIC NEEDLE and syringe. My heart stammers. My eyes can't believe! Giselle and I lunge at the same time. I win out. Giselle screams!

"Give me that!"

"No!"

"Give it to me! It's mine!" She pleads as if she has a right to own it.

"No!" I scream back. "Why? Why, Giselle?" I beg an explanation as she pounces angrily to floor. She pulls along the sheet as a wrap around her half dressed backside. She runs for the bathroom and slams the door. I use my shoulder as a wedge to shove inside.

"Why?" I ask it again.

"I can't take it no more!" She throws herself on the toilet seat with her face in her hands, and Giselle begins to cry. "I'm tired. I just want to be with Mommy."

I'd looked so forward to Giselle's stay, and only Lord knows the pain of our long distance throughout our years. My arms fold around her shoulders to buffer her sobs. Blind eyes can steal a peek inside her gaping heart. But, I look at her now and I look at my babies. I can't have her getting high in my house. I have to let her go.

It is useless talking to my husband, when on the one day he decides to come home early he disappears behind the bathroom door. The spray of the shower is recognized. But, the door stays sealed too long. I shove it open.

"What is that smell?"

"What smell?" Delbert asks.

"That smell!" I want to know. "Are you smoking crack?" I ask with alarm.

"No! I ain't smoking crack! This ain't crack, its cocaine. You know I wouldn't smoke no crack. It's coke. See," he says, showing two white pebbles in his hand.

"It don't look like coke."

"It is coke. It's just cooked, that's all. Try and see for yourself."

"I don't want that mess. I heard about that CRACK – people getting hooked on it and keeling over from heart attacks." I am angry. Don't know which makes me madder, Delbert doing drugs in the bathroom or Earl coming around.

"This stuff ain't gonna hurt you. Do you think I would give you something to hurt you? Try it." Delbert insists. "You know I wouldn't give you no crack. This ain't nothin' but coke. You've snorted cocaine before." I look at my Delbert with disgust. And yet the pipe in his hand makes me curious. "You can't get no habit from this stuff. Only difference in this and cocaine is you smoke it."

And suddenly, it occurs to me. So, this is what keeps you from me every night. It has been so long since Delbert and I have shared anything together. I accept the pipe into my hand. Delbert loads. Touches it with a flame and instructs me to inhale.

"I don't feel anything," I tell him.

"You just blew all the smoke out," he laughs. "You have to hold it in." He then strikes it again. Until, like the swirling of the cloud of smoke vanishing inside my lungs, he vanishes, too. Visions of Delbert are gone. He has faded and absolutely nothing other exists inside this gap that separates me from time. Only silence inside a peculiar space, where I have entered into momentary quiet.

I used to read my Bible faithfully. Now it seems the very day I received that God forsaken crack-pipe, my Bible lay face down on the back of the toilet bowl. It's where I first put it down, when I slipped into the bathroom to have a puff. Scripted on a legal sized page of paper and pinned to the outer door of our apartment is the Notification of Eviction. But all that Delbert can entertain is how we will get our next blast.

In front of a little shop on a corner, I take refuge under the awning at "Loretta's Frame Shop." The proprietor of this little shop is a friend of a friend of a friend. Hers is a picture framing business. But it is not pictures or frames that come to mind. I huddle inside her quaint storefront seeking shelter from the pounding of the rain. It pours like buckets from a sky that opens with a crash and glows with a flash of light. To pretend that I am shopping would be pointless, when even the washing rain can't mask the tears dripping from my eyes. Ms. Loretta smiles.

"I have a friend," she says. Before steering me clear across town to a human service organization, where the pending eviction is stopped. My rent will be paid IN-FULL, thanks to a little lady named Loretta, "a friend of a friend."

We pile into the car on just another day when a blazing orange rug tossed on the roadside catches my eye. It is not a new rug. It's not a great color. But "hot" orange seems better than no rug at all. I struggle to drag it three flights up. The weight of it challenges my tolerance, and determination pulls the load. Finally, I reach the last step. I yank the piece onto the landing just outside my apartment door. My keys jingle in my hand and I turn the lock. I pull harder, struggling to bring the old rug through the open door. Then quickly drop it onto the living room floor.

Suddenly, there comes an awful feeling in the pit of my belly and when I sit on the stool a steady flow of blood surges into the toilet bowl. Blood clots empty my body, too big for me to imagine they could fit the canal from which they drop. Plop, another and another crash into a pool of water behind a closed door. It feels like forever until Delbert arrives to drive me to the hospital emergency room.

"Why'd you wait so long?" I vaguely hear them say.

"I don't have a phone."

"Her hands are really cold and her blood count is low."

There is talk of blood plasma, a transfusion or something, I think. Suddenly, there is silence. Nothing more do I remember. Nothing more do I hear.

There is no Delbert. As a matter of fact there is no one, some twenty-four hours later. I awaken - ALONE – with transparent tubes stuck in my veins. I stare into a raised ceiling. Suddenly, I think of my babies and wonder if they are all right. A nurse appears to remove the needles and the tubing. She tells me that I am free to go home.

"We called your husband, Mrs. Gilliam. He is coming to meet you." She smiles and disappears.

I raise myself to sit at the edge of the bed. I reach for my clothing folded in a chair. Within minutes the nurse returns.

"Mrs. Gilliam, your husband phoned the nurse's station. He is sending a taxi to meet you."

"Thank you." Again she disappears, just like the escaping minutes on a considerably large wall clock. The late afternoon ticks away. The dusk of evening fades into night. I decide to mosey into an outer corridor.

"Excuse me," I call to the desk attendant. She is flipping pages on a clipboard and preoccupied with a telephone call. "Did anybody hear back from my husband?" I interrupt.

"Mrs. Gilliam!" She is surprised. "Are you still waiting on that taxi?" She places her conversation on hold. "Let me check with the other nurses to see if they received a call." I go back inside the room and have a seat.

"No, Mrs. Gilliam. Your husband has not called," she says.

"Can I go? I really gotta get home."

"I know you want to get out of here, Mrs. Gilliam," she smiles, "but we can't discharge you unless somebody comes to meet you. I'm sorry, it is against hospital rules."

Block upon block I walk in chilling weather after slipping away and onto a waiting elevator, unaccounted for. Finally, a half-block from home, I see him. DELBERT is walking a path toward me. We pass shoulder to shoulder along the walkway. He doesn't stop to greet me. As a matter of fact, Delbert doesn't stop at all. He only pauses, when I demand to know who is keeping the kids.

"Keonis!" He answers defiantly.

Keonis? I think silently, while you go off to play the lottery and to pay homage to the liquor store. I just lost our baby and no tears have been shed, just my own.

Some days later, snow whirls outside my living room window. It looks like a massive sand storm caught up in a gusty flow of freezing wind. Keonis is away at school and a distressing blizzard causes havoc through the quaint city streets below. Indoors, I keep watch over my babies, sure not to interrupt their noonday nap.

Ding-dong, the doorbell rings. In walks Benjamin, the Building Superintendent. He is no less, a family friend. A County Sheriff's Officer follows him close. We are in the midst of a major snowstorm, for God's sake. But it don't matter that my babies are asleep on the sofa. The news is executed swiftly and arrives with little surprise.

I dawdle clumsily between rooms. I think of the photographs, birth records and other keepsakes, never unpacked from a suitcase and stuffed inside a closet. Not since the day I moved in. I no longer have a single baby photo of Keonis. Delbert took every last one of them with him when he ran off to Charlotte, North Carolina. I haven't seen them since. I slide the bag out of the closet and along the floor. The Sheriff's Officer watches me and fidgets with impatience.

"Now look here ma'am, I can't stay and wait for you to pack up your stuff. Thirty minutes is all you got," he adds sternly.

"Don't worry about that," Benjamin says. He points to the heavy carry bag. "I'll move your belongings to the basement for a few days. They will be safe until you can figure where you will go."

I awaken Janiah and Gerald from their naps and hurry to dress them. I then watch as Benjamin carries my two tired bundles out into the cold for a seat in his warming car. Soon the Sheriff fixes a huge padlock on my door. But when he exits the building and drives out of sight, Benjamin quickly sneaks the kids back inside. He stays with them. Hiding them in the warmth of the building's cluttered cellar.

My feet sink deep into the snow and I battle the winds of a frigid storm. I dial Katrina's number. Ring, ring – ring, ring. I can hardly see for the snow melting on the lids of my eyes. I make the celebrated connection from a pay phone a block away.

"Hi Katrina, its Edwina. Can you get a message to Delbert for me?"

"Delbert is here. Hold on for a second, Edwina." She puts the receiver down and yells his name.

"Hello," he answers, when he is supposed to be at work.

"Delbert, the apartment is padlocked. What should I do?"

"Did Keonis come home from school yet?" He asks.

"No."

"Where are Gerald and Janiah?"

"With Benjamin. He sneaked them to the basement."

"Go back to the building. I'll be there."

Soon Keonis arrives, but no Delbert. Benjamin leads us outside the building and to the bottom of a steep, snow-iced fire escape. He watches as Keonis, my agile son makes the climb. Keonis heists the unlocked window and slips inside. Benjamin takes Janiah into his arms. I carry Gerald. With one look up, we realize that the possibility of falling is just not worth the climb. Benjamin takes the chance of being discovered by a nosey neighbor, when he uses the spare key left to him by the Sheriff's Officer. Sometime later, Delbert straggles home.

The weeks add up in a virtually vacant apartment. Our furniture is locked in the building's cellar. On short notice, Benjamin sends word ahead that somebody wants to see the place. I turn the oven off. I grab the kids. Benjamin shows the place and when they leave, we go back inside. I wonder what people must think about a vacant apartment that smells like homemade biscuits. I don't worry too much trying to figure it. I only hope they hate the place and never decide to move in.

CHAPTER 12

HE "WUVS" ME — HE "WUVS" ME NOT

Get your mind off your troubles and set your sights on somebody else's trouble or something like that. I heard that said before. Then the world won't seem so dark. I try visiting Aunt Tessy, so sick she can't hold her head straight. Aunt Tess don't part her mouth to take up food from the spoon. Aunt Tess don't suck the straw I shove between her parched lips, neither. She is full stretch on a hospital bed rolled against a sidewall in her and Aunt Trudy's living room. Aunt Tess don't do nothin', 'cept lay there and stare at the ceiling. Aunt Trudy says Aunt Tess is fading away in her final stages of cancer; one of those things that can't be fixed. The hours zip by. Day is near its end when I mosey on back across the street to Geneva's for a night's sleep. I lie down next to Delbert on the floor. Come early morning before I awaken, Aunt Trudy rings Geneva's doorbell and shares the bad news. Aunt Tess has slept away.

I think of Aunt Tess and the way I'd last seen her. Fixated and absent, the same as the day before. Her eyes were wide open, but her spirit already gone. Hmph – kind of like me. Only now, Aunt Tess' bosom don't rise and it ain't no more pain in her heart. In some ways I envy Aunt Tess for that. I ain't got time to be givin' to no funeral. Today is time to meet the train.

"One day you are going to wake up and find yourself all by yourself."

I have warned my husband. I gather the kids, and Delbert sleeps, plastered, in a snoring drunk. With a silent glance I bid him goodbye and hurry to a neighbor-friend who wisps us away in a waiting car. With Keonis, Janiah and Gerald by my side, the rail car rushes forth on its track. And like our speeding train, a burning pain journeys alongside.

Got bad news today,
real bad news.
But for some reason
I refuse to cry.
Lost a loved one
I was real fond of.
A precious part of me has died.
But I was cool,
Tuff-enough
to take the stuff,
tears and sorry words.

My heart felt light,
At peace with night.
I'm soaring like a bird.

Can't quite explain,
I hid the pain.
For what?
I don't know why.
All I know
is what I know,
and I refuse
to cry.

It has been twelve miserable hours on a Greyhound to Detroit, Michigan. It looked to me, 'fore I left Jersey, like spring was on the rise. Not no more. The bustling streets are snow covered, and it ain't yet stop coming down. I toss my duffle bag over my shoulder. Lift my carry case and drag the kids to meet sister Celia at the station. She's been kind enough to wire me the money and offer me her warm home to stay. We embrace, my sister and me, then little arms reach as Keonis, Janiah and Gerald get a kiss from their Auntie, whom they will soon come to know. It has been many a year gone with my big sister Celia away in Michigan. I wasn't more than a snot-nosed kid in grade school, by the time she moved away. Twenty-some odd years later, and sisters from the same womb, we don't know much what to say to one another. We make a bit of small talk. Chatting about this and that, after never having shared much more than a fifteen-minute conversation over the telephone. I love sister Celia and sister Celia loves me. Sisters or none, truth is one don't know doodly squat bout' the other. Celia bends to throw one of my big duffle bags over her shoulder. I grab the other and we press on to pile the junk in the trunk of her car.

The drive is short as we pass by crumbling and abandoned buildings. Celia points out the old broken down *Motown* spot. It is he remains of a palace and humble beginnings that once stood as an icon for *Marvin Gaye, The Supremes and Martha Reeves & the Vandellas*. Now it is just a shambles, set on the wrong side of the track. Before long I am directed to a dumpy little house. It is the house *Aretha Franklin* grew up in. It is a bit of history thrown right in the hub of dingy, dilapidated, run-down disintegrated, Detroit, Michigan. But, when we pull to the curbside in front of Celia's, it is apparent that my big sister has worked hard and paid her dues over the mounting years. My sister Celia owns a little house on a tree-lined, suburban street. Now what do you know bout' 'dat? Nothing about this place reminds me of the hell-hole I just blew out of.

Does Celia eat off the floors? This place is immaculate. Everything is spotless and everything has got its special little place. Discomfort looks me square in the balls of my eyes and asks. Is there a place for me? When Celia opens the pantry, I think my sight has betrayed me. All the food spilling into the seams of the closet gets me cross-eyed. There is food covering every shelf in the refrigerator, food in the top compartment of the freezer and extra food in the basement. More stuff packed away in a deep freezer, too. I haven't seen so much stuff, not since I was just a kid back in Jersey. But, now I ain't no longer a kid-girl, and I wonder if Celia knows 'bout 'dat. I pull out a cigarette from my purse. One of my long Kools dangling from my lips. Just when I'm about to fire it up, Celia cuts me a sideways glance.

"Can't smoke 'dat in here," my big sister Celia says.

"Huh!" What you mean, sister Celia? –I can't smoke in here. I am full fledged and grown."

"I didn't know you smoke," Celia admonishes, sarcastically. "You shouldn't be smokin' no how. But if you want to smoke, that's your business. But, you can't do it in here. You have to go outside."

Celia, girl, don't you realize its seventeen degrees outside – and its snow on the ground." Good sense tells me to mind my thoughts and to watch my mouth. I keep my mouth shut and don't think my thoughts out loud. Just throw my coat over my back, fumbling with the buttons to fasten to the neck. Then OUTSIDE I go. The door slams shut. I am a full-grown woman, sister Celia. Grown women don't go outside to smoke. Not even at Geneva's, do I go outside to smoke. I inhale the ice of winter and I choke. My fingers ache, and just now an icy wind snaps my neck to remind me. This here ain't Geneva's. This is Celia's. And I guess Celia got a right to run it anyway she please. I chuck my cigarette and squash the butt. Then hurry my icicled, fudge behine' back inside the heat of my sister Celia's cozy little house.

The kids are getting along just fine and making themselves at home with their little cousin. Celia's four-year old son, Harold is near as big as me. Little Harold weighs eighty pounds and darn-near stands to my shoulder. And Little Harold wears pants 'bout big enough for my thirteen-year old Keonis, just not as long. That little Harold has got the cutest and chubbiest of cheeks I have ever seen. I pluck his little forehead playfully, then, run so he don't push me over and roll on top of me.

Celia has prepared a heartwarming dinner of savory roasted chicken and it is the first good meal I have eaten in quite some time. Afterward I help her to empty the sink of dirty dishes, after the evening meal. Later Celia shows me to the bedroom. It is where little Harold usually sleeps, with fresh linen and a TV set high on a dresser top. Wow! I can't believe we will be watching COLOR TELEVISION tonight!

"Time to rise and shine!" Come early morning, Celia throws the bedroom door and hurries me out of bed. She does it the next day, too. Rushing me in a hurry. When I find Celia sittin' at the breakfast table with sleep in her eyes, and lookin' like morning come too soon, even for her. I snap her mug shot on Kodak film, with her Aunt Jemina rag tied in a knot on her head. Then I glue it with a caption, "The WARDEN," square on the front of the refrigerator door. Now Celia can see Celia, same ways I see Celia. But Celia don't think so much is funny 'bout 'dat.

"Good morning."

Oh Lord, here come Celia soundin' like de master.

"Get up Edwina, its time to rise and shine."

"Why can't I sleep a little longer, Celia?"

Always gotta stay busy, doing 'dis and seeing 'bout 'dat. We've got things to do, places to go, people to see. And Celia don't stop talkin' – that's because Celia ain't tryin' to hear nothin' I got to say.

In the coming weeks Keonis takes hard to a major adjustment as an eighth grader in a big city school. There is talk 'bout kids slicing one another with razor blades. Me? I'm busy running round with sister Celia and hitting all of the major radio stations. I'm trying hard to find a much-needed job. Celia drives me to every station in Detroit, Michigan, not to mention parts of Ohio too. Meantime, she helps me onto the rolls for city welfare so I can keep a dollar in my pocket and help replace the food we eat. Honest, I know what Celia does is right, but I'm dog-tired. Still, Celia say first we work, then we sleep.

Then, uhh-oh! Celia done let her hair down. I ain't lyin'. Sister Celia cooks some popcorn. Sister Celia fries some shrimp. Then, sister Celia pops in a video-tape inside her video cassette recorder.

"Have you ever seen *The Color Purple*?"

"No Celia." These tired eyes ain't seen, *The Color Purple*. These tired eyes ain't seen nothin' 'cept, ruby red, now since you don't allow me to sleep late.

Well I'll be damned, and slap me silly, 'cause Celia done told me to kick my shoes off. Celia done kicked off her own shoes, too. Celia and me has got our feet propped. Poppin' shrimp, eatin' corn and kickin' back on Celia's living room sofa, all covered in suffocating plastic. Celia, girl – you is living the life. Go on now, sister Celia!

Watchin' Danny Glover play that mean-ol'-Mista in *The Color Purple* puts me in the mind of Rupert Thurman Jordan, me and Celia's daddy. Mista is killing everybody's joy. He's bucking little girls, plain like day. My sister Celia is heated mad. She frowns her face and her mouth wads in a ball, just like her daddy. Then she gets sad and cries watchin' Mista, until — oops, Sister Celia's lips done slipped and say a cuss. Wishing she was a big grown man and wanting to jump inside the television box and punch Mista for what he done to "Sealy." "Sealy" is just like me and sister Celia, when Sealy don't know she pretty 'til somebody else come along and tell her so.

There goes March and heading into April. There are still no jobs and no callbacks, neither. I take up time writing poetry, 'bout my Delbert and stuff, when Celia does everything she knows to get me out to meet new friends. A new thrill in my life, that's what Celia says I need. But all I ever think about is Delbert, while taking up time, taking long walks up Eight Mile Road, a major throughway in the heart of dimming Detroit, miserable, Michigan.

It don't move me when spring is here. And I don't look for blooming roses come early May. Long walks, gold-tooth men, museums and even a visit to a Canadian zoo, don't make no luster inside this spirit gone cold. I ain't moved watchin' country bumkins fling jerry-curl juice off the rings of their curls. No. It don't make me hot to trot, hot in my spot and it don't make me cum none, neither. I'm just home sick.

Hope moves away with an empty heart.
Packing a teardrop before she parts.
Suitcase of sorrow, slung over her back.
Heartbreak for breakfast and afternoon snack.

The telephone rings. It's my Delbert, separated by the many miles, but carried closely inside my heart.

Delbert says, "Please come home, Edwina."

Celia says, "Don't listen to a word he says."

Delbert says, "I got a place for us to stay."

Celia says, "He'll say anything – just to get you back."

Delbert says, "I love you Edwina, really I do."

Celia screams with anger. "Think with your head, not with your heart." Her eyelids flicker like blinking lights. Celia is mad as hell, maybe madder than hell, because nobody ever comes to visit, until there is trouble. Then when trouble is over, nobody never stays. Celia's eyes run water and the heat of blood rushes her face.

"I'm sorry Celia." No matter that you encourage me. I've got a Greyhound ticket in my hand and as soon as school is over, I'll be on my way.

The Greyhound coach rocks from side to side as I walk the center isle. I am going to freshen up and put on my new sundress I got from the K-Mart store. With two hours left, until arrival, I know that spring has sprung. I can't wait to see my Delbert. Delbert honey, I am on my way!

Finally we pull into the bus station and smack into the middle of a June heat wave in New Jersey. Then there is the train and a taxi ride before I finally arrive. I find Melinda upstairs in the bathroom, crouched on her knees and hand-washing clothes over a hot soapy tub. Sweat pours down her cheeks and stings her eyes. She waves the back of her hand across her brow. She wrings her wrist and grins, before standing to greet me.

"Hey Short-Cakes!" She says, tenderly surprised. Since leaving North Carolina along with Sylvester and Katrina several years ago, Melinda has matured a lot. She moved back in with her mom and now has a child of her own. Melinda's boy is three years old, same as my boy Gerald. She and I embrace.

"When did you get here?"

"I just got here. The door was open."

"Where are the kids?" Melinda smiles with candid affection. Her ebony, smooth complexion is glowing and she blushes beneath her deep-toned skin.

"They're downstairs."

"Really? Keonis, Janiah, Gerald!" She yells their names with excitement. When they come running, she gives them a great big hug.

"Where's Ma?" I ask. Geneva, my mother-in-law, rarely leaves home. I am surprised not to find her sitting in her favorite chair, next to the window in the dining room.

"Ma had an appointment," she says. "You know she's been sick a lot lately. Simone took her to the doctor's."

Katrina is the oldest sister. Simone is the next and divorced for the second time around.

"Where is everybody?" It is highly unusual to find the house empty, when all day long the door swings open and the door swings shut.

"Well ...," Melinda says. But I interrupt, when truly what I really want to know is, why is Delbert not around.

"Where is Delbert?" I ask.

"Short-cakes," Melinda replies, "I haven't seen Delbert since last weekend. He's been staying with some African chick. Well, I think she's African or something?" She laughs. "I don't know. She's got an accent, that's all I can tell you."

"Really?" I say, trying hard not to sound hurt, when truly I am.

"I wouldn't even worry about it if I were you." Melinda quickly changes the subject. "So what's been goin' on with you?"

We talk and laugh, but my mind stays on Celia. She was right, since the HOME, Delbert promised – AIN'T. As a matter of fact, Delbert has pretty much moved out and gone to stay at his hussy's house, as Melinda tells it.

In the late afternoon hours when Simone and Ma return, I greet them with a welcomed hug.

"Hi Edwina." Geneva's eyes light up, so excited to see me. I extend my arms and wrap them around her. Before I can let go, Simone reaches under the dining table to offer a bit of friendly fire.

"Have a drink, Edwina."

"Simone," I say, "it is 3:30 in the afternoon, girl." Simone laughs.

"So what"? She chuckles. "Have one anyway." She throws a chunk of ice inside a glass and fills it half full with rum.

"When did you get in? Where are the kids? Have you all eaten?" I enjoy spending time with Simone and Geneva. I'm especially happy that Ma is feeling pretty good there, despite her doctor's visit.

"Ma, did the doctor say it was okay for you to be drinking that stuff?" I ask.

"Well, he didn't tell me not to." Geneva giggles light heartedly. Revealing several gaps where she is missing teeth. She lights a cigarette, when the doorbell rings. It is her daughter, Lynette, another sister-in-law. Lynette is married and moved away. Next Katrina and Sylvester stop by. Soon after, Katrina's ex-husband Fitzgerald walks in, and before long Simone's ex-husband, Kenneth, too. Fitzgerald smiles quietly and slips a bottle of rum from a long brown paper bag.

"Thanks Fitzgerald, you didn't have to," Ma laughs, "but I'm glad you did." She giggles.

Everybody is fond of Ma. Divorced or not, nobody seems to be able to stay away. Afternoon rolls away and evening pushes through. We laugh and we taste, wasting the day away.

Sometimes the bell rings. Other times the door just pushes open unexpectedly. There is merriment and a steady rumble of conversation. It is apparent that it is Friday, when brother-in-law Neil shoves in tired and worn. Another couple hours go by, until Dwight pops in with his girlfriend, Mary Anne. Wanda, the youngest of my sisters'-in-law, has also arrived home from work. She brings with her an old schoolmate, who gets no introduction. Jeanette is a neighbor, Wanda's co-worker and close friend.

"Hey everybody!" Jeanette yells. Unlike Wanda, who half-heartedly acknowledges the group of familiar faces. Wanda reaches toward Ma and across the dining table to dump an ashtray full with butts.

She exclaims, "Mommy you know you are not supposed to be drinking?"

Geneva laughs playfully. "Wait a minute," she says, while looking at me. "She thinks she's my mother." Geneva winks her eye and splits a devilish grin. I smile, sip my rum and keep my mouth shut.

"And Simone," –Wanda admonishes her older sister –"you ain't no help."

Simone sighs. "Hmmph." Her neck snaps and her eyes roll. "I know she ain't talking 'bout me," she says, ignoring the remark.

Wanda returns an intense glance. Her nostrils flare as she calls to her friend, "Jeanette, I'll be right back." She gives an offhanded glimpse of disappointment to her mother, then walks away.

"Jeanette, would you like a drink?" Simone offers.

"Oh no thanks, Simone. If I have a drink, I WILL be drunk!" Jeanette snickers, tickled by the notion of it. "I have to drive."

"Oh," Simone asks, "Jeanette, have you met Edwina"

"Yeah, she says, reaching to embrace me. "We met."

"Hey Jeanette," I smile.

"Are you and Wanda hanging out tonight?" Simone asks.

Jeanette giggles. "Yeah, we're goin' to the club. AGAIN." She giggles some more, a little louder, since partying is obviously what she does best. Wanda and Melinda hang out nearly every weekend and today is no different. "I'm going home to change clothes," says Jeanette. "Tell Wanda, I'll be back in a couple hours. It was nice seeing you, Edwina." She leaves out.

I wonder where I will put the kids down for the night's sleep. Until Ma directs me to the room at the top of the stairs. Always when there is no room left in this little house, Geneva finds space inside her heart. Some will sleep on the sofa, others on a chair. Keonis will make his bed on a hard wood floor between the dining and living rooms. I'll sleep with Gerald and Janiah on a skinny double-bunk-bed, slapped tight against a wall. Night has fallen and the kids are fed. Following a quick bath, I put them into bed.

Just as they begin to settle Dwight saunters in. His fingertips are snapping to a tune that rings only inside his head.

"Hey Edwina! It's good to see you!"

"Hey Dwight!"

He mutters, scatting a melody to an old jazz tune. After a quiet couple of seconds, Dwight repeats again. "Yeah, it's good to see ya, – good to see ya."

"You too," I say, when really I am thinking to myself, "You just said that."

"You have to forgive me," Dwight says, "if I seem a little distracted." Dwight is always distracted, unfocused and distracted - except when it is something to do with him and his music. "I got this gig over in Newark, tonight."

"Hi Uncle Dwight!" Gerald bursts excitedly, rubbing his eyes and suddenly sitting straight up in the bed.

"He-e-e-y Uncle Gerald!" Dwight playfully hollers back.

Gerald is amused. "Uncle Gerald? I'm not your uncle. You my uncle."

"Lay down Gerald," I say. "Your sister is sleeping and you should, too. It's time to get some rest."

"But, I want to talk to Uncle Dwight!" Gerald calls quickly, "Uncle Dwight …"

"You can talk to Uncle Dwight in the morning, Gerald," I say. "Goodnight."

"Listen to your mommy, Uncle Gerald. We can talk tomorrow."

"Mommy, how come I can't talk to Uncle Dwight?" Gerald asks softly.

"GOODNIGHT Gerald," I say.

"Augh," he says, before suddenly thrusting his back flat in a lying position.

And again Dwight begins to scat. "Dee-dit-dat …," then quickly stops to ask, "Edwina, where is Delbert? I didn't see him when I came in." Dwight stands at the bedside, reaching over our heads to the top bunk. That's the place where all of his stuff is stored, including his saxophone.

"Dwight," I answer rather casually, "I was hoping you could tell me that."

"No," he says, without a care. "That Delbert has got a mind of his own. And as a matter of fact, he's always been that way." Dwight laughs, while clicking open and snapping shut attaché cases and rumbling loose pages. Soon, Dwight leaves and shuts off the light. Five minutes later he returns. The light clicks back on.

"Yeah Edwina," he says, as if he'd never left. "I got this gig over in Newark, tonight."

"Oh yeah!" I say.

"Yeah, Edwina. I'm playing with some cats out of Brooklyn, who used to play with George Benson. They are bad, Edwina. These cats can really play."

Suddenly, the door slams at the base of the stairwell. Footsteps drum the steps. It is Billy, one of Delbert's younger brothers. The voices of him and his friend echo through the tiny hallway.

"Hey Sister-in-Law!" Billy shouts with a great big grin. He quickly acknowledges his oldest brother Dwight. "Wass-up Dwight," then, looks again at me.

"Edwina, I didn't know you were here."

"I don't think anybody knew I was coming," I reply with a smile.

"Johnny this is my sister-in-law, Edwina," Billy introduces me. "You already met Dwight," Billy adds with a sarcastic and a nonchalant wave of the hand.

"Hey, man?" Dwight calls.

With nothing more to say, Billy turns to walk away and keeps it moving.

"We'll talk later, Edwina."

"Okay, Billy. Nice meeting you," I say to his friend, who answers, "Yeah."

There is the squeaking noise of the ladder unfolding in the hallway and the patter of feet trailing off into the attic. The attic is not only the place where Billy sleeps; it is also his little retreat. The place he goes to kick his heels and to wind down when the workday is done. The floor creaks overhead. The stereo turns up to an earsplitting level. Its tremendous volume spills through an open window and can be heard throughout by people on the sidewalks and neighbors on the opposite side of the street. Blaring music and good times is a part of the everyday with Billy's arrival home.

"As I was saying," Dwight continues. Again the outer door, just at the bottom of the stairs distracts him. A voice calls.

"I'll see you'll later." The door slams shut. It opens and shuts twice more again. But, before Dwight can tell me the rest, Mary Anne yells from the bottom landing.

"Dwight. We better go hon' if we're gonna make it on time."

"Okay, I'll be right down," he yells back. "Edwina," he says —"we'll talk." Then he calls again to Mary Anne. "Just let me grab my saxophone."

He swings his horn by the neck and locks it into its big brown leather case and finally the light clicks out, one last time. There is the thunder of Dwight's feet pounding down the steps. Then at the same time he pulls the door to go out, he finds Aunt Rena approaching the outer porch. I hear him say.

"He-e-e-y, Aunt Rena!" It is Geneva's sister visiting from New York. "It's good to see you … good to see you. How are you? Come on in," he says excitedly.

"Hi Dwight." She giggles softly and pecks her nephew gently on the cheek. "Where is your mom?"

"She's right there in the dining room. Go on in, Aunt Rena. Ma will be glad to see you." With the door parted and holding the doorknob in his hand, Dwight hurries his words. "I wish I could stay, Aunt Rena, but I got this gig over in Newark, tonight, me and these cats out of Brooklyn. Mary Anne is waiting for me. I've got to go. I'll see ya' later."

As Aunt Rena makes her way inside, people are coming and going. You never quite know who is in and who is out. I sit quietly, until, despite the chaos, little Gerald falls to sleep. I stay a while longer to make sure he is sound, when just as I am about to tip away, Jeanette returns.

"Hi," she says. "Wanda ain't ready yet, so I thought I'd come up and talk to you. You don't mind do you?"

"No." I say. But, Jeanette is just eighteen and a friend of Wanda and I wonder what it is for me to say. Jeanette looks to the bunk, where my babies rest.

"Your babies are gorgeous, Edwina."

"Well, thank you Jeanette," I answer proudly.

"Edwina, I know that you don't really know me. Well," she says, "– we met but we never got to talk and know one another. But, I am really glad I got to meet you. You seem like a really nice person, Edwina. I'm just glad I got to know you for myself."

"What are you talking about, Jeanette?" I ask.

"Your kids are beautiful and you are a good mother. Delbert had me believing you were a whore. Somebody who didn't care nothing about her kids. He said that he took Keonis from you because you didn't want him anymore. "

"That's not true."

"I know it's not," Jeanette answers. "Well, now I do."

"Well Jeanette," I say, "I am glad to know you. I appreciate you sharing the truth with me."

"Oh, no problem. I see you always closed inside this little room by yourself. You look so sad, Edwina. Don't let him kill your joy. If you ever need somebody to talk to, you can talk to me. I'm Wanda's friend, but you don't have to worry about anything you ever tell me getting back to Delbert."

Jeanette reaches her arms to give a hug.

Jeanette walks back down the stairs. With one more look at my babies, I quietly tip away. I find Melinda just outside the open bedroom door. She fidgets before a big wall mirror, getting ready for a night at the club, fixing up her hair and her slacks all at once. She tugs the hems of her pants over her bare feet, zips the fly and buttons the flap.

"Melinda," I ask.

"What's up Short-cakes?"

"Does Dwight sleep on the top bunk?" I ask.

"No." She laughs. "Dwight is staying with this white chick in Pennsylvania. You met Mary Anne, didn't you?"

"No. I saw her, but nobody introduced me."

"She's supposed to be his girlfriend. But she's stupid and he treats her like shit."

"I was wondering," I tell her, "because he kept coming in and out of the bedroom. Back and forth," my hand waves in repetition.

"Don't pay Dwight no mind, Dwight is crazy." She giggles playful and sarcastically.

Dwight still plays the local clubs, doing gigs around town and stuff. The same as when I met him. Yet still he has not made it into the big time. Dwight and Kevin, the other musician and the youngest brother in the Gilliam family used to share that little room. But Kevin amazingly moved away to study at the Berkley School of Music, somewhere up in Boston.

I change the subject.

"Melinda, would you keep the kids for me tomorrow? I want to get away and go to Atlantic City for the day."

"Go on, Edwina. Enjoy yourself. Delbert is enjoying himself. I'll keep the kids. You deserve it."

Later and into the night, Vernon surprises everybody, when he shows up dressed like the C.E.O. for some sophisticated operation. The construction industry must be doing all right over there in Brooklyn, where he lives and works.

"Hey! Edwina!" he calls eagerly, with a twinkle in his eye. He flashes his wallet and a confident grin, while casually exposing "dead-presidents", squeezed tight on top of one another. Clad in a designer suit and exclusive tie, he laughs deviously and pulls from his hand a fresh bottle of rum. "How are you?" He asks, eyeing me up and down. "Look at you," he giggles. Vernon gently touches my arm. "You look good girl!" Chuckling, he pecks me with a kiss on my cheek. Vernon is still Vernon. "Let me fix you a drink."

In the morning the house is quiet, except for Vernon's snoring. His business suit is disheveled. The laces on his shiny leather shoes are loosed around his feet. His mouth wags wide open and his head presses back, where he sits on the sofa fast asleep. His nose crinkles and snoring stops for an instant, while he reaches to slap a nagging fly, threatening to interrupt his snooze. Billy slams the door behind him as he rushes out to finish his week's work at a retail store. Aunt Rena has taken the bus back to New York City. Geneva is up early, even before me and the kids. Neil is still asleep, I think. There are so many people, the only one I can truly account for, is me. Melinda and Wanda haven't long ago come in from the club. Melinda is sleepy. Although, she is prepared to keep the kids, just as she promised.

After he eats, Keonis gets off to visit a neighborhood kid. But first I warn him not to get too far from home. I am off to catch a bus beside a cluster of senior citizens who get a discount fair. Ten dollars pays for the ride. Most of that is shelled back to me in tokens. I use them to feed the casino slot machines.

So, I've been told, when a machine gets hot, you win big. I watch the little old lady next to me as she gathers coins by the handful and shoves them in a plastic bucket. Every time she pulls the arm on her machine, coins pour out. Finally she leaves and I slide over. I am not so lucky. My fifty bucks are gone. And that means I will spend the last waiting hours walking the boardwalk. But then it starts to rain. So much for getting away and good times. I'll be glad when the day is done.

The sky stands clear when the big coach reaches my stop to exit. The sun has returned and the rain is done. Finally, the instant I walk around the corner, I see Melinda and now Gerald and Janiah, playing together and standing just a little ways off from the porch.

"Look Gerald! Look Janiah!" Melinda calls. She motions to the street. "Here comes your mommy!"

The pair turn around in amazement. Then take off running. They crash into me and wrap their arms around my legs.

"He-e-e-y," I laugh, "slow down!" I greet both of their grinning faces with a great big hug.

"Where's Keonis?" I ask.

"He's at his friend's house," says Janiah.

"Yeah," says Gerald, "at his friend's." He repeats playfully.

"Mommy, where you been?"

"Yeah Mommy, where you been? And where is my daddy. How come my daddy didn't come home with you?"

"Did Delbert come home?" I interject.

"Nope" Melinda answers quickly. She changes the subject. "How was it? Did you have a good time?"

"It was okay. Not what I expected. I just needed to get away."

Later and when dark settles, I have my seat on the porch. There are familiar cars pulling in and others pulling out. There are the same ol' faces, except for the driver of one vehicle. It is a woman I have never seen before. She pulls over at the curbside on the opposite side of the street, a couple doors away. The headlamps dim out.

"That's your husband, Short Cakes." Melinda tells me.

"Huh?"

"That's Delbert." She says with confirmation. "He's with that lady. That African lady, Tilla or whatever her name is. The one he's been living with."

"What does she look like?" I ask curiously.

"Nothin' special," Melinda says, nonchalantly. "Being honest," she adds, "she's not cute at all. She looks kind of old. I mean, too old for Delbert."

"Do you think that Delbert cares for her?"

"I don't think so, Short Cakes. From what I know, she is just looking for somebody to marry. So she can get citizenship in the United States. Her family was going to pay Delbert to marry her, but he turned it down."

Soon the car door opens and Delbert steps onto the walkway. I bend forward to steal a peak of the woman who's kept my husband away from me. And now he leans into the passenger side window to share another word, before the vehicle zips away. Melinda and I continue talking as Delbert casually makes his way up the steps to the porch. He walks straight past us. He doesn't speak a single word.

In the weeks ahead, naturally I get discouraged. But compassion ain't long comin' when companionship comes inside crystal rocks inside a glassine bag.

I'll see ya' later Delbert, POOF – he's gone!

"So, you're just gonna take my kids away from me, again? Huh, Edwina?" We argue back and forth before my apartment door. "Can't I just see your new place?"

I finally got this place for me and the kids. I'm happy to be starting back working nights over at WMSP. And I'm glad too, for my couple-of-hours, two-bit job as a counter-girl at a little ol' drug store. With Keonis starting back to school soon, and Janiah entering kindergarten, I need all the work I can get.

"Don't I deserve to know what kind of place my kids are living in?" Delbert asks.

I turn and walk away. He follows through the tiny vestibule. We exchange words. Until finally, I let him in. The children are delighted. They greet their daddy with a big embrace. All except Keonis, who is more leery of the man he knows as Dad. Watching Delbert sprawl across an uncovered mattress, prompts me to remind him, "Don't get too comfortable, because you won't be staying."

"I know that," he answers, with a grin. Discreetly uncovering a couple vials of crack he's been holding in his hand.

The following week on Friday, Delbert rushes eagerly through the heavy paned doors. He strides like a man holding a million dollars. Soon and already there is this arrangement. It is sort of like a reunion between two pitiful peons. Laughing in the face of stupidity and cohabitating under a facade called love. It doesn't take long before Delbert quickly disappears behind the bathroom door. Each Friday on payday and hurried like a storm, first Delbert and then me, fading behind an empty wall.

Two pebbled particles topple from inside a tiny transparent zip bag. They are set flush on a wire screen. No words are spoken, when a glowing flame swells. It is followed by a sizzle and then a cloud of smoke. I hold my breath.

Tick-tock, tick-tock. I can't read the time on a big face clock. I float inside the seconds, until a spine chilling feeling comes to snatch me away. WHOOSH! I disappear. It's like groping in the dark in an unfamiliar place. Suddenly, somebody flips the switch back on. Silently, I pass the pipe to Delbert. He torches, then inhales. Striking a light, he's gone. Just like me, Delbert has slipped away. But soon we return to logic, when Delbert takes another bag from his pocket. And although the pipe exchanges back and forth, I feel like a bucket with a huge hole in its hull. Or like drinking the ocean, and somehow I'm thirsty all the time. My heart pounds with wanting. Until, the miniscule rocks and the money from a whole week's work peels away.

I run off to the DEALER, the crack dealer, to ask for credit. Delbert says that I am more likely to be obliged, than he.

"Favor for flavor," Delbert says. "Tell him I will pay him next Friday."

"What's up?" I holler, cool and casual, to a young brother posted on the block.

"What you lookin' for?" He saunters toward me, eyeing me all the way.

"Favors," I tell him, uneasily. "Can I get two on credit?"

"Do I know you?" he asks, peculiarly puzzled.

"I'm Delbert's wife. He sent me. He said that you would let me get credit, until he gets paid next Friday."

He nods in agreement. Then, leads me to an abandoned house, where I wait for him to retrieve his stash. But, I look at him. He looks at me – then he unzips his pants.

"Oh no! You've got it all wrong?"

"You asked for favors, didn't you?"

"That's what Delbert said."

"You ain't been getting high for long, have you?" I just look at him, stupefied. "You don't even know what to ask for. You asked me for favors. Do you even know what that is?"

"No."

"You're asking for drugs in exchange for sexual favors. No baby, I can't give you no credit, but you better be careful out here. Somebody else would take advantage of you."

The night is long. Summer is waning and September is coming in without any fanfare. Today it ain't Friday, but today is payday!

"Didn't you get paid today?" Delbert asks me.

"Yeah," I reply.

"Do you wanna' get somethin'?"

"Let me see what I've got left, after I go to the store." Beans and biscuits are all we eat lately, begged and borrowed from Aunt Bea.

"Can't you just get two?" Delbert insists. "Give me twenty dollars."

"I can't. I just told you there is nothin' to eat."

"Twenty-dollars ain't gonna hurt."

I'm like a baited fish. Sipping on rum and inhaling. Suddenly comes a tremble in the base of my spine. Jerking and slowly sliding my back, down the length of the wall. I grab for the wind, trying to hold onto something, anything to stop my fall. C-R-A-S-H – I hit with a thump. Well, at least that's what Delbert tells me; I don't recall nothin' as I was gettin' up from the floor.

In the early hours of the morning, while Delbert is away, a County Sheriff's Officer raps on the door.

"Where are you staying?" Delbert asks.

I haven't seen Delbert. Not since he left me and the kids, standing in the streets, after we lost just one more place to live. Keonis got so angry that he rode his bicycle all the way to the other side of town. He finds his daddy sitting comfortably at his Grandma's. It is dark outside when Keonis finally returns. His daddy sends him back with a ten-dollar bill and a message for me.

"Tell your mother to buy pizza and climb back in the window. I'll meet up with you'll later."

During a visit to the studio to pick up a small paycheck, John Werzhiemer, the morning announcer offers me his keys. It's registered, insured and he is lending it to me.

"Pay me two-three hundred dollars – when you can."

I'm exhausted from sleeping on the studio floor. I am tired. Always being careful to get up and out before daybreak, so the morning newsman don't see. I'm tired of bumming, begging, and asking for everything little thing. I will give the kids over to stay with their daddy at their grandma's. I won't ask nobody no more 'bout letting me spend the night. I'll just park that car. Lock the doors and lay my head in the seat. When the week ends I'll get a good shower at a poor-man's motel, where nobody will bother me.

My mind says one thing. But, I do the other. I drive to the street corner, and three guys rush my window all at once, fussin' over who's gonna make this sale.

"What you want?"

"I got this one."

"How much?"

And when my money is spent …

"You can come back and stay here with me. My mother don't mind." Delbert tells me.

"I mind Delbert! I mind! It is not your mother's job to take care of me!"

Melancholy,
Belly full,
It aches
with folly.
Stupid actions,
lacking passion and concern.
She'll learn,
Discern,
Melancholy.

CHAPTER 13

FITZGERALD

Delbert rears in his seat. He watches from a chair on the porch, while I press hard to twist the remaining wheel lugs from the hub of my flattened tire.

"Umph-umph." I stand still for just a second. I catch my breath, and try again. Then, one more "umph." It CRACKS. Soon my exposed hands clench the icy handle on a metallic jack. The early mornings are pretty cold. Autumn pales and winter takes her place without any fanfare. Clickety-click-click. The higher the heavy vehicle rises from the ground the more I strain. I push and then, stop, before finally working the bumper into the air.

A car rolls down the empty throughway. Fitzgerald's gleaming face reflects through the front windshield. Katrina's ex-husband still lives a few blocks away. He gives a tap on the horn, then stops to offer a hand. Fitz, clad in camouflage jacket, a flat topped hat and a pair of black leather boots strapped tight to the ankles, swings open his door and steps out. He giggles at the sight of me. Delbert is unstirred.

"Edwina, what the hell are you doing?" He snickers with juvenile tenderness. He pokes me with his finger and playfully nudges me aside. With straight-backed posture, the enlisted

Sergeant of the U. S. Reserves gives Delbert a holler. He waves his hand in an informal, friendly salute. Then right away he begins himself to man-handle the job.

"Hey man," he yells, "why ain't you down here doing this?"

Delbert returns an off-handed snort, twiddling complacently with a nagging facial hair in the chin of his short-cropped beard. With a pathetic nod, Fitzgerald falls to squat at the side of the car. All the while a gentle smile stripes his face. I stand near. When, in a whisper, he asks. "What's wrong, with Delbert? Why ain't he doing this?"

I shoot him a sideways glance from the corners of my eyes and he knows. I'm sure that Fitzgerald already has it figured. After all, he has known Delbert a whole lot longer than me. Fitz grew up in this neighborhood, just 'round the corner from the Gilliams.

The heavy tire lifts away from the wheel and into the palms of Fitz's strong hands.

"Where's your spare?" He asks. I point him to a tire packed deep in the trunk. He lets go a light-hearted chuckle.

"Edwina," he looks at my naiveté through gentle, but receptive eyes. "This tire ain't no good. What size are your tires?" I think for a moment. But, gosh, I don't know. Again, he chuckles, this time for the silence of uncertainty in my face. With an eye of scrutiny and finger laid aside his nose, Fitz quickly reads the numbers etched inside the hub. "Fifteens," he mutters, when a thought comes to mind. "I've got a tire to fit this at my house. I'll go get it. It will just take a minute." Fitz smiles. "Ya want to take the ride with me?"

In a glance, it becomes apparent that Delbert has wisped himself back into the warmth of the house. Fitzgerald parts the door of his idling vehicle and I step inside. We drive off veering left at the intersection. In just about two minutes, already we are there. I am content to sit in the car. But when Fitz offers me to come inside, that is exactly what I do.

"It's frigging cold out there," he says, blowing his breath inside his cupped hands. "Can I get you a cup of coffee or anything?"

"No thanks Fitz, I'm okay. I decline the cup of coffee. I don't even take a seat. He leaves me to stand alone in an open kitchen area for the moment's wait. Fitzgerald soon returns.

"How do you put up with him?" He smiles.

"Guess I'm used to it," I reply, shucking the question. We part to leave through a rear door.

"Did you have a tire?" I ask.

"I already loaded it in the trunk." Again there is that confident smile. We head back to his car and right back to the business of changing tires. Fitz finishes the job and refuses to take a nickel for his hard work. I thank him and he goes along his way.

Two days later, my car hood is raised. I should be at work. It is Fitzgerald again who hot-wires the engine. SPARK! — It sounds, just in time.

Whoosh! That's the sound of cars spinning past me while I upset the flow of traffic. The transmission is stripped. *She* won't push past thirty-five miles an hour. *She* doesn't do reverse either. Then a bald tire goes-pop and sends me flying around a brick wall, while under a bridge on a major highway. There is always something with this car. And for Fitz's help, all Delbert can ask is, "Are you screwing Fitzgerald?"

Today is Saturday and I am glad for it. I can take a rest from the strife of going and coming and focus on equally important things. Like the prospects of moving out of from Delbert for the second time, again. The paperwork is been authorized for a rent-subsidized unit in a three-story house, without Delbert's knowledge, of course. I'm hoping that me and the kids can move in sometime today. All that remains is getting my hands on the keys. But with afternoon pushing into night, I'm still waiting to hear back from the landlord. I decide to give him a call. The telephone rings and rings and rings, same as it has all day. Finally, a voice echoes on the line.

"Darn-it!" It's just another automated message.

"Hi this is Mr. and Mrs. Carrington. We are in Florida for the weekend." My heart falls with disappointment. "If you would like to leave a message, please do so at the sound of the beep."

I hang onto the receiver and listen for the tone, when, I hear. "I am leaving this message for Edwina Gilliam. The apartment is ready and you will find the keys in the mailbox. Enjoy your new apartment. I will talk to you when I return." I shriek, mindful not to stomp the floor too loud. The prospect of moving out from Delbert makes my heels go clickety-click.

Later on and through the fog of night, Delbert sleeps. I watch closely before I ease out from a small space in the bed next to him. I grab my waiting bags, then tip-toe down a flight of stairs. I start the engine then tiptoe back inside. I nudge Keonis, before sliding Janiah from her daddy's nuzzling side. But when I return for Gerald, I notice that he nestles beneath his daddy's limp arm. It is slapped flat across his tiny chest. I move Delbert's arm, when suddenly, he takes a deep, loud breath. Be still, I tell myself. Until soon a gust of air breathes a rattle through his nostrils and he starts to snore again. I ease Gerald out of the bed, then tip-toe down the stairs and gently pull the outer door shut. Suddenly it flashes open beneath the dimmed beam of a streetlamp projected overhead. I feel a tug, when Delbert snatches the kid away. Cussing and swearing, he disappears back inside the darkened house.

"I'll be back baby. I'm comin' back to get you," I vow, snubbing his daddy's angry confrontation. I flip the gear and drive away.

Early in the morning the phone rings inside the spacious studio, where I work on Sunday mornings at WBLJ.

"Good Morning WBLJ, Edwina Jordan speaking."

"Let me tell you somethin', bitch!" he scoffs. "You ain't never gonna see this boy again!" My heart pounds like the moment in the day when Delbert took Keonis away. "I promise you." His words sting, firing a current the course of my spine. "Payback is a bitch!" Cold hearted, retaliating words – "and revenge is a mother-fucker. Don't you forget it!"

And even though I know Delbert hasn't got two wooden nickels to rub together, the telephone rattles in my hand. He can't travel on the weight of lint-balls. And that's about the most he carries inside his raggedy pockets and even less inside his rattling head.

"You ain't never gonna see this boy again."

Slam! The receiver pounds and shatters my listening ear. But I won't be unnerved by Delbert. I pick up Gerald, when I get through at work.

It has been a week now since I moved out. I call on Fitz to drive me to the Salvation Army Store. I've got furniture and no way to get it home.

"Edwina, who is gonna help me carry this stuff?" Fitz asks, bewildered. He glares at the length of the stairs leading to the second floor.

"Me."

"You?" he screeches. He looks hard and long at my one-hundred-twenty pound frame.

"Yes, Fitz. ME!" He smirks, a befuddled grin. Then scratches his head, and gives over his able bodied arms. Together we lift the bulk of the hefty object.

"Ya got it?" He keeps yelling, as he hauls the front-end of a steel-framed, sofa-bed, up to the second floor. Then, we drive back to the store to pick up beds for the kids. Fitz hurls them, single-handed.

"Edwina!" Fitz exclaims, the apartment door flies open. "Look!" He says softly. He points to two oversized socked feet lifted at the end of the reclining chair. The very same chair carried in just thirty minutes ago. A pair of rancid, run-over shoes set nearby. "Ain't that Delbert?" he whispers. I sneak a quiet peek. Sure as day, Delbert sits comfortably reared. His arms bend at the elbow, his hands tucked beneath his head. "Call me." Fitzgerald says in a whisper, then, leaves out the door.

"So what you doin'? You screwing Fitzgerald now, whore?"

"I'm not sleeping with Fitzgerald. He helped me to carry the furniture. You are no help. Why don't you just get out? Nobody invited you anyway." The kids huddle close to their dad. They gawk at the both of us.

"Leave Delbert! Get out!"

"No!" Gerald cries, "Mommy why you hollering at my daddy?"

"Daddy, why's Mommy hollering at you?" asks Janiah.

"Ask your mommy," he tells her.

"Daddy, you gonna sleep here with me, tonight?" Yes, seems the only answer Gerald wants to hear.

"Your mommy don't want me here."

"Why Mommy? How come Daddy can't stay with us?"

"Daddy, can you sleep here? I want you to sleep in my bed with me," cries Gerald.

In the days to follow I watch Delbert make himself the more comfortable. Weekends he minds the kids. It ain't easy living with Delbert, but tonight he can baby-sit. I've got to work a holiday shift.

"Chestnuts roasting on an open fire," it is my most favorite rendition of *The Christmas Song*. I cue another record on the opposite turntable, when a red bulb shows bright on the studio wall. The light is activated by an incoming telephone call.

"WXLV, Merry Christmas!" I answer the line with the feigned excitement of holiday bliss.

"I hate you! I hate you!" Shouts of burning anger spit through the telephone receiver. A screaming rush of cursing insults surge into my ear. They are fired hot off the blazing tongue of my angry sister-in-law. "You slept with my brother Vernon and now you are sleeping with Fitzgerald too."

"I am NOT SLEEPING WITH FITZGERALD!!!" I scream back.

"I hate you! I hate you!" Simone yells bitterly. But now I hear another voice. It is the soft and tender words of her daughter who has taken over the call. She assures me.

"Don't listen to her Edwina, my mother has been drinking. She doesn't mean what she says."

Eventually we conclude our call only to clear the signal for another incoming line.

"Hey Edwina!" It is the cheerful uplifting voice of Fitzgerald, my friend. "Merry Christmas!"

"Hi Fitzgerald!" It warms my spirit to hear his voice. "And a Merry Christmas to you!"

"What are you doing tonight?" He asks, with the height of excitement in his tone.

"Working, Fitzgerald. I'm working."

"No Edwina, I mean when you get off. It's CHRISTMAS EVE!" I can just about see his smile through the receiver.

"Nothing," I tell him, "Nothing."

"Let's go out and have a drink or something."

"I can't do that."

"Why not? Is 'Foolio' still there?" He laughs and so do I. It is a perfect description. I laugh so hard my sides ache.

"Yeah."

"What time you get off?"

"Midnight"

"How you gettin' home?" he asks.

I never cursed that car with all her trouble, but I knew it was just a matter of time.

"Is your husband coming to meet you?"

"I'm walking home, and no, he is NOT coming to meet me."

"I'll pick you up."

"Thanks Fitzgerald."

The night flows with the anticipation of Fitzgerald's coming. I turn the key and lock the big glass door. Then hurry on to meet him in the darkened parking lot.

"So, where are we going? Are we still going out for a drink?"

"Thanks, Fitzgerald, but no thanks. I can't do that. My kids are expecting me at home."

"I thought you said that Delbert was watching them?"

"He is. Still, if I don't come right home, it will only bring trouble."

"You sure you don't want to go have a quick drink?"

"I'm sure, thanks just the same."

"I don't understand that guy." Fitzgerald starts in on a conversation that takes us from one thing to the next.

"Edwina, tomorrow is Christmas and I noticed that you don't have a Christmas tree." After driving a couple blocks from my apartment he pulls over to park. Still we talk of other things. We share like experiences and of our relationships, having married into the same family. I try to figure why Katrina let such a nice guy as Fitzgerald get away. Then before we know it, the better portion of an hour has slipped away. With so much more to be said, a flowing figure sways side to side with a hasty step. Suddenly DELBERT is standing at the passenger-side window of the vehicle where I sit.

"Busted!" he screams.

"Busted? What do you mean busted"

"BUSTED! – You are BUSTED, BITCH!" He says it again. Then he turns briskly and walks away.

"Edwina, I had better take you home."

"Yeah," I confirm.

"He's not going to try and hurt you or anything, is he?" Fitzgerald asks with due concern.

"Fitzgerald, I don't put nothin' past him."

"Do you want me to come inside with you?"

"Yes, walk me inside, please."

Delbert disappears inside the apartment, just moments ahead of Fitz and me. I follow several steps from Delbert and into the bedroom. I find him fuming and sitting at the side of the bed. Fitzgerald tiptoes to the kitchen, where quietly he waits. The instant Delbert sees me he throws toward me. I dart like lightning and my panic brings Fitzgerald running into view.

"What's the matter with you man!" He shouts at Delbert. "What you hittin' on your wife for? She hasn't done nothin' for you to be hitting on her."

Confronted – MAN to man, Delbert says absolutely nothing. Fitzgerald leaves, only after getting the assurance it is safe for me to stay. But, now, with Fitz gone, Delbert rages on long into the night.

"I'm gonna see to it," Delbert's yells with deep-set, bitter hatred, "that these kids are taken from you, whore. You no good bitch."

"If that's the way you feel, Delbert, do us both a favor. Get out! You're not supposed to be here, no-way. This apartment is for me and the kids. NOT – YOU!"

"That don't give you no right to fuck my brother," a sin he'll never forgive. That was twelve years ago. "And now you're screwing Fitzgerald."

"You can think what you want Delbert."

"Why don't you just admit it?" he screams. "You know it's true."

"What is it, Delbert? Are you still sleeping with Tonya? Is that why you are so convinced that I am screwing Fitz?"

Finally, he leaves, but, when all is quiet, Delbert comes back. He presses in with a couple vials of rock-cocaine.

"Where's the pipe?" I fetch one, and while the kids sleep we blast. But when it is gone, hell breaks loose all over again.

"You gonna give me some, bitch?" I shoot a snooty glance and don't look him in the eye.

"You can smoke my shit, bitch, but you ain't gonna give me none?"

"Get out Delbert. LEAVE – NOW!"

"Fuck you. I hate you and I hope you DIE."

"Get out! GET OUT!'" I demand in a screaming rage. "Delbert go, before I call the cops!"

"You want me to go, bitch? I know you got a restraining order on me. Do you want me to go?" He screams to the tops of his lungs. "I'll go. But, let me tell you one thing, mother-fucker! The ONLY reason I'm leavin' is because if I stay, I will fuck your little ass up and I don't want to go to jail. I'll be back. I PROMISE. You can mark my word. But, you won't keep my kids." The door slams with a BANG!

And with the dawning giving birth to a sun soon to rise, I watch his figure disappear into the distance. The shadow of a man is all he is and the donor of children to my womb. But, I can't control my tears.

Delbert chimes the bell, three days later. Keonis is away at school. He spends his day as a freshman in high school. Janiah, the now first-grader is down for a late afternoon nap. I listen closely. My eyes fixed on the closed door. The television is silenced. Gerald, nearly asleep on my lap, reclines with me in a chair.

"Sorry to bother you." I hear him convincingly say. "But I just forgot my key." My neighbor leaves out. All is quiet. Tap, tap, tap. I hear his feet, coming through the narrow stairwell. "Edwina!" he shouts my name.

"Mommy," Gerald is awakened. "That's my daddy." With my finger I shush his chatter. Then, CRASH, the apartment door flies. It is forced open with the kicking of Delbert's feet.

"Get out! Get out!" I yell. He runs toward me. Get out! I scream, while he snatches Gerald up and away. I take off running down the stairs behind him. The two of us sounding a clamor, like a stampede of wild horses. I grab for my baby, but Delbert shoves me to the floor. I yell for my neighbor. "Call the cops!" Delbert drops Gerald. He takes off running and disappears.

Things have quieted, now. Since, Fitzgerald comes to check on me, nearly everyday.

"Have you heard from 'Foolio'?" He asks. Then we laugh so hard it hurts.

"No Fitz, not in a few days."

"What is wrong with him? He's lost his mind, Edwina. You are a good woman and he don't know how to treat you." His head falls and shakes pathetically. "You deserve so much more."

"I slept with his brother, Fitz." I'm sure Fitzgerald has already heard all about it. Everybody knows, because Delbert made sure of that. "Delbert never forgave me."

"But, damn, Edwina, how long ago was that?"

"Twelve years, Fitz – twelve years."

"He's fucked-up. He's never appreciated you. Hell, you don't do nothin', except go to work and come home."

"I know Fitz, I've have tried – and it ain't like he's been the best husband to me. He's still sleeping with Tonya, I'm sure of it and they've got two kids together."

"What!"

"Yeah," I say solemnly.

"Let him go Edwina, what good is he? You have got to let him go. He's silly just like that damned sister of his." He shakes his head in disbelief. "Here I was stationed overseas and that wench is sleeping around. Then I'd come home she's got a frigging TV dinner in the oven." He giggles and then the conversation shifts. "Edwina you need to get a phone. If that crazy nigger comes in here and tries anything, you can't even call for help. You need a frigging phone. How much would it take to get you a telephone in here?"

Then Valentine's Day arrives. The telephone rings and to Fitz's invitation for an evening out, I say absolutely, yes! He arrives soon with a heartfelt card, just for me. But when dinner is through, it is apparent that Delbert has left a calling card of his own. The kitchen window at the fire escape has been left ajar and the phone wire ripped from the wall. Fitzgerald is furious. He reads a bitter note. It was left by Delbert and scribbled on the Valentine's card that he'd just given to me.

"Frigging coward! You have to divorce him Edwina." And, it is now that I know it is true.

In the weeks that follow, the divorce proceedings have begun. Fitzgerald visits faithfully. He slips by after the kids are asleep and before he gets off to work as a truck driver. He is by my side. Afternoons, when his day is done, he comes again, always to see about me.

"Edwina, let me ask you something."

"What is it, Fitzgerald?"

"I heard it, but I didn't know if it was true. So I wanted to ask you for myself."

"Ask me Fitz. What is it?"

"You are not getting high, are you?" Whoa – I can't believe that Fitz is actually asking me this. But, I don't hesitate to tell him that it is true.

"Yes, Fitzgerald, I am getting high."

"What the hell are you doing that shit for, Edwina?" I have no words with which to answer him.

"Did Delbert start you on that shit?"

"Yeah, Fitz, he did." My head hangs low, when I ask. "Who told you Fitz – how'd you know?"

"Your sister-in-law, your sister-in-law told me." Why did I ask, when I already knew? Everybody knows everything about me, Delbert has made certain of that.

"You gotta quit, Edwina."

"I know Fitz."

"Why are you doing it?"

"I don't know. It just happened. I'm sorry I ever started. But it ain't so easy to quit."

Come Friday afternoon, I visit Geneva. I miss her. I miss Delbert, too. I think a quick visit won't hurt and it would do the kids good to see their grandma. I arrive to see everybody hanging-out, on the walkway. Delbert sits on the front steps and Ma favors a seat on the porch. I make idle chatter with this one or that, while Delbert enjoys the kids. After an hour or so, it is time to go.

"Let's go Janiah and Gerald. It is time to go." Janiah is ready, but Gerald – IS NOT! He is always content to sit on the stoop in his daddy's lap. I wait a couple minutes. Then again, "Come on Gerald, we've got to go." He hugs his daddy and says goodbye. Suddenly, Delbert throws his leg out from under. His awkward foot thrusts straight for my face. I jump back in the knick of time – then RUSH him. I charge angrily and hope to slam his head flat against the cement floor.

"Leave Edwina! Just go!" Geneva screams in a panic. I hurry out of there. A cloud of dust peels from my tires. Smoke seems to blow out of my ears, while I drive. My speeding car leans, as it presses around the corner. I need to talk to Fitzgerald. I find him showered and changed and heading out of the door.

He says nothing of my ordeal, just, "Why do you bother to go over there?" He is non-sympathetic and hastens me away.

"Go straight home, Edwina. Give me a call when you get there."

I call him. I call Fitz, the second I come inside my door. Come nighttime his phone is still ringing. Ring-ring-ring, all night long. Then it is Saturday morning, – ring-a-ling-ling. No answer. When comes time for me to get off to work early Sunday morning, Fitz arrives, just in the knick of time. I angrily hop inside his car. Then, I see it. A baby girl's hat tossed in the back seat.

"Oh that. It belongs to ..." He tries to explain and I don't listen. Nothing he can tell me from here on will make me think otherwise. Eventually, we arrive at WBLJ. Fitz pulls over and lets me out.

Come late Sunday night and early into Monday morning, Fitz slips by for a "night cap." We share a little time before he begins his morning drive. He drops eighty bucks on the nightstand for the telephone bill, then departs. And suddenly – I feel, again, like a two-bit whore. I hop into my clothes the second he's disappears and hurry to the west end of town for a few bottles of crack to bandage the pain. Next night, he comes again, and by now it's something else, I be needin'. Well, Fitz – one hand washes the other – if you know what I mean.

"You know what Edwina, this thing between you and me, just ain't working. It has been close to a year now and I've been thinking about it. I have spent X-amount of dollars, you wrecked the frigging car, pawned the necklace I gave you and I've been giving you money to pay the telephone bill and the frigging telephone is turned off. What the hell are you doing? I had something else going when I met you, and I gave it up to be with you. I can't continue like this. I am done, Edwina, it's over between us."

Really it is okay, Fitz. I've been hurt before. You drive me around in your big truck, fingering brand new cars and say, "Edwina, how would you like to drive that! Edwina, don't look back – cause this is your year."

I believed in you Fitz. But now, it is clear to me that the something else, you had going before you got with me – NEVER QUIT. You ain't been so honest yourself.

"I'll see ya later Edwina."

"Yeah, – later – Fitz."

CHAPTER 14

FLYING HIGH

One year later, and in December my truth is more frigid than the season's change. Sensations of death take residence in the length of my stiffened bones. If I should lie down with a mound of dirt to cover my flesh, they would surely declare that I am dead. Although, I expired long ago. My diluted spirit has betrayed me and left me spent, like an empty sieve. Daunted eyes reveal parched remnants of overdue tears, like a rusty spigot that leaks no more. Every sordid immoral fiber has been swallowed and spit back in scattered pieces of callous laughter and disregard. My pride and dignity have been laid to rest. I don't know if I am living or dead. There is the threat of snapping that single tangled knot that dangles at the end of that one frayed thread. It is all that keeps me connected to the distant notion that maybe, just maybe, I had better HOLD ON.

Pork-chops sizzle in a cast iron pan. They are the makings of a hot evening meal and will set next to steamed white rice and stringed beans. Gerald and Janiah, stripped of their school clothes, set out to play before the afternoon sun goes down. Keonis makes merry music in my living room.

"Boom! Boom!" It sounds like thunder under the rug. The door pulls shut at four o'clock in the broad day. Where are his school books? I see no homework, pencils and notebooks, now when school is in? One more – Boom! I can't take it no more. Quickly, I throw the door to find Keonis sitting on the floor, Indian-style, with his legs folded. His fingers slide up and down the controls on a noise box, making stereo sound. A couple of his friends have joined him and gather to warm the sofa. Not excluding Harvey, who is a couple or few years older than him. Harvey nods in recognition of my presence and not a second off beat with the timing of the music.

"Hello Ms. Gilliam," he smiles suavely. His arm extends the back length of the sofa cushion. A lighted cigarette dangles loosely between Harvey's thumb and forefinger. On my coffee table, lies an ashtray, full with cigarette butts. At his feet, sets one empty, the other half-full, bottle of beer.

"Nah-nah-nah! Boy you ain't grown! I ain't having it. It's time for your friends to get their hats. Shuffle out. Git to steppin'. Let's go!" I send them on their way.

Then comes a knock upon my door. Fitz's rig is parked at the curbside. He smiles softly and so do I. But he looks better going than he does coming. Now go away, Fitz. Don't go away mad – Just go away.

The days and weeks tally. Divorce proceedings have ended. I sit alone wallowing over a marriage, never meant to be. With the progression of Keonis' defiance and the aggression of my addiction, I sit him down to talk. But the breach between my firstborn and me only gets wider. I ponder my affairs and what comes to mind is the exhibitionist who takes his pleasure in the last rail car on a slow moving train. I envision my old button-front dress, where not even the rippling wave formation at a nudist beach could hide my shame. I contemplate the companionship of the Corporate Computer Executive, who shovels his entire paycheck inside a glassine pipe, then blows it all away in the course of a night. He is no different, than my blue-collared buddies with far less to spare. Suddenly, there sounds a noise at the outer window.

"Keonis, I don't appreciate you coming in here at 2:00 in the morning. You are JUST SIXTEEN! What makes you think that you can sneak in and out anytime you please? It is only God's grace you don't slip and bust your fool head wide open, entering through a second-story window. Look at you! You are drunk and vomiting all over yourself. Can't so much as leave the stool, 'cause ya don't know if you're gonna puke or shit. But you're home safe, and I am thankful for that."

I move through the upper stairwell as Tyrell, my landlord, rushes in. We meet again in the foyer of my shanty apartment, today. The first of the month, "Mother's Day," some might say. It's a day when moms receive a welfare check, creating long lines outside check-cashing facilities in every ghetto across America. Out from my pocket I pull a small wad of bills. It is an even exchange for a month's rent with no change due. Also, Tyrell receives from my sweating palm a couple bills. I owe it to him to cover a small amount of cocaine that he'd extended to me.

"You alright?" He asks. "Do ya need anything?"

"Let me get two." Tyrell passes off a couple small packages wrapped over in aluminum foil. Several more bills leave my hand.

"That's some good shit. Ya know that?" He looks at me. "Ya know that?" He says again with spurred excitement. My head lowers to a mound of pure iridescent white powder. He unwraps it before my sight.

"See! I'm tellin' you, that is some GOOD SHIT! Taste. Taste it!" He insists. The tip of my index finger wipes cautiously. I dab my tongue to discover the numbing effects of great cocaine.

Suddenly, without announcement, in sweeps a man into the vestibule. It is my neighbor Dirty Mark.

"Edwina!" He shouts my name with breathlessness.

"Edwina! Edwina your sister is in the hospital!"

"In the hospital?" My focus turns to the weight of the news. Tyrell, my landlord is unfazed. He shouts angrily.

"Mark, close the door, man, we takin' care of business. Can't you see we takin' care of business?"

Mark is persistent. "Edwina! I stopped by to see Giselle and ..."

Tyrell interrupts. "Look Man! Close the door. I ain't playing. We takin' care of business. Tyrell abruptly pushes two more packets into my hand. "Here." He says. Packages I haven't asked for. "You don't have to pay me now. And, call me if you need some more shit. You hear?" I am distracted. "You hear?" he shouts.

The transaction is finished. Tyrell is still rattling over Mark's intrusiveness. I run the length of the stairs, stash the cocaine and scurry to the hospital. But before I leave my block—

"Hey!" I hear a voice calling. "You know when you moved on this block, I wanted to get with you, but you wouldn't talk to me. And now, I wouldn't have you. You oughta' leave that shit alone. Look at you! You're losing too much weight. You're skinny."

"Mind your damned business," I say beneath my breath to a meddling neighbor.

"You're going to keep on doing that shit," he yells, "until it kills you."

"You know what?" I tell him rather smugly. "I'm not going to be doing this always, 'cause God got something better for me."

"Ahh", he waves his hand in disgust. "You ain't never gonna quit that shit. I ain't never seen nobody get off that shit and stay off." I ignore him and get on my way.

I encounter Delbert a few blocks away. We pass shoulder to shoulder. He snubs his nose as if there is a funk in the air. I speak coldly. He says nothing. But after I have passed him, he quickly pauses in the walkway. He turns around and stops to stare and to have a look at me.

"Who's keeping the kids?" He asks haughtily.

"The kids are fine."

"Who's watchin' 'em? It better not be one of your crack head friends."

"Don't you worry about it. You don't pay child support and you don't take care of them." I turn and walk away.

"Crack head." He shouts. "Fuckin' whore. I hate you. She's a whore you'll. She fucked my brother." He screams for all to hear.

I am entranced by the sight of tubes flowing from nearly every hollow in Giselle's body. And where there is no hollow, punctures have been made to accommodate. My eyes well with water and my feet don't move. My mind scrolls back to when Giselle again came recently to stay with me. Janiah and Gerald were getting acquainted with their auntie and they loved her the more, because she sneaked them candy, when I'd say NO! I won't forget how we together did the 'remember when' thing, sharing forgotten stories from dwindling moments long past. Rewinding time and revisiting silly memories with heartfelt giddiness. Two adult women, playing like little children never fully grown. Giselle stretched across my bed, clad in pajamas. The two of us laughing so hard we darn near pissed our seats.

Then suddenly, I relive the horrid recollection of wiping Giselle's tears from her emaciated cheeks. They flowed like the great falls of Niagara. I hear her pleadings over and again.

"I want to die." It is a painful episode taking hold in my scull and playing-back like a bad re-run of an old movie. Then came the confirmation spoken from her own parched mouth.

"I HAVE AIDS. And all I want to do is DIE".

Her weeping ripped my gut like barbed wire. I struggled to keep from splitting inside. Her pain is mine, as I too am dying. Watching her is watching me. Watching her is watching Mom, and Minnie and Dad. I can't do this all over again. I look at her and see my own demise.

"I want to be with Mommy." Then, like an echo, "I want to be with Mommy!"

"NO! NO! Please, Giselle – don't do this!"

I leave the hospital to call Nadine from a nearby telephone booth, then, ramble the way home. She boards a transit train and arrives just thirty minutes later. Inside my muddled apartment she stays at my side. Her companionship is well taken, but really, I have had my share of pain. And – ALL I WANT — is to get high.

Nadine, God bless her efforts, tries to talk me out of it.

"Why don't you just have a drink with me," she persuades, as together we walk to the liquor store to get her a bottle of Vodka to quell her nerves. Cautiously, she maintains her balance with the aide of a walker and a bullet still in her spine. She cops-a-bag for me, then reluctantly indulges, just a little, to mask her own addicted shame.

I inhale the tube-like barrel of a long stemmed crack pipe, when all sense of being STOPS – in a single gasp. My body throbs and my torso throws to and fro. Then – suddenly, I am – released – with a thud, onto my living room floor. But, with little fear and less apprehension, I take it AGAIN, to my mouth and inhale. Another huge puff of smoke swirls into my lungs, while my little ones rest in an adjoining room. Then it's gone. The "stuff" is gone, leaving me disoriented and weak in the knees.

"Edwina," Nadine yells, while setting her emptied glass on the floor between her feet. "Edwina, why don't you put that shit down and get some sleep." She orders me. I do, in my own time. I stretch out to the floor. But my restless body welcomes no slumber. My heavy eyelids flutter in the night. Until finally, just finally, somehow and eventually God arranges for me to sleep.

In the morning, bedside visitation is granted Cedric from Trenton State Prison. He's got a choice – see Giselle now – or after they put her in a pine box. He opts to see her now. I shudder at the sight of him approaching Giselle's bedside. Death walks beside his withering frame as he drags the length of weighty, merciless chains, too heavy for the carrying. Linked-shackles about his ankles and wrists clank and rattle with the short-distanced parting of his feet. He is devastation personified.

Brother's jaws are hollowed and his cheekbones jut beneath vacant eyes. But when he smiles, I know now that it is him. Cedric — that same mischievous kid who always teased and pulled pranks on me. - Mommy's baby boy, Mommy's only boy – my dear brother, Cedric. He tickles Giselle's feet and calls her name, hoping she might reply. Then together, we three, Nadine, Cedric and me, gather with a staff of medical professionals to discuss life's chance.

"The only thing keeping her alive is the machine. It's doing the breathing for her. There is no oxygen going to her brain."

We listen before the decision is made, and the ventilator is unplugged. Three days come to pass, when Giselle slips away.

I have telephoned Celia, who is many miles away, in Michigan.

"I have tentatively arranged the funeral for Wednesday. Unless it would be more convenient for you to get here on Thursday or Friday," I cry. Her stinging reply draws through the receiver and burns inside my ear.

"I won't be there." She says with no elaboration.

I am numbed and don't know how to respond. "Okay," I say. I close our conversation and hang the phone.

Once the body has been prepared, Nadine and I go to the funeral home for a previewing to make sure that it has been adequately preserved. Adequate? Inadequate? Neither means very much to me. Our sister has already gone. Giselle is presented in one of my favorite dresses. Two hundred fifty dollars is had from Social Security. Some pocket change is donated by a neighbor and provides an extremely moderate floral arrangement. It reads, "From the Sisters." And I am grateful to the local flower shop and its elderly, back-bent, proprietor, who said yes.

I embrace Aunt Trudy, "Hallelujah!" and Aunt Mildred. Aunt Tess is no longer here. Uncle Melvin doesn't show up for funerals, anymore. Uncle 'Lonzo with his drinking, lives on the streets, he probably doesn't know that Giselle is no longer here.

A couple of my cousins have come. Aunt Bertie; Aunt Bea and Aunt Tootsie are here.

It is the evening of the funeral and Nadine sits on one side of me and Uncle Buster on the other inside a dank double room. This is the same funeral home that put Minnie, Mommy, and Daddy under. It is a place where my sobbing is not contained. I think of Minnie and I wish that she were here.

Soon I stand before a crowd of condescending sympathizers. I defend my dead sister for having been an addict and especially for dying of AIDS. But nobody could know, Giselle was entirely so much more to me. She will be cremated. But her urn of ashes I will refuse. There is nothing on earth that could substitute my fondest memories of my baby sister, my friend. My Dear Giselle, I will truly miss you.

Following the funeral, a handful of family members return to my apartment for a small gathering. When they have gone, the telephone rings.

"How did it go?" Broken and bewildered, I struggle to answer.

"Everything went okay." There is silence. Then I say, "Celia you hurt me."

"What do you mean?"

"You were not there for me."

She interrupts barefaced and unashamed, cutting with a razor sharp tongue.

"Steven said that I should come or send flowers, but I decided not to do neither."

I interject, tearfully, "Who is Steven?" I have never heard that name Steven.

"My fiancé," she replies with haste, then resumes. "If Giselle chose to live like she lived, and die like she died, then her soul probably went straight to hell. And as far as I am concerned you are all dead!"

With respect to the ill health of brother Cedric, I somberly reply. "Celia, I could go first, or maybe you, but in the event that it is neither … would you be there?"

"NO!" She states emphatically. "If I die I don't want my body flown back to New Jersey. I have a plot right here in Detroit."

"Well, thanks," I say, "I just needed to know. In the event I am faced with this again, I will know what I should do." I hang the phone.

LETTER TO CELIA

My Dear Sister Celia,

The wisdom of patience has become your grace, etched through the passing of time. You tried to fix something that was not yours to be had. Time is the greatest of all healers, but not without mercy. To God be the Glory, now and forever more.

No, sister Celia, don't you believe for one idle second that I harbor any bad taste in my mouth for you. My level of perception only leads me to understand through God's eternal wisdom, that you were hurting too. We all have a different level of tolerance, when dealing with these sort of things. "You are a tough nut to crack," as they say, my beloved sister Celia. But, I accept, I forgive and I understand the reasons why.

> She is a cruel teacher
> That experience,
> but, she teaches what she knows.
> And, she is graceful by the wisdom,
> learned among the pros.

A bit of love – inspired by you. I will forever, be grateful to you and I pray God's grace and adoration upon—ALWAYS.

The door opens and the door shuts. It seems there is always someone coming or going.

Is anybody here with you?'

"Just the kids"

"Where 'dey at?"

"They're sleepin'"

"Where's your pipe?" I inhale.

"I didn't know you were goin' through so much, Edwina." He exhales. "I didn't even know that Giselle was sick until I ran into you over at the grocery store. Damn, why does it have to be our family?" The pipe trembles in his hand. He holds it away from his mouth and speaks gently. "I sure do miss your mother. That was my buddy, 'Butch,' my favorite sister. We used to call her that when we was kids." For just a moment it is silent. Uncle Buster changes positions, then again begins to speak. "I think that's why I take to you so much, Edwina. I mean I love all of you kids, but of all Annie Belle's kids you remind me the most of her." He passes the pipe to me. "Here, put some more on there for yourself." He motions to the tiny white pebbles lined up atop the table. I load the pipe, strike a light and inhale. "I just hate," he says, "that she got caught up with your father. He was a mean ol' fart. I hated his guts. So many times, I just wanted to put my foot, straight up his ass. But, I miss 'Butch'. I really miss her. You're sweet, Edwina, just like her. I'm just sorry that you're goin' through all this shit. When is the last time you heard from your sister Celia?"

"I talked to her a couple nights ago, the same night as the funeral."

"And what about your sisters, Alfreda and uh-uhh?"

"Who, Nadine?"

"No the other one – Uh- uh? Damn!" He snaps his fingers impatient with himself. "What's her name?" It's been so long that Uncle Buster can't even remember our names.

"Who? – Rhonda? Do you mean Rhonda?" I ask.

"Yeah" he answers. "How come she wasn't at the funeral?"

"I haven't seen nor heard from Rhonda and Alfreda since …" I sit quiet for a second, trying to count the years. "It's been eight years." Again I am silent, before I tell him, "Uncle Buster that bothers me. The last time I saw Alfreda, she was shootin' drugs and living over in New York, using her apartment for a 'shootin' gallery.' Rhonda was shootin' up and trickin' and to tell you the truth –I don't know if they are living or dead." The air gets still. I pass Uncle Buster the pipe. He inhales, and I talk. "I miss my mother and Minnie and I miss my father, too."

"Yeah," he says. "I know how you feel, Kid." I know Uncle Buster understands, 'cause Uncle Buster just lost his wife. "It seems like our family is gettin' smaller and smaller."

"Now, Cedric is sick," I say.

"Huh?" Uncle Buster looks like he just saw a ghost.

"Yeah."

"Oh shit!" he shrieks.

"Cedric has AIDS. He thinks he got it from Giselle." A tear falls from my eye.

"Don't hold it in," Uncle Buster tells me. "You have to talk about it and let it out."

I change the subject. "You know, Uncle Buster, it's a funny thing, me and you sittin' here gettin' high together."

"That's life, Kid. I didn't even know that you were doin' this shit. Until I ran into you over at the spot the other night."

"Well – same here. I never thought you'd be doin' it neither." When the stuff is gone, I call Tyrell and Uncle Buster orders more, until …

"Ya got any money, Edwina?" he asks.

"No, I don't get nothin' else until the first of the month."

"And I don't get paid again until Thursday. Look, I'm gonna go see if I can borrow somethin' from a partner of mine. If I git my hands on anything, I'll be back. You gonna be up ain't cha'?"

"I'll be up.'

"All right – I'll check you later, Kid," Uncle Buster says. And then he leaves.

It is Saturday night. Same old stuff – getting high and liking it. Uncle Buster don't make it back. But Lance stops by. We laugh, talk trash, smoke coke and sup on lust, until the euphoria transforms our beings into tasteless, careless, lack-luster trifled remnants and filthy human beings. Our existence is reduced to rubble. The flesh we wear ain't worth the sack of bones it's layered on. Later Aunt Bea's daughter, my *sizzin'* Theresa, drops in. When she joins us, the pipe now travels in a circle, instead of back and forth. Suddenly, three thumps pummel my door.

"I'll pop a shell in your ass!" It's Lance's wife, with a strong-armed female doing the mouthing for her.

"Get out, NOW!" I scream. Lance and Theresa are not fazed. They don't move. Them women ain't afraid of all my hollering. They push their way against my weight and force in through the doorway. I run back up the stairs and hollering, "I'm calling the cops!" I start dialing and that's when they take off running, back down the stairs. A lone black and white arrives, while Lance, after stashing the drugs and his pipe, sits casually on my living room sofa. Theresa wanders about in a state of euphoria.

"Who called us? Did you call the Police?"

"Yes."

"What's your name?" Then the officer talks into a two-way phone and a voice calls back full with static. I realize, they are talking about me. "We've got a bench warrant for your arrest on an outstanding fine you never paid." Then my house phone rings. The officers let me answer it. A male voice whispers low.

"Is this Edwina?"

"Yes"

"Did you call Police Headquarters?"

"Yes. Who's this?"

"Don't say anything," the voice whispers. "I could get in trouble if they know I am making this call." Two officers, stare me in my eyes.

"I work for the Police Department." I recognize the voice of an old classmate, now working for the cops and looking out for me. "I heard the call, when it came in. Don't answer your door. They have a warrant for you." I say nothing. The line gets quiet. "Did you already let them in? Did you let them in, already?"

"Yes." My wrists are adorned with silver bangles as soon as I hang the phone. Theresa and Lance stay with my sleeping kids. I am escorted away.

"Have you got anything on you? Bend over and spread your legs." Eventually, I am escorted up the stairs to a common area where four women bunk. Here is my stay for the next couple nights. With one phone call allowed to the outside, I dial Fitz. He assures me he will handle it, Monday morning.

Monday morning, I am released to the streets. Somebody paid my bail. And, with no means of transport, I am free to go. I make my way to a lower lobby and plead to use the desk phone. No connection is made. Fitz is not at home. No answer at my apartment, neither. Where could Theresa be with my kids?

Standing in the courthouse lobby, I notice a man in business attire. He stands out. Beside me, he is the only Afro-American here. He wears a long trench coat. It hangs loose with a belt dropped on each side. A felt hat rests on his head. His shoes gleam like new money. For a meager second we make eye contact. Then I breeze through the outer doors and disappear into the courtyard. I have my seat on a cement bench and watch the passersby. I wonder if I should begin the hike down the main thoroughfare. It would be hours to walk and already, my feet are chilled in my bedroom slippers. My bed-jacket doesn't keep me warm. Then again, there he is in the long tan trench. It is worn by the same man I'd noticed inside vestibule.

"Do you need a ride?" He asks, while I stare at the prominent creases in his pleated trousers. His leather shoes gleam with a double shine.

"What's your name?"

"Edwina, Edwina Gilliam. Well – Jordan, I recently divorced."

"I'm Derrick, come on. Where do you live? I'll take you home." During the drive we talk.

"What are you doing out here."

"Well, I had a minor domestic problem at my home on Friday night. It turns out that I had an outstanding warrant. So they arrested me. That's crazy, huh?" I say nervously. "I call the cops to handle it – and they decide to arrest me." Jesus Lord, please just let this man take me home. No where else, just home.

"Do you live in this town?" My discomfort leaves me to ask. I make the effort to sound spontaneous and relaxed. He seems a normal guy. I reason with myself. A businessman dressed in business attire.

"Not exactly," he says. "But, I live nearby. I am a doctor's assistant at the hospital there."

I'm nervous as can be. Fifteen minutes into the drive he pulls over.

"Why are we stopping?"

He says nothing. Flip – he opens the glove box and removes something. But I can't see what it is. My heart races, when his door flies forth and he walks swiftly. He snatches open the passenger side.

"Come on."

"Huh?"

"Come on." He says, pulling me by the hand. "I'm not going to hurt you." He says, before walking me straight in the front door of a cheap motel room. The door locks. His clothes peel as quickly. He tears me out of my belongings and flips me like a pancake, once and then twice. He pushes some money into my hand and we leave as fast as we arrived.

I have just arrived home, when there sounds a patter up the stairs.

"Ernestine!" I say, uneasily.

"Hey." She speaks off-handed, dissecting me with the slant of her eyes.

"Ernestine, where are my kids?"

"The kids are fine," she mocks.

"Ernestine!" I say firmly. "Where are my kids?"

"They're all right – I told ya!"

"Where – where are they?" She blows a haughty stare.

"Ther' in school. – OKAY!" I know she has been drinking. She sighs, nonchalantly. "So", she says, "you just got out?"

"Yeah."

"Where's Theresa?" I ask.

"She's locked-up. She stole your television – girl. She got busted walkin' down the street with it in her arms."

Come another Monday morning I smile and say good morning to Janiah and Gerald and I give them a hug.

"Good mornin', Keonis." I say. He mutters something, keeps on walking and ignores me when I call his name.

"Oooh!" whispers Janiah with her mouth hung open.

"Janiah, go get your brother. Tell him to come and eat."

"Oooh!" Again, she says, "Mommy! Keonis said that word."

"What word, baby?" I thought I'd heard it too, that four letter B-I-T-C-H-word. The word I chose to ignore.

LETTER TO KEONIS

I pay a visit to your room and find you with your mouth clenched and arms folded stiff across your chest. I unfold your arms, and you leap for me, like you're hauling off on one of your school friends. I don't wish to hurt you boy. Just only want to tell you of my struggle. We tussle, arm in arm and I hold you to the floor. I love you, Keonis And it ain't a day on this earth that I would intentionally visit my indifference upon you.

BITCH – the door SLAMS! I inhale a deep breath. I exhale and let you go. Then I begin to cry. And even still – I love you.

A box-like vehicle pulls to the curbside. It has big parking mirrors and a state insignia painted boldly on the sides. Out steps a tall, skinny, woman with glasses that sit on the arch of her nose.

"Mrs. Gilliam?" She calls me by name, and thrusts a business card in my face.

"Yes" I reply.

"My name is Mrs. Davidson. I am an investigator for the Children's Services Department. Can I speak with you for just a moment.?"

"I'm gettin' ready to go meet my kids from school," is my clever reply.

"Well, we need to talk. I'm here to investigate a claim of child neglect against you.

Extension cords drape the ceilings, pulling power from the apartment downstairs. The electric company disconnected the service months ago. The cupboards shelves are empty, and the refrigerator might as well be a closet for the lack of refrigerated goods it holds.

I'll need to inspect your apartment as a routine follow-up on this claim."

I'll be damned if you will. I think deviously.

"Who sent you?" I say.

"I am not at liberty to divulge that information."

"Well, I don't feel obligated to share my personal effects with you neither, Miss Lady – whoever 'da hell you are. My thoughts keep quiet.

"You need to let me in to see your apartment. If the claim is unsubstantiated, I can close this case."

"NO-O-O!" I answer her LOUD and clear! "I'm not giving you entry into my apartment."

Mrs. Davidson winces. Her bushy eyebrows raise. She glares superciliously over her thick-square rims. But, I return the haughtier stare. I'm not doin' it. My babies are ALL I have.

"I'll need time to speak to my attorney."

Oops! An intentional monster-sized pretense just slipped straight through my teeth.

"I'm runnin' late, Mrs. Davidson, I've gotta go and get my kids."

I hurry on, and upon reaching the school I don't see my kids. The library – I think of the library. I told them it is a safe place. They know to meet me there. But I don't find them. I make my way to Ernestine's apartment several levels up in the high-rise apartment, just across the street. There is no answer. And again – tap-tap, no answer.

I file a missing persons report only to learn later that they were hold up in Ernestine's apartment all the while. Her oldest boy, Hasaan, pressed his hands to cover their mouths while I stood knockin' outside the door.

Ernestine once asked me.

"Edwina, don't you know that shit stinks?"

Well, Ernestine, I wasn't sure what you meant. I'd never been asked that before. Now I know. Yes, shit has got a stench like none other. I have since learned all about the stench of shit. And as a matter of fact the stench of shit makes me think of you.

I trusted you to watch Janiah and Gerald the other night, so I could take the train out of town the next day to do a day's work. Gerald cried so hard, I took him with me. The next day, Gerald and me are runnin' late and tryin' to catch the train, when we see Janiah and Kahlia. You turned your own daughter and mine out to the streets. I didn't recognize Janiah. Her hair was unbraided, cut with a scissor and stood straight on top her head. I didn't send her to you lookin' like that. The clothes you dressed her in were not her own. They fell off her shoulders like a curtain on a rod. They hung long on one side and past her knees. Her shoes flapped like a hobo's, too big for her feet.

"Mommy I know where Keonis is," Gerald and Janiah told me that.

"Where?"

"At Aunt Ernestine's."

"Where is my son, Ernestine? Where is Keonis."

Now you show me a letter that Delbert mailed to you, saying he wants you to come to court and testify against me. What is wrong with you, Ernestine? You been conspirin' with Delbert and Katrina all the while.

I hurry to confront Katrina. Her son Dwayne, shrewdly meets me in my path. He smiles snidely and pleasures himself with spitting words of unpleasant truth.

"You wanna' know where your son is, Edwina?" He says crudely. "He ran away to Pennsylvania to live with his dad. He said that all you do is smoke crack. He even wrote a song about you." Dwayne giggles cuttingly. "You'll hear it," he jeers. "He hates you Edwina."

I hurry past him. And move straight through the yard and up the back steps to deal with Katrina.

Is it irony or treachery? Child Protective Services visits. Ernestine hides my kids. And Delbert, who hauled ass out of state more than a year ago to avoid paying child support, is now sittin' right here, inside Katrina's apartment.

"You need help, Edwina." Delbert plows into me the minute I see him. "I'm going to take those kids from you. Katrina's going to help me."

He speaks calm with confidence and a drink in his hand. My eyes fill with angry tears and I am ready to explode. My gut tells me to hold my peace, listen and know the truth. Delbert's voice slurs with the influence of strong drink.

"That's right, Edwina." Katrina says.

I boil inside, because I know Katrina don't want my kids. If she could collect the state check without the bother of them, we would not be having this conversation.

"I will help him." She adds. She raises her brow and flaunts a haughty glare.

"I guarantee you," Delbert boasts, "'um gonna take 'dem kids."

His arrogance overwhelms me.

"Look at you Edwina," he goes on. "Why don't you just admit that you're a crack head."

Delbert resists the truth, that he introduced me to this shit.

"You are smoking crack, you committed adultery with my brother. You're unfit. Accept it. No court is gonna give you custody and you know it. Just give the kids to me. You'll make it a lot easier on yourself." He jeers maliciously. "Suit yourself, Edwina," he giggles. "I'm gonna get them anyway."

LETTER TO ERNESTINE

Ernestine,

Toby is angry that I still tolerate you. He asked me once.

"Edwina, do you know what Ernestine thinks of you?" He was so angry he was screaming and big veins popped from his neck. But I had no idea that he would tell me —"ass-wipe – that's what she calls you Edwina, a fuckin' ass-wipe." Why Ernestine? I thought we were sisters, two peas from the same pod. I thought we looked out for one another.

Where were you when your babies came knocking at my door to ask me, Aunt Edwina, have you seen my mommy? So many days and so many nights, I took them in for you. I recall in the darkness of night, watching them from my window, plowing playfully in the mounds of snow piled like mountains, in a parking lot across the street. I called them in for a home cooked meal and a place to sleep.

But life ain't fair, and nobody ever said it was, Ernestine. When you were homeless, I even shared my apartment with you. Face it, Ernestine, you need help with your addiction just as much or more than me. I nearly despise you, Ernestine, but God won't take kindly to it. So let me pray for you instead, as you go on your way.

CHAPTER 15

THE "MOURNING" AFTER

The amalgamated scent of sulfur from kindled matchsticks fuses with the hum of burnt wick and candle wax. A frayed bedsheet is a scarf for the air that seeps past the window frame. It sways with the howling of the winds. I shove a gentleman caller over the doorsill and back outside into the hours of the night. Then return and have my seat on a hardwood floor.

Staring through the dim of a flicker and the lighting of a crack-pipe, I see my babies, tucked tight and warm. They huddle beneath blankets donated by the Goodwill Store. At their bedside, stands the borrowed peak from an artificial Christmas tree. It measures seven to eight inches is all. A handful of silvery ornaments adorn the synthetic branches, where it sits inside a cardboard box, wedged with newspaper to help it stand.

Christmas has arrived inside this little room. Janiah and Gerald arise to greet the dawn of Jesus' birth. A stuffed, fuzzy face on a white rabbit for her and a brown teddy for him, brings a squeal; thankful for so little. Their wide-toothed faces smile and bring water to my eyes. Then I wonder how my firstborn is spending his Christmas day. Keonis? Is he happy and does he think of me?

My heart crumbles to think, Mrs. Davidson, from the Child Protection Agency came to take my babies away from me. My sight ponders the wires extending to the ceiling as they divert electric current from the apartment below. The refrigerator is a chilled and empty, hollow box, except for a small chicken, set aside for frying on this Christmas day. It is a day without tinsel. It is a day with no shiny wrapping or bows.

My eyes rest for a moment on the kitchen oven with its door swung low and parted. An oven that has burned its course and no longer gives out heat. I look down to the coldness of the splintered hardwood floors. Then I remember Larry. A friend I met in passing and who has given me a key. My babies gather their little stuffed animals to tuck tight under their arms and we make our way under a gray and frigid sky. Several short blocks away, I find it. Larry's little place. I shove the key. The lock turns. I don't know what or who I might find on the other side. When Larry arrives he finds us waiting, smilin' and waitin'. We are happy to have heat and a warm pillow on which to lay our heads.

Early comes morning, and while Larry is away I dismiss the distaste of idle thoughts and plow ahead. I confront the cold to stand in line for a couple loaves of bread. To my delight are added a couple pastry rolls. I return to prepare a dinner meal of beans over seasoned rice; food from Larry's cabinets he didn't know he had.

My blessings are counted for today. A little flavor and a bit of love brings this place to resemble "HOME." Larry is pleasingly surprised, the instant he steps foot in the door.

"You didn't have to cook!" His face lights up like a florescent bulb. "Where did you get the food?" I'm smiling. He's smiling. Larry smiles so big the walls grin back.

"From your closet," I tell him. Still glowing, Larry suddenly remembers something that he is supposed to tell me.

"Oh yeah, Edwina, I ran into your sister today and she said to tell you …"

"My sister?" Larry doesn't know my sisters. "What sister?"

"She said her name was Erna ... Ernestine, – or something like that."

"Oh, you mean Ernestine." I'm still smiling. "I didn't know that you know Ernestine."

"I don't."

"Well, how does she know you?"

"I don't know. Just listen." He quiets me. Let me tell you."

"What?" I say. I can't imagine nothin' being so urgent that Ernestine has to send a message through Larry. She don't know Larry. When I get through with all my busy talking, Larry takes a deep breath.

"Your sister said to tell you that your brother died."

Then comes silence, utter silence.

Larry apologizes.

It is now that I reflect on some of my last conversations with brother Cedric. And I ponder how he had called to tell me that he was sick and always to warn me of my reckless ways.

"Hello."

"This is New Jersey Bell. I have a collect call from Cedric Jordan at the Trenton, New Jersey, State Prison. Will you accept the charges?"

"Yes, I will."

"Go ahead please."

"Hey Cedric"

"What's up Sis!"

"Not too much Cedric, I miss you. I haven't heard from you since Giselle passed."

"Yeah, I know. What you been up to?"

"Same ol' thing, Cedric, you know."

"Edwina, you're not still getting" high are you?"

"Yeah."

"I kinda thought so, 'cause I call and I can't catch up to you much, lately. You ain't trickin' or nothin', are you?"

"No," I reply, hesitantly.

"Cause you know you don't have to do that, ya know. You're too smart for that. How's my little niece and nephews doin?" he asks.

"They're doin' okay."

Brother goes on to ask about his own children; two daughters, Fran and Charlotte, by two different women.

"Edwina, do you ever run into Jeanette?" Cedric always asks about his kids. "I have been tryin' to get her to bring Charlotte up here to see me, ya know. But, she tells me that Charlotte don't want to come."

"That ain't right," I tell him. "How she gonna leave a decision like that with a little kid?"

"If you ever run into her, please try to talk to her. I really would like to see Charlotte."

"Oh yeah, Edwina," he remarks as though his memory were just jostled. "Get a pen and take down this number. It's Lorraine's sister's number, she's raising Fran now." Lorraine is Cedric's other baby's mother. Fran's mom, Lorraine, passed many months ago. "With me sick and all, I want you to get in touch with Fran, so she can know who her family is. I miss my kids, ya know."

The number rolls from his lips and I scribble it among many numerous entries in a little phone book. He continues talking, when comes a gleaming smile that shines straight through the telephone receiver.

"Hey Edwina, check this out," Brother exclaims, before wailing into a melody. He sings a song for me, and I must admit, he sounds pretty darned good. When he finishes, again he is smiling. I can feel it clear as day. "I didn't tell you I could sing, did I?"

I smile back.

"Nope Cedric, you didn't." We laugh aloud, something we have not done together in such a very long time. I miss Cedric already and I know that one day the phone calls will end.

"I really miss you Edwina, and I love you."

"I know. I love you too, Cedric," My tone is soft and broken. This is sounding final and it makes me sad. In many ways I don't know what to say to Brother. One day there will be no ring-ling from the telephone operator at New Jersey Bell. He will be leaving. Hello and goodbye. Hello and goodbye. I am sick and tired of saying hello, just to say goodbye. Suddenly,

Brother changes the subject as he does often, racing in and out of enthusiastic conversation, going from one subject to the next.

"Edwina!" he says eagerly.

"What!" I'm excited, wondering what Cedric might say next.

"Do you know what I really miss?"

"What's that Cedric?" I smile.

"Fried chicken, I miss fried chicken. Do you think you could get up here to bring me some? It don't have to be home fried, bring me some Kentucky Fried, or anything. I just got a taste for some fried chicken."

I say I will. When all in the same breath I make a million and one excuses, why I can't get there. In my heart I know that I will never see Cedric again. I love him too much to see him so sick. Besides, I am running from myself so hard that I don't have time to get chicken, money to buy chicken, nor do I desire to make time to willfully subject myself to the sickening pain of watching Brother die.

"Well, I guess I better go. I know I can't run your phone bill up. I love you sis."

"Love you too, Cedric."

Neither of us say GOODBYE. We say, "See ya later," and we hang up the phone, for the very last time. I miss you Brother.

Brother called me from prison some time ago, to tell me that he was sick. He thought, maybe, he'd picked up the virus from Giselle, exchanging needles and works. Says he just got dizzy, one day and passed out. There is no burial. Cedric has already been cremated, where he expired at the Trenton New Jersey State Prison.

I move out of Larry's apartment some weeks later, just in time for Mrs. Davidson of Child Protective Services to revisit. With pride I receive her presence at my ever-so modest, newly acquired first-floor residence. The electricity has by now been restored, in lieu of a written agreement to satisfy the outstanding debt. The kids are healthy, happy and clean. They greet Mrs. Davidson playfully in socked feet and pajamas. Mrs. Davidson is so impressed that she leaves before I can take the honor of inviting her to inspect the fullness of the cupboards and refrigerator. The investigation of child neglect is terminated. CLOSED! FINISHED! They say that God looks over babies and fools. A babe, I am not. Blessed is your faithfulness.

≈≈≈

On this unforgiving, sweltering August afternoon, an entire church congregation has not so randomly encamped on this drug-infested street corner to holler glory. I had no way of knowing that this is no better neighborhood than the one I'd left behind. Drugs are being sold from my very doorstep. Dope peddlers hold their posts around the clock. My asinine vulnerability gives me convenient access to the center core of hell.

Standing on the high reaching bleachers, the choir sings. Two humongous loud speakers reverberate shouts of hallelujah praises through an echoing microphone. And there is talk about driving out the devil.

I can't deny for a solitary second, that I love the rumbling of the bass, ear-shattering as it is. It feels good to my body, and even better to my famished soul. It follows my arrogant, pattering feet and dances me all the way up the block to buy a bottle of crack.

There he is, my boy, Bugsy, on his bicycle.

"Hey Bugsy! What's up!" I ask, while I'm trippin' on the music all the way. "You holdin'?"

"No, he replies, "but my partner down the way is."

We talk a bit, of old times, his family and mine, before he grabs my few dollars and spins off on his bike. I ease leisurely back to the front stoop where I wait and take in some of that old fashioned spiritual flavor. It reminds me of better times. Soon, Bugsy rolls-up, returning on his *too-little for him* bicycle with his baby in a harness strapped to his back. We discreetly make the transaction, to the clanging of tambourines. Then I toy with Bugsy's baby's chunky cheeks and talk, dumb baby talk.

Suddenly, three plain-clothed officers, grab hold to Bugsy's bicycle bars. He attempts to swing a U-turn in the walkway. First words out of his babbling face, "I ain't got nothin', I got my baby with me!"

Somebody's watching me – Narcotics Under-Cover Agents? They've been watching all the while. They turn him loose, let him go, then run straight for me.

"Yeah this is the short babe in the photos," they quip.

They recognize me the second they squeeze the cuffs about my wrists. I go down with a vial and a stupid crack pipe stashed in my oversized pants pocket. Busted — IN FRONT OF AN ENTIRE CHURCH CONGREGATION. I can still hear the music.

"Swing low", white patty-wagon — comin' for to carry me to jail.

For multiple hours I lie, locked in that wretched, stinkin' cell. Inhaling the pungent fumes of an exposed urinal next to the solid wooden slab, where I rest. Eventually comes the transport, down to the county jailhouse. Alongside a slew of notorious drug dealers and addicts, like me, who'd also been popped over the long weekend. After my preliminary check-in and change into a green suit of attire. An oversized, cocky-framed, wide shouldered, mannish-looking guard, with short, wiry hair escorts me to a little room with a tiny barred window. It sets high on a top floor of a tall building. My roommate is a young woman. Unlike me, she has been before the notorious Judge Hale one time too many. Three days pass, before I have my say before the hard-nosed, sister-woman, Judge Hale. She despises repeat offenders.

"Judge Hale, your Honor, my name is Edwina Jordan and I have never been in trouble. This is my first offense. If I see the light of day, it will be my last offense. You won't see me no more."

The processing of paperwork is a matter of several hours, until I am released. Six months probation, it cost me. That's hilarious. I can get high Thursday afternoon through Sunday nights. I can leave the shit alone three days on Monday, Tuesday and Wednesday. I can see my Probation Officer on Thursday morning and if she needs me to piss in a jar – no problem, I will.

"Short-Cakes," Katrina's message is delivered straight and deliberate, "Katrina said to tell you, you are not to take them kids NOWHERE.

My kids are inside and I stand outside, uninvited into Melinda's apartment where Janiah and Gerald have slept the last few nights. I stand watchin', listenin' to her give orders from Katrina, from behind a closed screened door.

Then, I think. Katrina is right. I am incapable – careless and incapable. Yet, I'm afraid. Afraid Child Protective Services will give my kids over to the two people who despise me most. I'm angry, brutally angry.

"Now don't get mad at me," Melinda says. "I'm just givin' you the message. If you decide to take them kids you'll have to deal with Katrina. Now, that's on you." She disappears.

Seated on the stoop out front is Melinda's live-in boyfriend, Gary.

"Edwina", he says, "'Dem is your kids. I wouldn't leave em. Take your kids with you. She can't stop you. I don't care what Katrina say."

"I'll be back." I tell Gary, before I turn and walk away.

"Da-ding-a-ding," sounds a little bell on the back of another screened door. It is the entryway inside a little corner store. It's a small store that sells gum and candy, among other things. The young gentleman here knows me. He trusts me with a few odds and ends, until I make it to the Welfare office tomorrow morning to get my welfare check. He fills my bags with a little this and some of that.

'Da-ding-a-ding." I leave his place and head on home. There, I prepare an adequate meal, then go back to Melinda's to get my kids.

"Mommy, where was you?"

"I wanted to come home, Mommy."

I listen as my babies fire questions. I sit them to the table for an explanation and a bite to eat.

"Mommy was locked up. I was arrested and put in jail."

"Why?"

"How come you was in jail?"

"Because I did something that I was not supposed to do. Mommy has a drug problem and when people do drugs they go to jail. I want you both to know how much I love you. I'm sorry." I grab them close and hold them silently in my arms.

"I love you mommy!"

"And I love you. No matter what anybody ever tells you – you remember that – I love you."

"Now, let's say a prayer and then let's eat."

With the kids returned to school, there comes a rat-a-tat-tat. I scamper to the window and I part the tattered slats on the chord-strung-Venetian-blinds. "Nah, can't be." It has been too long since I had a legitimate visitor. NO WAY! I was bettin' on it being Tyrell or one of his cronies, come to call.

"Uhh-uhh, nah", say it ain't so. It is Celia. It sure nuff' is. Not today, not now. Not like this. "Oh No-o-o!"

If I could crawl under the floorboards, I would, whoosh away, like a bad episode of Minnie Mouse. If Celia sees me, she'll swear she's seen death warmed over. Must I open the door? I debate with myself. I can't leave her to stand there, after she's traveled from over six-hundred miles away. Sure, you gotta open it. "Darn it!" – Say cheese! My frown becomes a smile turned upside down. The knob turns reluctantly, and the hinge swings back.

SURPRISE! I think to myself, as Celia peers in the face of iniquity, personified. I look at her and she stares back in full consumption of what I am not. I simply smile, when to evaporate would be so much more comfortable. Everything I fear has come unveiled and magnified under scrutiny. Celia can't digest the haggard sight of me. I'm a hellified, grueling disclosure that brings a twitching in her eye. She glances quickly, at my disgusting non-radiance, with my hairs on end, then, turns away.

The house is – well – shabby – and Celia can't wait to step foot back outside the door. I can see it in her face. We embrace. And, our words are few, after all of four years. She brings with her the heart shocking, uplifting news that Alfreda is in town. Alfreda is in town! Nobody has seen, nor heard from Alfreda in all these long years. I thought Alfreda was dead. I nearly go through the ceiling. Celia offers me the ride to see Alfreda, but I'm shamed with her lookin' at me. She turns and walks away.

I take the long walk instead and soon, I am poundin' with all my soul, beatin' the chocolaty flesh of her exposed left upper arm, I squeal her name from the top of my lungs.

"ALFREDA, ALFREDA" … I can say no more.

"STOP hitting me!" She screams with a pained and tender smile.

I can't hold my peace. It is not an apparition. Sheer joy, is what it is. SHEER JOY! To see her in the flesh makes me act like a pure idiot. I want to pinch her or maybe pinch myself. I can't believe my eyes!

"YOU ARE ALIVE. I am so THANKFUL … SHE IS ALIVE!"

The news she bears is even greater. Rhonda is alive too – sick with HIV. Yet I thank you Lord! She is ALIVE.

As shamed as I am at the sight of myself. Still I smile a barefaced, true-hearted, full to the gut, smile, nearly from ear to asshole. That is what I feel like. A total ASSHOLE. What have I done with myself for all of these years? Before me, is my sister. She is healthy and whole, free from the affliction of addiction. It's needless to ask her the question. "Do you still get high" I can't believe my sight. Alfreda is thick with the good gifts of life and it is apparent. Forty-two years old and she's been blessed with a bundle of joy. She holds in her arms a beautiful, healthy infant baby boy. My eyes are loyal and my sight is true. I am ecstatic beyond definition, in spite of myself.

A light of discomfort dares to expose me, haggard and worn, with esteem the measure of a caterpillar or more likely an inchworm. Because when I shed my skin, I can never hope to be a butterfly. Alfreda's camera snaps and snaps again. My sister, Alfreda has always loved to catalogue photos of the family. Clickity-click, click. Mirrors of negativity caught on film.

Then, spit out as confirmation of self-neglect and unadulterated stupidity.

CLICK, CLICK, CLICK. CLICKETY, CLICK! I wish that I could CLICK my heels and stop the image marked inside her little mechanical box. I hate having my picture taken. This time as before, I twist my face like a contortionist to purposely distort the image. My hand flies over my face to spoil the view. Zoom your lens elsewhere. There is no beauty to be mirrored here, from inside nor out.

For all of two days I will have my family to surround me. HOMECOMING! Celia, my Lord, has found her way home. Alfreda, after eight long years, has finally come home. Rhonda ain't here, but she can sure' nuff get home if she wanted to. And Grandma is going home. HOMECOMING! – a melancholy occasion, inevitably marked by loss of life. Sadly, my maternal grandmother will be laid to rest come morning.

And the day arrives when I see faces I thought I might never see again. Uncle Buster is here, Uncle 'Lonzo and even Uncle Melvin. My aunts and my first cousins, fully-grown, bring second cousins and third cousins. And Aunt Trudy, bless her decrepit hallelujah soul. She's still praisin' the Lord and tellin' the whole wide world "God lus' ya!"

I've got family here I didn't even know I had. – Gapped teeth, yellow teeth, crooked teeth, green teeth, rotten teeth, no teeth, false teeth, gold-crowned teeth. – Put a kiss right here! Give me love! You *is* still my aboriginal family, SMOOCHH! Nappy headed, bad breath, funky armpits and all. I love you, too cutie. Come on over here and give your cuzz' a hug. Now back it up a little, I'm getting' nauseous!

Embraces and hugs extend to all comers from every avenue. Kinfolk rekindle old relationships and talk about the past with no point of reference for current affairs. We haven't seen one another since that last morbid gathering. We are an abandoned bunch-of-folk who pale in the light of good times and who misconstrue hardship as the "good ol' days."

"The good old days?" Twisted talks of beatings with leather straps prompt undetected, bitter tears masked in a giggle or a grin. Some travel far, by train or plane. While others embark from a block or two. But, when it's all said and done, all will separate, departing forlornly to some respective hollow, desolate place from whence we come. But, we will meet again for the next ominous, homecoming. How asphyxiating.

The instant I inhale, it strikes me like none other. Visions of the FEDS closing in or perhaps the company I keep, equal the FEDS. I'm going BANANAS! Call me schizoid, irrational and no doubt, totally paranoid. But I know the signs of rude reality. My heart thunders, like a marching band. I've an uncanny notion I will drop dead in my tracks. Hell is kicking up dirt 'round my heels. I S-C-R-E-A-M! Satan is chasing me into hysteria. – I S-C-R-E-A-M again!

More panic! I race from one extreme of the house to the other. My heart won't slow – and "I beg you Lord – PLEEEEESE, let me see my kids – ONE MORE time!" I hear them – they are screaming for me.

"Ohh! Ohh-ohhh" – Tears stream my cheeks, and I SCREAM! – I want to see my babies! NOW! Before, I keel over and DIE! My feet won't stand still, they dance and they run, hysterically. Suddenly – I stop to grip the inside knob at my front door. It doesn't open. I run some more, the length of the house, beating a path into the bathroom, then, plunge heedlessly into the tub. I snatch hold to the long stemmed neck of the shower bar. It snaps – I scream AGAIN, but this time through an open window, while standing in a dry tub.

"Call 911, somebody call 911!"

Flashing red lights and sirens appear. I sit frenzied, feeling like a babbling lunatic and the total paranoid fool that I am. Janiah and Gerald arrive with tear- filled eyes to tell me of the heartless bitch, my trusted crack-smokin' neighbor Leslie. She tried her best to drown them at the neighborhood pool. And still it ain't enough to make me quit.

Little did I know that you, Dear Lord, were anticipating my call. Perhaps it had to do with my meeting with Aunt Trudy's daughter, Cousin Jennifer, last night. I ring her from the booth down the block.

Lord, forgive me, but that cousin of mine has got a way of making everything a Christ-mission, just like her mother. She twists the burden of loaning folk money into an opportune moment to tell idiots like me about the Lord. In her heart she knows that I don't have an ounce worth of good intent for the asking.

"You need to get them kids into Sunday School." You got 'dat, Cuzzin'. The kids go to church, you go home accomplishing what you aimed for, and I get mine. I'm sure you understand.

I stand watch to see the box-like, white vehicle veer away from the curbside on a Sunday mornin'. No quicker than the broad black lettering, that spells out – "Church Van" abandons my view, I zip into my jacket. I slap my stupid-looking hat over my matted hair, and haul ass to the walkway. My ignorant, agitated feet pound against the cold pavement. It is a swift and hurried trip to the corner and back.

In an instant the process begins. My hand sweeps my pocket for the familiar feel of the crack vial, stuffed deep inside. I skillfully remove the plastic cap between my thumb and forefinger. I watch in anticipation as the soft white rocks slide onto my dresser top. I hasten to the spigot for a few drops of water. Grab for a spoon and cigarette lighter, before setting the underside of the metal spoon ablaze. I marvel at the transition as the soft white mass dissolves into a bubbling syrupy patch in the center of the scorched kitchen utensil. It freezes solid, molded in a clump, perfect, like I'd hoped it would be. I raise the hand-made pipe to my lips. Put the fire to the mass and inhale.

My journey begins; transposing me into a paranoid, dejected, demoralized, deflated, disillusioned, recluse, – irrational and impeded, trembling copiously, while trying to set the pipe back onto the bureau top.

I hear talking – inside my head. "As far as I am concerned you are ALL DEAD. — Fuckin' ASS-WIPE" And, "I hate you B-I-T-C-

H! I HATE YOU! I HATE YOU!" Yes, Delbert – screaming and shoving his penis down my throat. Thoughts are summoned of my father, stripped naked on top my sister and straddling her plain like day. And the blue black fella' from Georgia, staring down over my head. Unzipping his trousers and shoving my insides. – Then Mr. Ellis telling me to keep hush and placing a hand between my thighs.

My heart pounds like thunder. The silence of death takes residence inside this empty shell. Then AGAIN – TALKING – INSIDE MY HEAD! You don't have to live like this. – You want to live – or do you want to DIE?

My bosom aches, "Oh Jesus," my knees go limp, "let me live." My legs collapse. "I want to live." I fall at my bedside, drenching the blankets with flowing sadness and breathing the stench of death. My fingers tremble and fold over my sobbing mouth as it hangs open with heaviness. The moments pass with nothing other than an uttering. –Don't let me die." My tears flow cold.

My spirit knows no peace, until suddenly all becomes totally quiet. "So quiet, you can hear a rat piss on cotton." My eyelids lift and I am bursting inside like a crumbled dam let go with the force of free flowing waters. I rise to a tingling in my spine. Now, MORE voices inside my head. At first from a distance, like somebody else talking to me. – LIKE GOD – saying – I don't get high no more. But the words are inside my heart. I hurry to a mirror, where I see a huge smile swelling across the face of a little girl. She speaks to me, plain like day. She tells me, "I don't get high no more." Her cheekbones rise and she calls a little louder. "I don't get high no more!" I look at her square in her face. I whisper back – "I don't get high no more."

With joy, I snatch forth a dresser drawer, removing everything. Plastic medicine bottles crack pipes, rubber bands, aluminum foil, empty vials, EVERYTHING, ALL THINGS, useless reminders of the habit that owned and possessed my soul. Another drawer slides open and another, until I hear the clickety-click of tiny glass bottles tapping the inner ceramic bowl inside the commode. One atop the other, they wade in a small pool of rippling water, and disappear inside a darkened hole. There comes a song – ringing in my ears, "When that Evening Sun Goes Down," and the chorus rings back: "Goes down."

When I recount with this foolish mind,
Dear Lord, the journey you carried me through.
That is when I know,
it ain't never my desire to see the evening sun down.
But in that day
help those of us who never learned the passageway.
One day too late
we rise up on a cooling board,
long after the sun done set,
and so far from the mark –
we don't even realize –
it's "sundown."

Hebrews Chapter 11 Vs. 1-

**Faith is the substance of things hoped for
and the evidence of things unseen.**

AFTERMATH

꙳

My unsuspecting co-workers at the local radio station pivot on the backs of their heels, when I tell them I'M BACK! – after three years gone. They have a good long stare at me. But, my giggling melts the air, when I throw my arms to greet each thawing face with a tremendous hug.

"Good Tuesday afternoon. This is Edwina Jordan filling in for Sandra Hendrix, over WXLV. It's currently, seventy-two degrees on this absolutely gorgeous April afternoon. Details on your forecast in just a moment, but first this word from ..."

With a click of a switch, my microphone shuts and the door to the studio flies open. In saunters a tall, slender gentleman with salted hair that shows from beneath the edge of a Texan-styled tall hat. He walks with dignity. He speaks with the authority of "folk-in-high-places." His low-riding boots are black leather and a shining buckle marks the outer arch of his foot. Slender pants fit tight and high around his waist. They are heisted with elastic suspenders. He slides a music selection into my hand and instructs me to play it. The door swings shut and he disappears. Soon he returns, this baffling stranger, just one last time to dismiss me. The station has been sold and handed over to the tall white Texan in the ten-gallon hat. My service is no longer needed.

Thanks to the Lord, the tax-paying public and the landlord who said yes, merely two meager months slip from view. I move from the familiar drug-infested neighborhoods I'd claimed as home. My next employment opportunity is at a YMCA as a driver. With a quick, lunchtime stop to the Beauty Supply Store I am pampered with more customer care than my due.

"I'd like to buy some curling irons."

"The gentleman behind you can help you with that." All the while I feel a really gentle and playful tug to the back of my hair.

We converse about everything, this gentleman and me. Everything except the electric irons I've come to purchase. Telephone numbers exchange hands. Perhaps he will give me a call this evening, when we both finish up at work.

Ring-a-ling-ling. I wait, deliberate and patient. I don't want to seem anxious. I stare at the handset still clinging onto the receiver. I don't dare pick it up until it chimes, just one more round. Then, finally, "Hello."

"Hi Edwina, this is Cardell. I'm the guy you met at the Beauty Supply store today, how are you?

"Fine thanks. How are you?"

"Don't you remember me from the 'Safe' Place meetings?"

"As a matter of fact I don't. Are you telling me that we met somewhere before?"

"I'm the guy who put the dollar in the basket for you."

I'd only been to one, maybe two Safe-Place meetings. Safe-Place, indeed it was. Narcotics Anonymous meetings, the place I'd retreated a time or two. Running from myself and trying hard not to get stoned. And yes, I do remember somebody reaching to drop a dollar in the collection basket. But I didn't look to see from where it came. We converse on a number of things with effortless flow.

Are you single? Have you ever been married? Do you have children?

Questions and answers, fire back and forth revealing a couple things we two have got in common, small children and addiction. Cardell is a recovering addict, just like me. Still, he hasn't asked the one question that I would expect to be the foremost of all. But, I gotta know.

"May I ask you a question, Cardell?"

"Sure."

"How old are you?"

"Um' twenty-eight, be twenty-nine in a month."

Twenty-eight? Cardell throws his words with a chest full of pride. BIG-MAN is just a baby', with milk still drying around his mouth. He's TOO YOUNG for ME. I had better let him know. It is better that he go running, now, than when he finds out that I've got an eighteen-year-old son. I don't know who this man is closer in age to – me or Keonis? Cardell jabbers breathlessly. In a moment I interrupt.

"Cardell." I call his name and he keeps right on talking. "Cardell," I call again, intent on breaking any connecting thought. "Cardell," I say, "I am thirty-nine years old."

"I don't have a problem with that." He answers me with not so much as a hiccup.

Fish are jumping inside a bubbling pan of fresh, hot oil. Cardell meets me at my apartment for lunch, reigning with a smile that gleams like the September sun. Cardell meets Keonis, who has come home to stay with me. They laugh, eat fish and everybody seems happy. We get together again and a couple times after, until Cardell has to leave. We keep in touch, while he attends an out of state trucking school, marking a path from east to west and honing the skills of his new career.

In the many passing weeks, the phone rings. To my surprise it is another trucker friend. Fitzgerald is on the line.

"He-e-e-y, Edwina, how ya' doin?" He calls my name excitedly, his voice reverberating through the receiver. He informs me that he has remarried and I am happy for him. I'm glad to know that despite all we been through, he and I can at least stay friends.

"I didn't know what to do for you, Edwina," he admits. "You kept on doin' that friggin' shit."

Following his announcement that he is in town, he stops by to see me. "You look good Edwina, I'm so happy for you." Fitz hugs me joyfully with strong arms that squeeze the breath out of my chest. He brings along with him a friend, who calls himself Chevy. Chevy is a smooth trucker-fella', with sprinkles of gray in his hair and caught between the aging of time. Chevy wears a 1970's "Coolie High" – fade haircut and a sporty, 1980's Applejack cap, tipped slightly to one side. He takes pleasure in driving around in a brand new car from the nineties and listening to just about every do-wop hit ever recorded. After all of the greetings and formalities, Chevy removes a bottle from a bag. The three of us sit and talk, while laughing and sippin' a social drink.

Then the doorbell rings. Having completed his training, in walks Cardell, to my biggest surprise. And now I've got three trucker-fellas' surrounding my kitchen table.

"Cardell, this is Fitz and Chevy. Fitz – Chevy, this is a friend of mine – Cardell."

"Hey Man! Nice to meet ya', Fitz calls warmly. Cardell, offers a cordial handshake, then takes his seat in the one remaining, empty chair. "I don't know if you drink – would you like a drink?"

"No – I don't drink," Cardell says uneasily, looking about the table and glancing back and forth at me. Fitz already got a wife. His newly divorced companion, Chevy looks thirsty, and he sounds like he's got plans for me. The more Chevy drinks, the more he keeps calling Cardell, Youngblood, creating an unspoken standoff between the two of them. The conversation flows, while I enjoy the company of my old and new friends.

In the weeks ahead, summer heats up. Fitz and me talk back and forth, as old friends do. Cardell keeps touch. And Chevy makes himself no stranger. He takes me shopping and on a daytrip to enjoy a splash at the beach and even takes me dancing. But as nice as he is, it's Cardell I like and Cardell wins over. And after four months of waiting, bugles blow in the bedroom, piercing the sound barrier. "The Saints Come Marching In," yeah, "The Saints Come Marching In!"

Well, the years toll, until Cardell and I marry. But after raisin' up three grown kids and getting married for this second time; it looks like hell is still kickin' up dirt round' my heels. But, when the evening sky looks dim, sometimes cracks and parts at the seams, I remind myself the sun still shines behind the cloud-fold. God is still watchin'. He's sittin' and lookin. Overseeing and taking notice how everything plays out. It is enough, that you kept me, Dear Lord. You've been a merciful Father and I couldn't ask for more. Thanks for the journey and the jubilation inside the pain.

Beloved think it not strange concerning the fiery trial
which is to try you,
as though some strange thing has happened unto you.
But rejoice
inasmuch as ye are partakers of Christ's sufferings
and that when his glory shall be revealed
ye may be glad,
also with exceeding joy.

I Peter Chapter 4:12

LETTERS
FROM THE HEART

LETTER TO CARDELL

Greetings Cardell,

May you be in perfect health and spirit.

From the experience of one "addict" to another,
I never wished to see you walk through this alone.
Abandonment is an unpleasant place to be. Funny thing
– you abandoned me. Dressed in your finest façade,
you speak the words, "I love you." But, you know what
Cardell, truth is, you are too busy fulfilling your own
worthless desires to love anybody but yourself. And
beneath that big beautiful smile is hidden, – a foolish
child inside the stunted body of an, unfeeling man. You
walk soft and never argue. Truth is, you have nothin'
to argue 'bout. Cardell does what Cardell wants, and
nobody gets in the way of that.

I reflect on our many, long night's conversations and
our time spent together. Sweet misery is what we have.
And Cardell, where comes the capacity to break my
heart? You take my kindness for blindness, and all the
love I could give is never enough.

Perhaps, my mission is not the union of marriage, but
expressly to tell you of the Lord? Well Cardell, Jesus
loves you and He sprinkles his grace with patience,

sparing you time to recognize His presence in your life. Nothing is to be had by your own might, and you will never conquer prosperity, without first recognizing He who strengthens you.

I will be praying for you, Cardell, despite your thinking you've got it all worked out. Praying that God will protect you and soften your heart. I am confident and faithful that one day you will give Him the praise he so deserves.

As for me, I think it best I clear the pathway. God has a mighty work to do in you. You will always be in my prayers, and, Cardell, I will forever love you. May God grant you strength and may His mercy be your portion.

LETTER TO ALFREDA

My Dearest, Alfreda,

Alfreda, look at yourself and see the strides you have made. You are a wonderful and intricate piece of perfection, a work of God's almighty art. He doesn't make junk. Stop blaming your environment when all goes wrong. And just for today – let the past be in the past. Daddy is no longer among us. And sis, he is no longer to blame for who we are and for who we have come to be. Let harmony be your blessing and you will experience His comfort for always.

Peace

LETTER TO RHONDA

My Dearest Rhonda,

You know the good works of the Lord, my sister Rhonda. I can tell through the things you say. Let your way be known by the things you do. You are not the only one who struggles with imperfections, but God knows your heart. He has been so merciful unto you. Be merciful unto yourself. Look how many years He has added to you in your sickness. Truly he has a great work for you and is lending time for you to get it right. Give Him the glory. Show Him honor. Stand and receive him as crown over your life. Do all these things, and He will NEVER let you fall. I pray God's mercies upon you.

So Long Nadine

Letter to Nadine,

Nadine, you are a beautiful and precious sister. You have been a friend who was there in times least expected. You have always accepted me with unconditional love. Now you are so extremely ill. I paid you a bedside visit today, following a call from the Intensive Care Unit at the hospital. Upon reaching the care facility, together with Janiah and Gerald, I pattered through a not-so-distant corridor. I discovered you far weaker than ever anticipated. I recall my previous visit, just days ago. I reflect upon a vivacious and feisty sister sitting upright in the bed and making a fuss about this or that. But, today is different. I unload the basket of white and yellow flowers to a table at your bedside. I position them toward the sunlight shining vibrantly through your window pane. Your head tilts less than gently against a pillow and tubes press upon your swollen cheeks. You know not that I am here, and yet I talk to you. Your screams are panicked and your moaning pins my spine. I can't say that I know what you are going through.

I used to ask you, "Nadine what are you trying to do? Are you trying to check out on me?"

"No," you would say, "I'm not ready to go nowhere, at least not yet."

I will miss those long conversations on the telephone. They became far few and in between when you neared your end. You gave up on yourself, Nadine. I was pulling for you. Your baby boy was pulling for you too. Did you hear his cry as he stood at your hospital bedside. He proclaimed with pride, "My mommy knows I am here, because she can hear my voice."

I had to tell him today that you were gone, that you had prayed and gone up to meet the clouds. His little hands lifted from his sides with a total sense of loss. And in his tiny words he said, "I want to see my mommy, but I can't. I guess I won't see her no more." His eyes are innocent, Nadine, same as we when we were snot-nose tots. I sure do pray that he won't hear the thunder we heard. And never see the lightening we saw. And may the warmth of a radiant sun, shine just for him always. Take care of yourself Nadine and thanks for the good times. I will hold them dear to me, until we meet again. So long Nadine, I will see you in the hereafter!

Miss You Toby

Your arms stretch around me as does your smile with a great big, loving hug. Together we go, arm in arm to a waiting hospital bed. You wave to the paramedics, greeting each and confirming with a kind word that you have finally made the decision to get your rest.

Still, your eyes long to hold on to an existence that is too late to grasp, too short to hold. Your affliction is not for lack of courage. It is time that sweeps you away. Your mouth opens. Your lips clap, one to the other. From them is uttered not a single word. You are too spent to speak Brother Toby. Your days are exhausted and you must go. Our last hours together were ominous. You made me laugh a lot, when in my gut I wanted to cry.

Who were those people? "They come all the time," you tell me, "two or three of them at a time." I pray they were angels, sent down from heaven, not to harm, but to help you on to a better way.

Rest in peace, Brother Toby, I will always love you, my brother, my cousin, my friend.

LETTER TO ERNESTINE

Ernestine,

My heart grieves with time passing for the years, months, hours, days and minutes, gone by without our reconciliation. Ya know Ernestine, my heart breaks at the notion that it must always be this way. You once told me, you didn't know why you treat me like you do. You admit it to me— you are jealous. Jealous of WHAT? We are two peas from the same pod; I am no different from you. One day your eyes will be opened, and on that very day, my arms will too. But, until God wills it, I wish you nothing but good and may you find your peace within.

God Bless you Always

LETTER TO AUNT TRUDY

Aunt Trudy,

Like the great oak tree, you are well up into your eighties and still preaching, forever teaching and still standing strong. There is ONLY ONE WAY IN! And it is – JESUS! Hallelujah! JESUS is the ONLY way. You shout it to the tops of your lungs until your eyes well with tears, sending tremors up my spine and a quake upon the earth. Aunt Trudy, your message has been well received and I thank God for you.

I didn't know that I had a right to get out of my marriage, until you set me straight. I will never forget our little conversation.

"Edwina, why do you put up with it?

"Aunt Trudy, The Bible says 'til death do us part. I made my vow."

"Edwina, let me tell you something," you reply. "Everything is not of the Lord's doing." You speak the words emphatically, "

You are one mighty powerful, little woman and my greatest gift on earth was your message to me, about a man named Jesus. Don't know where I'd be, had it not been for you.

Thanks!

LETTER TO DELBERT

Dearest Delbert,

Sparkling grays frame my temples and fine lines define my eyes. Any dream of perpetual love with you was simply a vision bestowed upon my inexperienced youth and now dried up like scorched waters in a low-lying stream.

But, now you say that you forgive me, as though you have handed me a white rose in the center of a garden. Stubborn, obstinate words overflowing out of a narrow-minded, belligerent, pig-headed, fool-hearted, ignorant old man, for I forgave you a long time ago. Little comfort do I find in your words Delbert, because soft words don't teeter on hard truth. Until you can put life in this body, or until you can take life out, it matters not a damn what you think of me. All fear of you abandons me, like steaming hot vapors from a whistling kettle. Forever I did wait, when you gave no rest. Forever I cried, when you offered no peace. Forever I am gone. And forever has always been a very long a time. I pardon you Delbert, forever. Be gone, not as in death, do it with peace in your heart. Forever and Always

A Letter From Satan

I saw you yesterday as you began your daily chores. You awoke without kneeling to pray. As a matter of fact, you didn't even bless your meals or pray before going to bed last night. You're so unthankful. I like that about you.

I can't tell you how glad you made Me that you haven't changed your way of living. Fool, you are Mine. You and I have been going steady for years. And I don't love you yet. As a matter of fact, I HATE you. I hate you because I hate god. I'm only using you to get even with god. He kicked ME out of heaven. And I'm going to use you as long as possible to pay him back.

You see, fool, god loves you. He has great plans in store for you. But you have yielded your life to Me. And I'm going to make your life a living hell. That way we'll be together twice.

This will really hurt god. Thanks to you, I'm really showing him who's boss in your life! Look at all the good times we've had: watching dirty movies and TV shows, cussing folks out, partying, stealing, lying, worrying, being "perfect" in every way (yes you've learned well how to make sure everything about you is perfect and expensive, and by the way you'd better have everything super clean for me; well everything but your soul). You are a true hypocrite (I love it when you allow me to flow through you to point out faults in everybody else –I guess it's because I've made you into something perfect), sexing it up and down, overeating, smoking, drinking, working roots, playing with My tarot cards and living your life based on superstition and astrology, staying away from any church with power (if you do find your way to church – I make certain you go to sleep and while you're awake you play a role, so only you and I know what's really going on behind that pretty/handsome face of yours), You brag, boast, listen to and spread nasty jokes. You, gossip, you're two-faced, backstabbing and feeding Me with Playboy and Playgirl pinups. Surely you don't want to give all this up; we've been together for too long.

Come on fool, let's burn together FOREVER. I've got hot plans for you. This is a letter of appreciation from Me to you, personally. I'd like to say "Thanks" for letting Me use you for all of your life.

FOOL, you're so gullible. I laugh at you when you're tempted to sin and give in – HA, HA, HA … You make Me sick.

Sin is really beginning to take its toll on your life. You look twenty years older. And I continue to need new blood. Go get them for me. I want to do to them what I've done to you and MORE! Teach some little kid how to sin or even better, – fill them up with your ridiculous fears and hang-ups so they can grow up to be just like you. All you have to do is smoke, drink, cheat, gamble, gossip, lie, fornicate, overeat, make excuses to miss church, party hearty, listen to the top 10 jams, scream a lot and put those stupid Christians down for not doing what you're doing. Do all of this in the presence of children, and they will do it too; kids are like that you know.

Well fool, I've got to go now. I'll be back in a few seconds to tempt you again so I can keep you from having any peace of mind – Ever. My wish is your desire – you only want to please Me. So whatever I want to do, I know you're ready and willing to at least try it, huh? If you were smart, you would RUN somewhere, admit that you're a sinner and live for god with what bit of life you have left. I intend to have My way with you until the very end. My way is to kill you or make sure you die at any moment, without Christ as the one in charge of your life. Anybody but Christ.

It's not my nature to warn anyone; but to be your age and still sinning is becoming a bit ridiculous. Don't get Me wrong, I do hate you but I know that you'd make a better fool for Christ. And you might find out something that I've known all the while. Since you love me so much, don't share this letter with anyone else, it'll be our little secret, OK?

Author Unknown

MOURNING GLORY

This ol' vine
ain't got time
to be sittin' on no sill.
I ain't no potted plant
no magnolia tree
settin' 'top a hill;
nor purple daffodil,
I'm not a poinsettia.
I coulda' been a pink carnation
or even somethin' betta',
like a white gardenia flower
or a simple water lily,
don't forget, forget-me-nots;
I'm not just being silly,
when a flaming iris I'm not;
I'm just a mourning glory,
a sun-dried weeping flower
in the dawning
of the early morning sun.
I could have been
an African daisy,
but I'd been crazy
to sit inside
a long stemmed vase,
upon a shelf,
all by myself,
when this ol' vine
got a story to tell.
What if I'd been a sweet pea
or potpourri
with baby's breath,
high strung,

like a Fuji mum
and smellin' my ego
like a perfumed
purple petunia.
But I declare,
I wouldn't dare
be a marigold,
pot of gold,
or undersold,
knowing what I know
and what I been told.
It ain't no daisy
nor buttercup,
no begonia
come springing up,
or weed try creeping up,
gonna choke my seed,
bleedin' me
out of my redemption.
No indeed!
This ol' vine
ain't got time
to be climbin' hills
and settin' on shelves,
through the rocks of ages,
flippin' pages
that fade too soon
to read the script.
'cause I gotta story to tell,
'bout a flower plucked
from the bowels of hell.
When the angels get to 'steppin'
and to ringin 'dey bells.
It ain't no time
for rippin' and runnin',
'cause I be

sowin' and reapin'
in the dawning
of the early
morning sun.

We are troubled on every side, yet not distressed;
we are perplexed, but not in despair;
Persecuted, but not forsaken;
cast down,
but not destroyed;

2 Corinthians Chapter 4:8,9

MOURNING GLORY

IS

A DEDICATION
TO ALL WHO HAVE GONE AHEAD
TO GATHER AT OUR NEXT
GREAT AND REJUVENATING

"HOME COMING"

Mom and Dad;
my sisters, Pat, Nora and Rose; my brothers, Eddie and Chuck;
Cousin Rea, Aunt Adelaide, Aunt Mary and Aunt Aggie;
Uncle Alford, Uncle Harry, Uncle Lester, Sr., Aunt Gert',
Uncle Marvin, Uncle Bobby, Aunt Margaret, Great-Grand-
Pop, Grand-Pop, Grand-Mom, Mother and Father in-law; my
sisters-in-law, Sheila and Doris; my brothers-in-law, Alvin and
Bobby; and my Dear Friend, Stewart

Printed in the United States
50142LVS00004B/109-162